D0458903

YEAR
of the
ORPHAN

A NOVEL

DANIEL FINDLAY

ARCADE PUBLISHING • NEW YORK

First North American Edition 2019

This is a work of fiction. Names, characters, places, and incidents are either products of the author's imagination or used fictitiously.

Originally published in Australia in 2017 by Penguin Random House Australia Pty Ltd.

Arcade Publishing books may be purchased in bulk at special discounts for sales promotion, corporate gifts, fund-raising, or educational purposes. Special editions can also be created to specifications. For details, contact the Special Sales Department, Arcade Publishing, 307 West 36th Street, 11th Floor, New York, NY 10018 or arcade@skyhorsepublishing.com.

Arcade Publishing® is a registered trademark of Skyhorse Publishing, Inc.®, a Delaware corporation.

Visit our website at www.arcadepub.com.

10 9 8 7 6 5 4 3 2 1

Library of Congress Cataloging-in-Publication Data

Names: Findlay, Daniel, author.
Title: Year of the orphan : a novel / Daniel Findlay.
Description: New York : Arcade, 2019.
Identifiers: LCCN 2018055716 (print) | LCCN 2018057803 (ebook) | ISBN 9781628729948 (ebook) | ISBN 9781628729924 (hardback)
Subjects: | BISAC: FICTION / Coming of Age. | FICTION / Science Fiction / Adventure. | FICTION / Contemporary Women. | GSAFD: Science fiction.
Classification: LCC PR9619.4.F575 (ebook) | LCC PR9619.4.F575 Y43 2019 (print) | DDC 823/.92—dc23
LC record available at https://lccn.loc.gov/2018055716

Jacket design by Erin Seaward-Hiatt.
Jacket photograph courtesy of iStockphoto.

Printed in the United States of America

For Mum, who has always encouraged me to write

0

There were a heat. Air hotter'n blud. Baked her skin as she moved. Dint carry much. Evrythin she had weighed against how far itd have to go. Count it. No ship, that were gone down a hole. No swag bar sum rounds that might help her get it back, the rest of it cast off an down the same hole. A bottle, drymeat, tea and a billy, four heavy rounds, scope, watercatcher, skully and wrap. Coat, boots, shirt an strides, more dust than cloth, woulda stood up on their own if she let em. Flint. Long knife. The shimmer come off the top of the cracked clay in the gully, always ahead, never gettin any closer. No seasons in the desert no more. Blud weight, blud money. It were a dead mans jacket she wore but that werent sayin much. Once and soon enough her boots was gunna be on sumwun elses feet. If they ever found her that was. She dint need no talent for seein the signs nor the scope to tell her that soon enough she was gunna be with the dust and dead and gone and on the wind. The System were near, she could feel the colour of it comin closer, but she figgered she werent gunna make it this time. On her heels were the Reckoner, she were near enough certain. Day after day walkin bad ground that she shoulda been sailin, waitin for a dust storm to hit that never come. Small mercies. Now this. The heat risin up outta the ground and cookin her boots. Nights of the clearest starstruck cold she'd ever seen. All the time, he'd been trackin her across the sand. All the way from the Glows an the Spirals an up out the earth. Past the bones of them Ghostet whatd come before her. Scavs an scouts an who knew. Along the flat snow roads where cotton bloom caught against the twisted bushes. Heard tell they was once tended careful, gone wild now. A score of days walkin back an that mara, that scaretale pickin up her tracks sumthin like the day after that. She'd hit the staked castouts on the sand late yesterday. They never put em out nearer than three days walk which meant she were gettin close. She eyed their dried up bodies but the rope an wood werent worth the takin. Dint have time for no scavvin now anyways. The fella followin her kept his distance in the heat of the day and closed the gap at night. Trailin her an wouldnt get shook. Makin up ground over the cracked an parched earth, never close enough to see clear through the scope but it was him sure enough. Whatever kinda thing he were. Loped steady, leaned left, carried weight on his right hip though sling, spear or blade was all rumour. Who knew? Years of hearin his name an she'd never believed he were a real thing. All them scare-tales they talked at the System said he et them he kilt. She'd seen plenny of bones down the Glows that mighta borne the truth of that out. Scavs strung from roof an bough an still more disappeared an never come back.

He were taller than her. A coat that mighta been near enough the colour of the soil or just covered in enough of it not to matter anyway. A soft slouch on his head, she could tell by the shape but maybe it were the heat haze and maybe it were dust but drawin a bead on him dint come easy an it never lasted. He were smoke, mixin with the sheoaks an bluebush, faded in an out of wadis until she felt the fear in her belly, sweat on her palms an kept movin. By her own reckonin it wouldnt be long now that she woke in the night with him standin over her or never woke again. All she

2

could do was keep gunnin to the System and pray the fellas who watched the sand saw her comin and cared enough to get the gate open. Pray for once she ran into another scav or hunters bringin in a load of roos an coneys.

He might not take her if she made the walls. Sum protection, for what it was worth, spillin from the trash and noise an firelight of other souls. Then again, there was rumours he were wun of them, that he walked among em in the circles of the System without care before fadin through the iron an disappearin into the red dust that clogged yer lungs an made ya spit up blud an weep forever, ya breathed it long enough. He were sumthin outta dust, outta whirlies an willie willies, and sumtimes she thought she were makin him all up. He were the boogeyman, takin kids an old alike, eatin up scavs that crossed him out Painter way, or Olympic way, or anywhich-way the tale got spun. They was stupid stories to keep the brainless shook and yungens scared. She'd never believed em but when she tried to focus the scope on him an couldnt she knew what it was. Never seen nuthin like it in all her years on the sand.

The aird been cold an clear the last few nights and she'd no need of her wrap, shipless as she were. Still, she'd slept with it stuffed in her mouth in case she cried out, though she reckoned she'd beat that habit a long time. All them stories but it dint change there were a fella trackin her an she dint like bein hunted. Dint sit right at all. There werent nuthin certain but wun thing, the Reckoner were coming.

1

Before

Were a day. Were just a day. Up at dawn an the three of em headed to the gully. Check the traps, see if any lizards or coneys had forgot their lernins an got strung up. Walkin always walkin. Mum an Jon with damp cloth over their mouths an she got the proper mask bein the little wun. Kept dust out sum but she still spat pale red. Out to the soaks and rockholes takin the plastic bottles. Check the traps, dig for roots and grubs, set up the sun stills lest the soaks come up dry. Then she an Jon set to scav an scav an scav. The near hulks had been stripped long ago an what mighta once been shacks was just shapes on the ground that came an went in the storms, old things lost to dust. Evry now an then though they found a spring or sum bit of plastic that were worth sumthin to the traders headed to the big camp. Screws were good, bolts better. They was buildin things thattaway. Walls an such the scavs said. Had a powerful need for things dug up an found. They was thirstin for bits of the old, whatever them fellas could get their hands on. Copper an steel were worth plenny. Salt an grub. They picked an picked. Were the ruin of an old farmhouse still standin a mile distant but it were a bad place an stripped clean anyways. More hulks out in the dunes, plenny of treasure left to find. Rust were slow in the long dry. Them sand scarred monsters from the old times still looked alright on the inside sumtimes. Now an then they still had fellas inside but most often they was stripped bare. Bones was good for carvin. Bone handles an bone knives. Leg bones the strongest. She an him knew where the good wuns was. Dint tell Mum evrythin he dint. Jon always made sure she brought home sumthin even when she dint find it herself. Out there an fetch me back what ya find. Make yerself useful. Evrywun's gotta have a reason her mum said but she knew she were alright. Mum, thin as a whip, bones standin stark against the sundarked skin. Only pretend hard. Lean, muscle like braided wire an the same dark blue, opalchip eyes she got told she had herself.

Mum found soaks an water for the scavs an told em what was comin in their days ahead. Told the futures of them what came tradin through on their way to the big camp, the place where they was puttin a system in place. Told em good enough that plenny come back, askin what the next season held, where they might comb the sand an cracked salt lakes for fortune. Plenny to be made outta things from the old before. Sum of them scavs had been comin their way for years, droppin little presents for their mum an her brood when the haul was good. Only pretend hard her mum was, she still stroked her hair till she slept when the night terrors and whirr-whirrs were on her. She listened in on what the scavs told her mum. Gettin harder they reckoned, hadta go ever deeper, ever darker for them things from the before. Sum went out an never come back. Down the deep dark they said, things you din wanna wake. Fear comin off em like stink as they told their tellins over the fire.

★

They was just comin back in from the hills, the mallee standin stark and black at their backs. Heatstained sky spite the droppin sun. Sweat beadin on her lip inside the mask. Pockets fulla wire an a coupla long black rubber strips that werent cracked too bad. She went in with water an Jon put the billy over flame an went to get their mum. She int emptied her pockets fore he were back comin in the door at a run. The sun low in the west an the shadows cast long. No mistakin what he was sayin, breathless an pale, eyes standin out sharp against his skin, hair the red of dust. It were their hour, wun of their hours.

Theyre comin, theyre almost here.

Werent no need to ask who. He'd come barrelin through the skin hangin across the entrance, an Mum were on his heels. Eyes wide, the whites bigger than she'd ever seen, sumthin stuck in her head she always wished she'd forget. There was only wun big space inside, no way out, no place to go. Mum pulled aside the mat on the hard packed floor, an openin in the dust that might be big enough for wun small kid, but only wun. She picked her up, lookin her hard in the eyes. The same eyes she got told she had. Her mums lips was pressed together in a white line, the cords in her skinny neck standin out an her fingers leavin bruises that was gunna outlive her. Her ma let go of her arm for a second, held her finger over her lips and and then laid her in the shallow hole, holdin her eye all the way down. Coverin her with rags, hands movin fast then pushin her down deeper.

Wun hope, they only seen the two of us. Wun hope.

Now the light went dim, the mat pulled back over her an her mum flingin handfuls of dust over it, buryin her in the floor, tryna cover evry trace. Mums last words in her ears fadin, just the sound of her own hammerin chest. She lay like a dead thing in the dark, an she figgered she was, knees drawn up to her chin, wun balled fist in her mouth, tryin not to shake. All too fast to follow. There were no heavy footfall, if stories was true them that was comin moved on bare feet an claw, teeth like long knives. Or mayhap were it boots of skin, bark and leather, movin like shadows over the floor of the desert, silent in the arvo haze with blades drawn, nuthin needin to be spoke.

Ghostmen. Out the dark men. Blademen, badmen, bludthings. Reckoner. All them names.

Whisperin names. Why? Shut up. Teeth chatterin. Could hear her brother an ma had gone out back into the open, both shoutin from a ways off, nuthin she could unnerstand. Her ma cryin out an noises of struggle, her brother's screamin wail that turned her blud cold. She lay still in the hole, she closed her eyes an ears.

When she woke she couldnt move a long time. She was cold with her own water that she'd let go all over herself. She dint remember doin it. Her knees was stuck an she pushed the rags aside an lifted a corner of the mat slow, dust drainin in onto her. There were no light, it were long dark. She couldnt hear anythin and pushed her way through the cloth, through the ache in her head behind her eye. She sat up painful from the shallow grave that werent wun an she could see starlight through the door. The skin were gone an the stark sand stared back at her through the empty frame. It were cold like it never were and dead quiet. She climbed out of the hole further, crawlin towards the outside, her fingers stickin to sumthin pooled on the sand. She knew not to cry out. By the stars she saw the shack was wrecked but not stripped. Them what had come barely cared for the dry snakemeat and hoarded oil an wood. The saved water was gone but the watercatcher were in wun piece and the dust were littered with bones barely cleaned. Sheaves of grass still restin in the corner like they always was. When she looked at em it were like nuthin had changed. From the door she could see the plain. There was no firelight, no camp close by. They come outta dust an went back to it. On the sand she saw more dark patches reflected in the starlight, sticky to touch. On small legs she tripped out into the dirt, feet bare, the silence louder than the noise in her head. She walked a ways into the sand an then lay down on her side facin the shack, seein the night clear through it, straight through the broken walls. Whisperin, the fear on her. Thinkin they were out there watchin, knowin they'd missed her, turnin around right now an comin back for seconds.

Mum? Jon?

She knew blud, she knew the Ghosts had come, the maras and sleep terrors had told her they would come. Mum hadnt kept the fear from her neither. The longer she lay there starin out into the dark the more she thought there was nuthin real strange about this except that she was still breathin an her ma an brother werent. Ghostet they was. Et by them things from the dark. Breath caught in her chest an she forced it back down so she dint let a howl go an give herself away. Her eyes dropped to the stuff that had been dragged out of the shack. Skins an jars thatd held bolts an screws, both empty. Scraps of steel an the rubber they'd brought back that afternoon. She looked through the shack at the frozen dunes an nuthin moved.

2

Before

He were in a foul mood this mornin. Another wun dead. Another wun taken out to the big burn pits where the waste turned into smoke. Smell of flesh an garbage crowdin him. Shoulda been used to it by now. Where did they find em? In this bludy place where there werent hardly any kids anyway they still managed to find a few an he was always buyin the weak wuns, a knack for pickin up yungens what was on their last legs. This fucken land. Dint have no name he knew of. Had been a desert since theyd started makin memories. Fucken Glows an fucken scavs an fucken cornerboys. He picked up the pace towards the middle, the boss was gunna come soon. The circles was quiet this time of day, that was sum small blessing, an the heat was workin its way up, sun still low enough to just be drawin a faint sweat. His feet scuffed over the dusty concrete, sendin up small red clouds. The shacks an sheds he passed was cobbled outta sheet iron and hessian. Scraps of wood an bits of hulk stitched together with tarp an rope into blind monsters. Heads of sleepers an drinkers an sniffers an smokers wakin bleary an sum not wakin at all. Sum what couldnt be bothered walkin to the well or the nearest soak was stumblin out back of their camps, he could see em. Collectin the water from under plastic scraps, pissin in the ash of last nights fire. Rubbish of bleached plastic and bone heaped around the doorways. Charms an icons, wheels an knives, all small and brittle. Precious few yungens an even less old. He passed em, roundin the curve of the big Circle. The System. He spat on the ground. Down the cuts he could see halfway across the ring road that looped all around the inside the wall, breakin only at the tyres built around the old water tower an pickin up again on the other side of them grim dusty stacks. They was the only things that stood taller than the leftovers, the fibro barracks half fallen in and ironroofed sheds in the middle. Stripped hulks an old concrete channels leadin nowhere. Leavebehinds that werent doin nowun no good. He turned down the hook, headin straight through the circles now on the new cut, seein the first of the hungry corner-boys wakin but they all knew who his boss was an better than to try anythin. Yeah keep yerselves to yerselves, he eyed them off an they kept his gaze, hands in their short pockets, sum of em swingin a careless verse back an forth between themselves, wakin slow. He were startin to sweat now, had been walkin a hot minute or so. His hands was damp an he patted his pocket again, feelin the shavings of gold wrapped in a plastic scrap through the cloth, wonderin if anywun would take em or if it was back to the Old Mans place for barter. Medicine, gold, clear wine, never knew what the scavs took these days. Whatever they could get their hands on the thick bastards, thinkin they was sumthin special. Werent nuthin to him, fools takin chances outside the walls, but he knew the Old Man kept em close. He cleared dust out of his throat, hackin hard. All the time wonderin what was gunna get brought in, if there was gunna be anythin up on the block that the Old Man would wanna take a look at. He hoped not. Was done choosin bad cattle.

★

10

They knew his face, knew that he'd be callin his numbers usin the hands, that he werent gunna be yellin anythin in a hurry, now or ever. That was well an good, more than a few silent faces in the System. When the boss showed up finally an watched two fellas go past on the block they knew he werent gunna be callin out either. Just left it to Karra. Hands was no good in a cipher but they was plenny fine for makin trades an whippin curs. Now the sun were up the heat were chokin, makin evry breath burn in his chest an even the little heeltoe steps of the sellers an buyers was draggin up enough dust to start sum other fella coughin in the back. Werent no moren forty blokes, just a quiet mornin, movin weight of wire, cloth an iron. Sum sellin old books but nowun was buyin. Usually rubbish these days, all the farmin an smithin an diggin books was long gone, hidden away. They was more story than anythin else anyway Karra reckoned. Werent nowun growin much out here. Werent the tools for smithin neither. Place were a fucken blight. What they had to go by was what was in their heads, for a long time now. What they had to trade was what they made or hunted or scavved an dust knew things was gettin harder out on the sand. All things even better to be in here than out there he reckoned. He remembered the walls goin up not that long ago, shitty things they was. Piled em around the Stacks an them tyres was gunna be more trouble than they was worth, mark him. He moved the stump of his tongue around in his mouth, workin sum moisture into the back of his throat as a yungen was dragged up onto the block by a rope collar. He could feel the boss straighten up an peer at the kid. Looked like a bag of bones but at least she had both her arms an legs. The scav what brought her pulled her up by the throat an her hands went quick to her neck as she got throttled. She kicked, showin them buyin that she could move. He dropped her back down hard on the packed ground but she dint cry out. Sumwun from over his shoulder spoke up.

I seen that yungen before. Its blud of that woman what casts the ash, the wun what lives outside the boundary, out towards the Glows. Looks myling to me.

The scav with the rope hawked an spat on the ground next to the kid.

Aint no fucken myling, look at her. Live as they come. Shes an orphan. Bluds dead. Her nearenough too. Ghosts et em, dunno how they missed her but here she is. Her ma was a clever wun, this wun might be as well.

Fucken scavs, had no idea. Karra knew her price was gunna halve at least. Ya dint mention the Ghosts on the block an ya sure as shit dint sell sumwun a clever bit of cattle. The seller werent a slaver though, Karra could see, just a scav from out in the dust whatd found a live wun. Knew no better. In here ya dint taint nuthin with Ghosts that was for sale. Out there it mighta been sumthin ya lived with but System fellas werent too keen to think on what was past the fence. He felt the boss tap his shoulder an for all his years servin he turned an looked at the Old Man, raisin his brows. The old fella was all hooded up spite the heat, face in shadow like it always were, a scatter of grey hairs on his chin an dust in evry weathered crack an wrinkle. He looked square back an nodded his head before turnin an makin his slow way through the gathered folk. Karra turned back to the block, not riskin a shake of his head, knowin that it could earn him a floggin but what was the Old Man thinkin? He stood still a moment more an then moved forwards through the fellas in front of him, diggin his hand into his pocket, feelin the scraps of gold there, shiftin them in his sweaty palm, his brow drippin with sweat an the heat startin to burn his pale skin that never seemed to darken. He raised his hand an the fella on the hammer pointed at him. Werent no other takers on this wun. First price was the last price. An for good reason. They was takin gold an bindings an a little clear wine. He waited ready to count and remember the price. The yungen had been pulled upright by its dusty hair now and stood swayin on bony shanks.

He could see proper now its palms black with dry blud and the eyes dark blue and flat in the burned an dirty face. Karra felt a shiver on him as her gaze drifted over the fellas in front of her. She were worthless, he knew it sudden. She was already dead and gettin work from her was gunna be impossible. He had an urge to warn the boss but the old fella was already away up the road. Concerned with bigger things was the boss, though dust knew what. He sucked in a lungful of scorchin air an signed a weight an number to the cando man runnin the auction and it were done. He had his self a stablemate, a dirty bruised orphan standin no higher than his hip. Dark hair bleached to dirty brown by the sun an covered with the taint of the Glow and the Ghosts. He dint trouble himself too much with them superstitions but they shat him anyways. Wun more thing to be thinkin about. He stepped up to the hammerman who looked like he couldnt fathom his luck an dropped metal on him an took the rope roughly, signin wunhanded.

Come collect the rest, word is bond.

The yungen stumbled and he dragged her sharp upright. Karra dropped his gaze down an looked into the eyes of the yungen. Nah, werent no myling. Near dead but live enough. He signed awkward again with wun hand, keepin a grip on her shoulder.

You speak the hands?

She dint give no sign of understandin. Ferfucksake. He sighed, air whistlin past what was left of his tongue. Course the bossd choose sum sand rat without no lernin or voice an couldnt fucken sign. Sum skinny vermin with flat eyes that werent gunna live to see seven sunups. Ferfucksake. He slapped the kid across the face, then again harder, snappin its head to the side, sumthin like shock cuttin through whatever werent happenin in its head. It half looked up at him, stick arms an hands like dead spiders comin up real slow from its sides an bless his fucken eyes it were signin at him. Slow as a loaded cornerboy but the scrap could speak sum kinda hands.

My mum . . .

He leaned down to her, stopping her hands with his own an signin slow an clear.

Yer mums dead yungen. Yer an orphan, unnerstand?

The kid dint move but she was lookin at him. He raised his hand to slap her out of her daze again.

I unnerstand.

She signed back slow an deliberate, face blank.

Good. That old fella what was just here, thats the big boss. Me, Im yer evryday boss. You belong to that fella an that means you belong to me. Yer gunna do whatever yer told, sun up to sun down an all the night between.

Dust driftin in her breath. A small nod.

Good. Now we're goin home, Im gunna show you yer digs an then we're gunna get you to work.

The kid dint move. Snakequick he clipped her behind the ear. He were startin to see there werent gunna be much cryin comin from this wun. Dint look the type. Yep, he could pick em. Least when this wun carked it, it were square on the boss. She werent gunna take moren a scrap of food here or there, were gunna be dead in a week give or take. End up on the pits like all them others.

Water?

He looked down half surprised at his charge. She dry swallowed the heat.

Water? This time she signed.

So ya got a voice do ya? Water is for them what work.

The yungen spoke again in a clear, low voice.

I can find the water. I can see the sound, me mum . . .

He leaned down to look at the kid again, but the voice faded to nuthin, lost in its breath again. It seemed like it was speakin sum kind of truth but the words were nonsense. It were a pretty small kid after all, mighta been lernin to talk, mixin up its words an made a bit mad by the sun and whateverd happened to it out past the boundaries. He looked it up and down and an then kneeled down so he were eye level with it. He kept the rope wrapped around his gnarled knuckles an signed slow for her.

We're goin back to the bosses place, theres water there. Stay in step an Ill take ya off the rope when we get back. Act up, Ill knock ya flat.

He dint wait for a reply, just stood up, both knees crackin and protestin, an started walkin in the old fellas footprints back to the homestead, tuggin on the rope whenever she fell behind. The foot track led them back out of the Centre, past hooks and cuts. He kept his head up, draggin but not too hard on the scrap, an she kept up good enough. The odd stunted sheoak, even in here, tappin down into sum lost water, more specked around the wells. If he turned he coulda seen the tops of the tyre stacks an the tower in the centre but he had no need to be rilin himself this early in the day. The tower, the tyres, the walls an the boss's place was sat all around him but he knew where he'd rather be. It werent on the wall, the Watch could have that all to their pissed selves, and it werent the Stacks with their stink an rotten faces an sharp knives. Nah, the Centred be good enough for him. Been in there plenny with the old fella, seen how there werent even much dust against the sills in the middle. Were cool in them old buildins too. Seen they had sum real old glass that still let the light in an werent crazed an cracked like most else around here. His mind were wanderin an he checked himself sharp. Quickest way to the lash. Aint had many stripes put on him but even once was enough. It were gettin hotter an he could feel the sweat drippin down his back. Sumwun musta brought in a load of roo an there were a smell of meat an brush fires as people got to cookin. No sign from the yungen though that she had a hunger, or anythin much else. Karras own mouth was waterin at the rank, oily smell of dust knew what fryin up but he never tarried no more with gold on him an business to finish up.

The Old Mans place rose up outta the shacks an dust like it were sprung from the soil but Karra knew it were put there not all that long ago. Were from before his time but werent no proper leave-behind, though it were made outta stuff from the before. Three big steel boxes pushed together, two end to end in a crookleg shape an wun on top makin an eyrie. He dint know how theyd stacked em but there werent no give in the thing. Just jagged cuts in the steel done with blunt saws an hammered flat, rust creepin on the chopped edges. Inside were holes and hung sackcloth makin rooms outta corners, an a partbroken ladder in the dark leadin up to where the boss kept the books an salves, all the strange things of medicine he'd collected over who knew how many years walkin the sand. Karra turned back to the Orphan but she werent lookin. He jerked on her lead an waited till she caught up, crouchin low on the sand next to her, tryna see it through fresh eyes. It were all he knew, an now it were gunna be all she knew too. Hadta remember his own awe when he first saw it. It were wun of the only places in the System that had sum kinda fence, rusted girders sunk into the dirt an strung with wire, the whole place a kinda warped three sides an sittin a hundred strides inside the edge of the big wall itself. A gate of corrugated iron and an awnin made outta burlap that he'd strung up an hadta clear of sand an dust evry other day. That were gunna be her chore now. The big steel boxes that made up the house was different colours, eaten an chipped by rust and the endless sandstorms, wun faded blue with Maersk on the side an Hanjin on the two rust coloured wuns. Old time words, musta meant sum big stuff back when and werent nuthin now. He'd heard sum fellas say now an again they was goin up the Hanjin when they was fetchin medicines an poultices an the like. He looked away from it, at the Orphan, who was starin slackjawed at the boxes. Musta been the biggest thing she ever seen. He took her shoulders an unhitched her from the rope, signin slow an careful when she were standin free.

This is yer new digs. Im tellin ya twice cos Im feelin real kind this mornin. The bloke what owns this place owns you an me. Whatever shit yer peoples mighta told ya about who ya was an what yer worth, ya can forget it. Theres nuthin special about ya an if yer like the last three yungens that come through here youll be dead in a week. Yer keep yer head pulled in an dos yer told while yer breathin. Stay outta me way unless I call for ya. You hear me clappin, ya come runnin. Unnerstand? Ya stuff up, or dont do what yer told, first Ill beat ya, then the lash.

His mouth filled with saliva an his back ached for a sec when he mentioned the catonine. The kid was lookin at him kinda dumb an all a sudden he couldnt stand her face no more. He cuffed her around the head, harder than he meant to. A perilous small kid, skinny wrists and legs, a halfwild thing from the waste, eyes standin out like opals, sharp bones cut outta its face. Clear though, he saw, she were lucky that way, the flies seemed to leave her alone. Most of them what came from outside the boundaries werent too bad, it were more System kids what came to see the boss with gummed up dusteyes. Werent gunna be too much heavy liftin goin on by the look of her stark shoulders. In fact it were just gunna be more work for him. The boss werent gunna have nuthin more but another wastrel an less on the plate for Karra. He grabbed it round the neck, fingers almost wrappin the whole way. He could feel the little nobs of her spine stickin into his palm. Coulda squeezed hard an saved em all the trouble. Werent gunna be long anyway he figgered. He pointed at the small pit next to the building.

Shit goes there, ya eat inside when I tell ya, an work starts now. Go inside an get a step an a stick an get the dust off that cloth up there. Then come find me.

She moved like he'd ordered. Stoppin for a second at the door just like he remembered himself doin the first time.

3

She dint know when she'd fallen asleep but it werent when she planned. Meant to lie still an keep watch but exhaustion took her. Had enough wits about her to wrap her mouth again an that were a small blessin itself. She'd dreamed again. Itd been happenin more an more of late. Bright an sharp too. She remembered slicin herself on brittle old glass as a yungen. Her mum'd cleaned out the cut with Jon watchin on an then she'd held em both close a moment. Tellin em to look after each other. She knew now why Mum an Jon'd been lookin at each other. If she'd picked up infection there were precious little to be done. The wound was clean though, she'd healed nearenough overnight, her mum lookin hard at her next sunup, turnin her wrist this way an than, mutterin to herself. Now she dint even have a scar to remind her. Hadnt thought of it in years but the look twixt her mum an Jon was fresh in her mind.

She were losin it mayhap. Not enough water, runnin ahead of the breeze she was. Had been gettin slack, leanin on the ship too much. She'd been on shanks pony most her life but now she were sailin she were slippin. Aint forgot her craft though. All day she'd been backtrackin through the gullies, draggin brush over her prints and stayin in the old water tracks. She wore boots trimmed with frayed rope, her tracks just marks in the dust that coulda been made by the wind. Near enough invisible she were, findin the riverbeds long dry an the hard ground. Learned that wun from the old scavs she had. Only cost her a finger an the nights in the cipher she werent gettin back. She looked down at the halfpinky on her left hand. Bothered her more than she let on. Theyd told her back when, water would always find the lowest ground and so should she. Stay off the ridges, watch your shape against the sun. Sumtime durin the day, she couldnt right remember when, she'd lost sight of the dusty shadow that tracked her from just inside the horizon. Not seein him at all, hours of loopin an backtrackin mighta been wasted. She'd know soon enough. Had been edgin her way towards the System and now it were only a day, maybe two from where she lay. In the cold just inside the boundaries she could tell herself for seconds here an there she was safe and there were no Reckoner on her trail. She thought of Block. If she made it to the walls she was gunna pay him a visit, owed him that at least. On top of all else he was her best buyer an the Wide Open Road meant sumthin to him as well. She was gunna need his help again if she was ever goin to get it back and even with all the blud tweenem it paid never to get on the wrong side of Block. The ground sumtimes wept the blud of those Block had sent down. She looked at her hands, even in the dark they had a shine, dint need any special eyes to see that. It hadta be no moren a few degrees but her palms were sweatin like she were down the Spirals. The foolin herself werent lastin. She shook herself, tryna fight the sleep an the long night comin.

4

Before

Block sat sharpenin his hook knife, watchin the backs of the fellas facin the sale. He stroked the pitted blade across the oilstone, feelin the burrs disappear, listenin to the edge come up. Without lookin down he grazed his thumb across the blade and then took a thimble of steel from his pocket. He rolled the blade over it, straightenin the sharpness, and then slipped blade, stone and metal back into a pocket of his dusty corduroy. There were a kid on the hammer today. A bony orphan dragged on a rope, knees like marbles. Dint often see other kids up for sale. His mind were wanderin. He spied the rich old fella that lived out near the wall. He were watchin the yungen on the block, an the bald prick that come an bid for him near evry other day. Plenny to spend the old rich fella did, plenny to lose, enough to spare a scrap or two for a hardup yungen Block reckoned. Sum metal gone to barter, then sum old gear, wire an such, an then Block watched the old fella bugger off back up the road. The kid got bought, no surprises there. Dragged off by the bald fella. He shivered in the heat. Next were a yung bloke. Blocks eyes flicked back and forth between the hammerman an them what was buyin. The fella were tall but weak lookin, skin a pale cast under the sun, hair like dirty copper. He dint seem to speak no tongue, come from the sand, a wanderer sumhow left out there he reckoned. Lucky to even be breathin. The trade on him picked up an then he were gone, weighed against clear wine, cloth an spars, hard tack. Scavver buildin a ship he reckoned an him cattle for wun of them cando fellas in the middle. Wouldnt wish that on nowun. The swap kept swingin back an forth, steel scraps for blud, glass for wire. Food an gold, trash an treasure up fer trade. More metal than regular, scavs musta found a vein out in the Glows an come to sum kinda parlay cos they was all bringin it in an dint look like no blud been spilled. Innerestin. Long while since a truce got held outside the boundaries. He'd heard tell it was gettin harder out there. Hadta go farther. Might be that he gotta head out an see for himself but not today he reckoned. Today he was gunna do his scavvin inside. He picked his mark while the sun were still low. There was enough trade goin on around the System, enough back ways, enough swapsie between block and pocket that nowun was ever gunna notice. Them fellas in the middle that was buildin up their wall was all worried about what was outside, dint look too close at the inside no more. They got it twisted he reckoned. Plenny to worry about on the inside. Block ran his finger along the string that ran into his pocket, all the way to the birds beak he'd just honed up. He was gunna eat tonight, nuthin more certain.

★

Block loped out tween two sheets of corrugated iron, wipin the blade on his cord, pale red on the inside of the hook blade. Sumtimes all they needed was yer voice an they was pissin all over themselves an handin over whatever you was askin. Yer money or yer life. Block licked his finger an ran it round the inside edge before droppin the blade back in his pocket. The sun were right overhead an even though they was just scraps he fancied he could feel the gold weighin him down. Couldnt figure why fellas was so fixed on it, ya couldnt eat it an it were too soft for knife makin, but moren more was takin it as guarantee on a trade. Whatever they reckoned. Let em try throwin it at him when he came at em blade up. See what comfort it gave em then. Dint matter, it were light an easy to lift. Suited him real fine. His walkin had took him back on the ring road, he'd hadta track the fella from the auction a fairways inside an he liked the feel of the sand on his right whenever he could get it. Three days back he'd pulled a coupla baby lizards outta dust and tangled grassroot, shards of egg still stickin to em. Cold-bluded an slow without the sun to liven em up an newborn, they was easy pickings. That were all he'd had an his gut knew it too. He trekked along the sand and patches of cracked white concrete, edges worn round by feet an the dust storms that rolled over without much warning. Sum of the littler cando men was startin their drum fires, and breakin out the racks of whatever coneys an bushmeat the trappers had brought in. Sum werent even pretendin, peeps just startin fresh on gettin out of it. There were a gaggle of nearblind leadin each other by rope. Fellas an lasses among em all had the dusteyes, weepin an swollen, nuthin much to be done for em an most folk left em alone. The wun what could still make out shapes was leadin the rest, followin their ears an noses towards the grills, beggin for scraps. Flies tracked em close, werent fussy about where they shat an ate an bled the blind werent. Sum of em looked like they was fresh outta the waste, fresh from out past the boundaries. Plenny of peeps still drifted in, there was walkers and runners out there still. The days of the monsters werent done, no matter what them big talkers in the Centre wanted fellas to believe. Block knew. Blockd seen. He wound the string around his finger, not concentratin on nuthin in particular, just watchin peeps dark an pale, all coated with dust an more dust. He looked down at his own wrists, tracked across with white scars. Standin stark against his skin where he'd worn the bracers. He werent sure what he looked like but he knew his hair were black an messy. He sheared himself with the hook blade on the reg, less for any wanderin hand to get a hold of. Daydreamin. Always got his head up in the sky. Moren half his trouble he reckoned. He stopped, feelin the gold again, looked around, seein a kid watchin him, its eyes milky an half gone an it werent five years old. Unlucky. He beckoned to it an it crossed the track, weavin between fellas that dint even see it, until it were standin in front of him.

Hungry?

Yeah.

Its voice was raspy, dust dry. A rattle in its chest like an old mans cough. Snot runnin free from its eyes an nose, trackin through the dirt an dust an runnin into its mouth.

Want sum grub?

It licked its cracked lips. *What do I gotta do?*

He smiled crooked at the kid. It understood. That were good.

★

The old drunk was wun of them that reckoned he remembered Winter. It werent true of course, couldnt be. The last Winter happened a long time before them what was born now and nowun could remember that far back. A long time ago the fellas who made the paper an roads mighta known what Winter was and who knew how far back that were? Now it were just the liars in the System. Sum of em mighta once known the trick of farseein and rememberin but nowadays they was just dusty old drunks what said anythin they could for a sip. Couldnt trust that. Not a word they said. Beggars and fools. Block knew most of them, had dodged through and stolen scraps from their tables an not got caught real often neither. He watched from behind a curtain of sacks, watched the kid stray a touch too close to wun of the drunks and the old mans withered claw reach out, snatchin at the scrap of drymeat he'd given the little wun. Block moved quick, steppin inside the leanto as the

23

old fella snatched at the wrigglin kid an then he was into his swag. Piss stained blankets, smell of rot, empty bottles, wrappers, faded pictures an finally what he'd come for. Honest paper, covered in words what he couldnt read. The kid dropped the roo an the old man claimed the leathery scrap an began to gum it down to nuthin. The kid legged it an Block slid outta the dark an back into the street. He met the kid on the next corner, givin him the rest of the food and sendin him on his way. In his pocket the old drunks treasure nested tight with the gold scraps, the leaves wrapped in a bundle. Block had the idea them things was important. He might only be a yungfella himself but if he made his self a thinkin man he was gunna run this place. He looked up an down at the hustle on the hook in front of him, seein it fresh. He was gunna get his due, no mistake. Sleep no more in the dust. Nuthin more certain.

5

She were almost there. Almost safe. Almost dead. Almost outta
water. Swingin the word almost in her head till it lost all worth.
Couldnt shake her thoughts of the wells. Drawin water out of the
ground never stopped seemin like magic. She knew she were close
to the System cos she could start to feel it in the ground under her
again. Her feet took wun shudderin step after another, meander-
ing, slippin on loose red dirt and gravel. A fly crawled into her
mouth an back out again. On the very edge of the horizon she
thought she could maybe see the top of the System. The land looked
near deadlevel on the way in but it were cut with dry riverbeds an
broken white concrete slabs an always took longer to cross than she
reckoned. Summa the older scavs called the run in the Bridge or
the Sighs if they was pissed but none of em could ever tell her why.
Sumhow the smell of people made it over the sand and she could
taste the familiar stink of the pits in the back of her throat. In the
stillness an heat she heard loose stones movin behind her and she
swung around, droppin to wun knee and draggin her bayonet out
of the sheath that hung from her waist. She kneeled in the dust for a
long time. Forced herself to take slow breaths and focus her driftin
vision on the heat haze and whirlies that rose outta the spinifex here

and there an from the edges of the old creek bed. Nuthin moved for a long time. She put the greased blade back and faced her nose at the System again, wishin for the thousandth time on her long walk that she had the Wide Open Road with her. Her fingertips hummed with the memory of catchin the breeze and blazin along the white roads laid down long ago. Instead she were marchin under a careless sun, away from the Spirals where her ship were buried.

*

She dint know when she'd fallen. She came awake at the bottom of a small gully, legs folded under her like she were a doll cut from its string. Her cheek was in the dust, little drifts caked against her lips, mask pulled down around her neck. She pulled her hand from under her body and reached up to touch her head, takin breath in fast when she found the lump. She dragged her head from the sand, liftin her gaze up where she thought the System oughta be, evry movement makin her gullet rise. Her eyes ached and she focused slow on a wall of dirt, knowin she was concussed, no use to herself. She were deep in the gully. It took a second to realise what she were lookin at, he were near the same colour as the shadow where he sat. A fella crouched no more than ten paces distant, face wrapped with a dark green dustmask under a wide brim slouch. His jacket she saw, it werent a cloak, hung past his hips and covered sandcoloured trousers and worn boots with sum kinda fur or fabric on the bottom. Trailin from his wrist were ropes of hide, made into a sling and his other fingers flowed a stone through over an over as he looked at her. Her eyes werent playin fair but what she could make of his gaze were open. Looked at her with no anger or any kinda feelin at all. Probably the same way she looked at game she reckoned. Not cravin its death, just needin to eat. He unfolded his self from his crouch like the wind had picked him up and came closer. She dug the heels of her hands into the ground an tried to lift her chest but the knock to her skull werent lettin any sudden movements pass easy. The

26

heat, the sand and the stranger blurred together, a pattern of light and pain that nearly made her blackout again. She felt like chuckin but there werent nuthin there. She retched, croakin like sum baby bird. A strange flush of shame. She saw that his boots made almost no tracks in the sand as he came closer. They was near enough like her own. Tracker boots, scav boots. She laid on her stomach, chin up as he came to her, breath pantin out of her now. He crouched in front of her, throwin a shade over her eyes an reached his hand out, takin her chin gentle under two fingers. She took in a sharp breath at the pain and the expectin of the blade across her throat but he dint reach for nuthin. All she could see was the sling wrapped around his wrist. His jacket stayed closed. The fear come up strong when she looked in his pale eyes above the mask, near colourless. Werent colour in him at all, he were bleached ribs an bones, but he were still walkin, still on his feet. A ramblin man. Her heart hammered through her coat but her limbs werent cooperatin and it were all she could do to brush the top of the bayonet hilt and imagine drawin it. His hands werent careless. Her head was set down and the soft touch of the sand echoed through her skull, a wave of sick comin up from her gut. When she opened her eyes again she saw a plastic bottle and felt his hand pushin her onto her side and the mouth of it put against hers. For a moment she thought of fightin but she smelled water and allowed herself to be fed a few drips. It had to be safe, it had to be. He could have killed her ten times over and there werent no need to waste water or poison on her. His hands were on her again, pushin her up so she were sittin position and then draggin her from the back of her coat into the shade of an overhang in the riverbed. She kept her eyes shut tight an it made it better sumhow. He leaned her back against the eroded hollow and crouched down in front of her, his hand on her chin again, tiltin her head this way and that. She blinked. He'd opened her satch an was goin through it, pickin out the shells an turnin em over. They was near enough the most perfect she'd found, still

had a light coat of grease on em. Bout all she had to show for
her trip down the hole. He put them carefully back in her bag an
looked close at her. She could feel his eyes rovin over her face and
against her will her eyes cracked open again, flinchin from the
light, the headache beginnin to throb so painfully that for a second
she thought he had poisoned her after all. She squinted through
her lashes, tryin to see what was happenin without lettin too much
light in. The fella took out the bottle again and topped it up a little
from another stashed in his jacket before puttin it in the shade next
to her. From another pocket he took a pair of field glasses all in
wun piece, scarred and weathered but clear in the lenses, and put
them on. He looked at her again but this time she couldnt see his
eyes. Then he stood and was gone from her sight, up and over the
lip of the dry creek bed, feet findin purchase on old roots, and then
she were left alone on the floor of the wadi, only the bottle and her
battered head tellin her it hadnt been sum kinda feverdream.

★

That night she made the gates. The Watch so careless she was on
them before they saw her, and her knocked about and stumblin
in the dusk like a drunk. She couldnt look offcentre, any glance to
the side made her bile rise and her head ring like a struck bell. The
outerman were young, scraps of beard on his face and his pike too
big for him. Always put the yungens on the outer.

Hold!

Shoutin out as he saw her too late. Panic turned to smirk when
he saw she were human enough, alone, an a girl as well. He put
his pike at portarms, werent no more than a pace from the walls
an fellas probably had him covered by now. Blades an slings up,
pretendin to earn their keep. She couldnt look to see. Far as he was
gunna figger she werent nuthin more than a scav comin in from
the wastes an a little worse for wear.

Open the gates. She was holdin her stomach down with evry word.
State yer name.

Nun of yer business.

You got a ship dontcha?

Yeah.

What you doin out there in the Glows?

Wasnt in the Glows.

Yeah you was. Wheres yer ship? What ya got onya?

Still out there. An nuthin for ya.

He sucked his teeth at that, whistled his disapproval.

Toll.

Speak on it with the Block.

She saw him straighten up a bit at that. Could smell the rank smoke comin from the inside. Rubbish turnin to ash. Animal to meat. Same place for evrythin an evrywun.

Gotta pay the toll.

Mutterin to himself now.

Let me through an a ladll come by an fix it up later.

Yeah thatd be right.

But he was done arguin an so was she.

Open up.

Spose I will. This time.

He slouched to the drum an knocked a pattern, each wun makin her flinch. She heard the bolts and wood gettin drawn back an the small gate set inta the big wun swung open. She squeezed past the outerman, waitin a moment as the next blokes sized her up an opened the inside wall. They was older than the kid outside, an looked sharper. Coupla fellas strapped with parangs an hide. There was plenny of swagger but it werent much and she knew it. Plenny of things out there past the boundaries thatd walk through that wall no troubles an that werent even speakin on the Glows. The little wall kept em safe, if only in their heads. She'd been over and under and through it herself but not with her head in this state and not wantin to get a length of trackiron spear put through her lungs.

★

29

She cleared the second door an put her heels on packed System sand an she were inside. Waited till they was gone an then put her back against the wall real gentle an let it take her weight for a second, makin sure nowun could see the shake in her knees. In her coat was a bottle she hadnt left with an on the back of her head were a lump she dint put there herself. These were things she knew. Precious else to show for a long trip out and an even longer wun back. Come back a lot poorer than she went out. Might be she dint want to go see Block just yet, dint have much for him but a scare story and she werent sure she wanted to be tellin it. The lamps were all gettin lit an the smell of animal fat an oil wafted from the stalls an shacks of the outer circle, light gutterin as a chill breeze came across on the dirt an iron roofs. Moths an bugs was swirlin around the big fires burnin on the wall but she knew the blaze was for show. Werent actually any fellas tendin them, it were just another way of makin it seem safe. From where she stood she were near-exact between the Centre, Blocks place and the Old Mans digs. Course, he werent there now but the big steel boxes still was, them rooms was gunna outlive em all. Sumwun else standin on the same spot she got lashed. Strange fucken days. Dint matter though, she werent goin anywhere near that place, Blocks or the Centre. A few things to work out before that. Block were canny anyhows, she dint need to be announcin herself. His eyes was all over the place, prolly already knew she were back an travellin too light.

Even the glow from the lamps made the corner of her eyes ache. What she needed was a liedown and to get a billy on. What she needed was her own place, needed to head into the Stacks. She walked slow along the dusty street on the inside of the first circle. They was all circles, just wun, two, three, four and soon until you got to the middle and the inner split with the big cuts, the wider tracks that ran across the tarmac cross an tower that skewered the whole joint. The whole place wun big crushed circle. Gates, soaks an wells, a kay across maybe, an more an more an more people

30

evrytime she came back inside. Evrywun sick. Evrywun always sick. Hardly saw any old folk no more. More an more was catchin sum kinda strange rot. Hair fallin out an teeth fallin outta rotten gums, just droppin in the sand. Stragglers from outside, comin in from other places she sposed. Boundaries werent what they was. Peeps dint often make much sense after theyd been outside for too long. Talked up all kinda beasts an whatnot. Scavs came back with plenny of stories about the Ghosts an the fella what walked with them, that bludy Reckoner. She touched the tender skin under the hair on the back of her head. Then there was the yungens, plenny more around than when she were a littlun but they was all weak. Plenny only fit for the Stacks she reckoned. Hard to believe but sum folks was puttin down roots. She werent sure about that, werent sure if roots was gunna hold in dust. She shrugged her coat higher up around her an took out her beanie, carefully slippin it onto her head an over her lump, tradin pain against the chill. Her bayonet an satch sat close to hand an most folks moved aside as she walked around the hook. She was goin a little out of her way to avoid havin to cross the Centre, was gunna have to zigzag a bit, but her eyes was strugglin and the light was that much worse where Karra an them cando peeps lived in the middle. Furthest from the walls, close to the deep well. Couldnt blame em, it were a good spot for most.

She made her way along, slippin the eyes of the hungry and the candos alike, fellas sparkin sumthin in the firelight, a hammer here and there and evrywhere scattered was shit and garbage, things waitin to get made into sumthin else. She reckoned her headache was gettin worse. Not many yungens on the cuts tonight, couple lads throwin lazy ciphers round the circle. She'd been out that game a while an sum. Their rhymes reached her ears an she stopped herself from listenin too hard, were an old habit an hard to kick.

★

By the time she'd crossed the System she were stumblin. The Stacksd climbed up an up an up above the ramshackle huts an scrap shacks made outta wire and drums an leavins from the scav piles, now they was loomin over her black like the great burned trees she'd run across now and then. The Stacks ran right up to the town an then spilled back into their own, the old water tower at the middle holdin it up or were it the other way around. As she got closer the light of the hooks an cuts at her back faded an by the time she stood facin the broken wall of tyres an could see the alleys an entrances disappearin into em it were like she was facin the deep dark all over again. Werent many fellas around but a lanky girl an boy stood backs to the stack, watchin her wary as snakes as she came up. The girl called out, uncoilin from her slouch, hands dug deep in the pockets of her too big overalls. *You lost?*

The Orphan looked up at her, headache needlin in behind her left eye now. The boy lazily reached up an arm an laid it on the shoulder of the girl whod called to her. He let her hang for a while, lookin her up an down before vouchin her. *Shes alright. Been here a while, aintcha.*

A nod were all the Orphan could muster. The girl spat on the ground and slumped back against the curved wall. She passed them into the Stacks, eaten by the dark, lit here an there by glowin paint splashed on the rubber walls an old fireless lanterns. It were easier to let her hands find the way in here than her eyes, trailin along the cracked an crazed walls, sum of them made from tyres three or four metres round an stacked high together, leanin together an closin off the sky at the top. They was caulked with rag an dust an bone an she always forgot how quick the cold dropped on her once she were inside. The narrow path she walked widened out, openin into a wider road an she half felt, half saw others passin her in the gloom. Eyes down, the way of the Stacks. Warrens an burrows on all sides an the scuttlin an calls of creatures she couldnt see. She pushed on further, stayin left, her coat brushin up against others an even with the headache her eyes started workin good and then workin too much. She kept em down anyways, the path openin again into a cavern that here an there showed sky past the towerin blackness. There was more lanterns, sum with flame sittin far from the walls. It were sumthin them livin out in the light couldnt even imagine she reckoned. This were the Stacks market, folk still needed to trade an sleep an eat, even in here. She saw more cornerboys leanin against the walls, cuppin smoke careful in their hands, just canvassin, eyes like glass. They dint even look at her. This were where she were proper unseen, this were her peeps. She walked quick as she could through the market, the smell of old rubber an heat crawlin and curlin inside her, easin her head. Dark doin wonders for her. Down another side alley, draggin her fingers against rubber that time an heat had turned to stone. Rubbish collected like sand drifts against the walls an small creatures scavved in the heaps. She pushed through the gaps, headin deeper, finally reachin the junction she was lookin for. She ran her hand down a stack that sat close, hardenin her hand an pushin it into a nearinvisible cut in the rings of rubber. She wormed her hand in an then pushed her shoulder against it, usin her arm to lever it open an scrapin through the brittle rubber and into the inner rim. Flakes rained down on her head as she felt her way in the total darkness. She walked clockwise a few paces and then felt for another cut in the rubber, peelin back a door, pushin though into more dark, hearin her breathin and then crouchin so she could reach an old casing lighter. She flicked it, castin a shallow glow inside the tyre stack, circles risin up into the darkness above her. She lit a tallow lamp, this were home. A bedroll an a metal box. Old paper an books she'd cadged or kept. Bottles of clean water an a sharpening stone. Her spare billy an a plastic bag of tea. She unhitched her bayonet an stuck it sheath down into the ground. Then she sat in the dust an took off her boots an footwraps, real slow, the stink of her fillin up the small space. She went through her satch, takin evrythin out, shells and the bottle she hadnt left with last, an put it all in the footlocker. She unrolled the swag an lay down, movin the blade

33

justso, close enough. Boots in reach. Too knackered even for a brew. She blew out the lamp, an pulled her coat round herself. She always forgot how cold it got deep in the Stacks, special when ya stopped movin. The heat in the day out past the fences, out past the long boundaries, it always made a kid of her. Were like she couldnt hold onto the feelin of bein real cold out there, no matter what the nights were doin. She rolled her head careful, avoidin the ache an the bump. She were gunna rest, just a little.

The dream come on her quick. She were little again, sittin in the shade of the leanto with Jon while her mum was makin a stew of leaves an yams an game. It were the middle of the day an Mum was singin real soft as she sat by the fire, stirrin it evry now an then but more often sendin her gaze far out into the flats, watchin the horizon.

She still looks for him. Jon whisperin to her as they played crosses in the dust.

Who?

Dad.

Dont remember.

Sumtimes I do. I can kinda remember his face. She tells me about him sumtime.

She took the game. Jon smiled at her.

Gettin better at this. Gunna be clever.

She remembered the feel of him warm an close like a pain. Him an her ma fillin her vision with all them dear things. Stew an crosses an dust an nuthin to tax em in the shadowless midday. Stirrin an stirrin, just dinner to look forwards to. She woke herself lyin on her bedroll in the cold stack, deep dark still an she could near smell the smoke of the cookin fire. She lay awhile eyes open, not tryna think on nuthin, just takin the measure of her thoughts, grateful when sleep took her again.

6

Shes back.

Block nodded. He'd thought so, felt sumthin on the wind.

She dint have no ship or nuthin.

Now that was interestin. It wouldnt have been easy partin her from the Wide Open Road. There werent many like that ship and even less in the hands of scavs and orphans. He leaned to the side of his desk and spat on the dirt floor as he thought the word. Old superstitions. Orphans was bad luck back in the day. How many knew that now? Orphans evrywhere.

She gone to the Stacks?

Yeah boss. Went in a little while ago.

Block sucked his teeth. His name carried sum weight there but he still dint send anywun in without a real good reason. Too many dint come back and nowun was ever talkin in the Stacks. He looked at the yungen in front of him, waitin patiently.

Done good. Go on then.

He looked past the vanishin kid at Cutter, who leaned against the door frame.

You want me to go get her?

Say what you liked about Cutter but he werent afraid of much.

Nah. Give that littlun sumthin to eat. Ya done good bringin him in, he's gunna make good eyes an good hands. Sharp tacker.

Cutter hacked a cough into his hand, the skin on his neck tight an strained.

Yer a fucken soft touch these days. Hadta work years for ya before ya threw me a crust.

Block half smiled, lookin at him close. *Feelin alright mate?*

Good enough.

Watch yerself, moren more gettin the waste. Hair an teeth droppin. Seen the Watch draggin em out to the pits.

I know it. Smell em cookin all night.

How many scavs we got on the sand right now?

Cutter thought a moment. *Four. Five if ya count the Orphan?*

I do.

Five then. Two on canvas, three on shanks.

What about the bald fella?

Last I heard he had ten out, five on the breeze an five on shanks. Hes sendin out moren more.

Theyre gettin hungrier. Five on the breeze huh, theyre buildin sum ships, moren they used to. Reckon the Orphan ran into sum of em out past the Boundaries?

If she did they aint comin back.

Block nodded. *Keep yer wits mate, keep countin em in an countin em back. Make sure our fellas is comin in an if they dont, that we know why. Unnerstand?*

Yeah boss.

Block smiled. *Good, well piss off then, an get that yungen sum food.*

Cutter heaved himself off the frame an followed the yungen out the door. Block looked up from his papers an watched his retreatin back. Was gunna have to keep an eye on Cutter. Plenny was gettin sick an not many was comin good. He werent gunna send him in after the Orphan neither. Fetchin her from the Stacks were his own job. He stared back at his papers again for a while, not seein the words. She'd come.

7

Before

A foot in the ribs woke her. Karra dint look back, knew she would be up and followin him if she wanted sumthin to drink. Water. It were all she'd thought about for months. From sun up each bakin day to the moment she drifted uneasy into sleep she dreamed of cool water. Now and then she could see the smell of it on the breeze and taste the sound of it in the back of her throat. Memories not her own comin to her on the Westerly. She followed him to the front room of the box, sectioned off by blankets draped over braided jute strung back and forth between walls. Day before she'd carried bucket after bucket of water back from the nearest soak. Ground the red saltbush fruit down to paste an then jarred it up. Cleaned the awnin an swept the rooms she were allowed in. Karra gave her a few mouthfuls in an old can and then set the topper back on the jug. It were cool an clear an tasted like soil an rust. She tried to savour it but her body got the best of her an she drank it down fast, cravin more. Karra stood a while, starin out the window to the yard, watchin the heat haze rise off the tin roof of the leanto. She waited for him to decide what she were gunna be doing. Finally he turned an signed to her.

Inside today. Put the marbles into tens for me an dont muck it up.

She let her breath out slow. It were wun of her favourites, most of all cause it kept her outta the sun. It were easy work, movin the red desert stones into bundles of ten and then groupin them in ten by ten squares. Dint matter that at the end of it she'd pour em all back into the bucket an start again. She dint muck it up much an it meant he were too busy to come up with anythin nasty for her to do. She knew her numbers well enough thanks to Jon and the work took only a little focus. It pleased him that she could count and he'd hinted that if she did it good and kept her nose clean he would let her count sumthin more and make up weights of powders on the slidin scale. She sat herself down at the table fashioned out of old heavy wood that Karra called sleepers. It were pitted with bolt holes and knots and she reckoned itd led a hard life. Out the window sumthin about the pitiless glare reflectin off the scrap and rubbish scared her and made her think about the destroyed shack out on the edge of the Glows. She werent even sure she could find her way there, even if she was free and healthy and she werent neither no more. No way to find where the Ghosts had cast aside the remains of her brother and mother and left their bones to bleach in the dust and heat. She couldnt feel much right now as she sat in the gloom countin but she knew there was a weight down deep in her, sum eyeless thing that twisted and lurked in the night and tried to wriggle its way up her gullet and out into the world. She was dreaming, dreamin in the day so deep that she dint notice the boss standin behind her, the only sound the dull clack as she counted the countless pebbles into groups of ten and slid them scratchin into bundles across the wood, careful not to lose none of em in the table.

You can count.

The boss's voice soft an low behind her. She dint reckon he'd ever said a word to her. She looked up at Karra sittin in front of her, his hooded eyes givin her nuthin. His fingers spoke.

Answer him.

Yes boss.

And speak?

Yes boss. I can speak, an count real good.

There were a soft laugh from sumwhere behind her. She had the sense he were movin around, talkin half to Karra an half to himself. His voice had a burr to it, like he had dust in his throat.

Yeah, you can count. What about your letters?

She shook her head. Why would she need her letters? Never did nowun no good, better to know where the water was, or where the game hid in the middle of the day. Jon woulda said different, he was tryna learn his letters. She stopped the thought from goin any further.

No, boss. No letters.

There was a long silence. She thought he might have left the room, it were so quiet. Finally he crossed into her view an spoke. *When you finish with her tomorrow, send her up to me.*

Karra scribin at the desk in the corner of the room gave nuthin away. Just signed his obedience, looked blankly at her and went back to his ledger. The boss nodded to himself and disappeared into the inner rooms where nowun followed. She watched him go and then looked again at Karra, unsure. He looked back at her again with a flat stare, black eyes in his duststreaked face. He pointed towards her stones. She counted.

★

The evenin chores took time. She emptied the bosses shit bucket into the small burn pit, swept the inside of the metal rooms and then swept dust into more dust in the yard. She beat out the sackcloth beds and then stripped naked and beat the dust out of her own clothes. Karra went into the Centre on sum bidding. Travellers an scavs had come and gone durin the day, sum on sand sleds, travellin with guards an cando men, others comin in solo from the waste, stayin a short time but headin back out heavy with trade, leavin papers, satchels an things from the old world with the boss. Sum of em talked about ciphers, plenny talked about the Centre, there were words flyin all over, landin around her, an she prolly only grabbed a couple down an understood what they meant. Today was the first time the boss noticed her she reckoned and definitely the first time he'd spoken to her. Still had a tongue but he spoke the hands like he was born to it. Sum of the fellas comin in that spoke only the hands, she knew they was sumthin to do with the ciphers or mebbe they was born silent. Was that what happened to Karra she wondered or maybe he was wun of them born with sumthin missin or sumthin extra like her mum used to talk about. They was rare. Kids was rare, but those what were born seldom came without sum extra blessin or curse. How did anythin get born out here? And who was them that did the ciphers? She thought of Karras blank gaze whenever she signed him sumthin he dint wanna talk about. He could do a thing with his hands to make em closed like a weathered rock, like sum wadi swept clean of evry scrap. Like just nuthin. Dreamin in the day again. She dint hear him behind her, only felt sumthin hit her hard on the back of her head and heard the ringin in her ears as she sprawled flat and naked in the dirt. She turned over and saw Karras shape standin over her. His hands was fierce and deadly.

You dont get nuthin for nuthin. Standin there starin inta space and shit to be done. Get yer threads back on an get back to sweepin.

He spat on the ground with a hack. *You got things to do. So do em.* She crawled to her feet. *Yes boss.*

He spat again and signed in short angry stabs. *Yes boss is right. You dont work and your throats cut and yer fed to the dogs. Unnerstand?* She nodded.

Get to it.

8

Block were patient. He thought that mighta been how he got his name but truthtold he tried not to remember. Still, his patience was wearin a little. A day and a half and no visit. The Orphan, he spat, the Orphan counted herself a friend. A friend? He dint know. They was closer than that. She werent a friend. She wasnt, he corrected his thought, she wasnt like any of the admen or the cando men that spouted shit into the air and made promises worth less than their lives. He'd seen her brought off the sand an bought for scraps. No visit though, and her missin her ship and dust knew what else. He sat in the gloom of his work room, at the back of the long tin shed that were once a tool store an now were stacked with bodies yung an old, sleepin at all angles. Workshops where they fit. The tarp that covered parts of the rustin roof strained against an early mornin gust and ropes dragged over the corrugated metal, thumpin in the ruts like the dull fingers of sum giant beast.

He looked at the sleepers that crowded his floor, the little wuns that worked for him and the even littler wuns he fed that were wun day gunna do the same. He were gunna be patient, had learned the word careful. Werent gunna just make a move and hope for the best. You made wun and you already knew what the next ten was evrywun else was gunna make. That was how you kept food in all them mouths. That was how you made a little space in the System. He looked out past the bodies lyin across each other on pallets and hessian and through to where figures darkened his door. He peered into the glare. Werent her. Just Cutter an Gus settin a mornin watch. He stood, bones crackin, an reached up to unhook the cloth that covered the hole in the roof. Sunlight streamed in, lightin up his desk, catchin the dust floatin in the air. He would wait. He was good at that.

9

She was dreamin fit to die. Hadnt dreamed this much in her life. She were back bein hunted across the sand but it werent just the Reckoner after her. Them hulkin eyeless things that stalked the deep Glows had come up to the surface an they was followed by mylings an maras, limbed like scorpions an with bludy maws like the Old Man used to tell her about. Trapped on the wrong side of the Sighs an werent never goin home. She came awake clutchin for her blade, thinkin she were back down wun of the deep holes, leftovers of dead scavs hung from the ceilin by the Reckoner by way of blud warning. Seen plenny of things she wished she hadnt. She looked around an she were in the Stacks, her things still scattered around her where she'd put em. Boots akimbo, bayonet stuck in the ground. She sucked down breath an wiped the sweat off her face with her wrap. Fever an hunger was eatin her but her head still rang. The day before she'd managed a bit of water and sum tack she'd had in her locker but then she'd sicked sum of it back up in the corner. She'd been weak, the ache still fierce but she was steadier now, her eyes was sortin themselves out. Hadnt pissed yet an that was always a worry. Thin grey beams filtered in through cracks in the top of the Stacks but she dint need it to see.

The rounded walls of her place kept out the noise of passin folk an most of the heat. She figgered it for early mornin, she were close to cold an welcomed it. Starin straight up she felt like she were at the bottom of a tiny spiral. She used to climb the walls of her stack near evry day an look out from her own private eyrie but the urge dint come often anymore. She were more worried about what were goin on down below of late.

*

She licked her dry lips, coughed an tasted dust. Today she would go see Block, he was gunna be pissed that she hadnt showed yesterday but all day it was all she could do to not remember the Reckoner lookin into her eyes and her waitin for the blade across her windpipe that never come. More than passin strange. She looked across the round room at the water bottle. It was real, he'd left it with her. She had seen sumthin out there but she dint know what. She'd fled the Glows with Ghosts followin, she only hoped the Open Road was hidden well enough. The ship were her life. She'd covered her tracks real good, covered em the way she'd been taught and between Block, the boss an the old scavs there werent no better teachers. She was weak though, and the Spiral a long way. She was gunna have to ask sum favours and they was from people she already owed a few. Still, she needed to get back out there and get the ship, without it she wasnt gunna cover no ground and no hope she'd find her way back to them locked doors deep underground. No proper scavvin an no way to keep at the old fellas task neither. Today was the day, she was gettin up. Either Blockd help or she was gunna have to cipher to get what she wanted, she could feel it, taste the iron in her mouth. They werent takin no soft wagers either, that wasnt how they did these days. She looked at the little stump on her hand. She werent no kid no more and they made sure she knew it.

44

10

Before

They travelled half a day out the System before the boss sat down. Dint talk on the walk but to point out the hills an animal tracks when they crossed their path. She int been outside in a long time an the space an the quiet of it soothed her though she'd never realised she were missin it. The clean air an all the rest. Sent her thinkin down ways she dint wanna go but she let her eyes stretch out to the horizon an just watched the mobs of roos in the distance an the scatter of scrub. For an old fella he covered ground good an by the time they made a day camp an the Orphan got the billy on she were feelin the walk. They sat a good long time sippin the brew fore the Old Man spoke an he dint take his wrap off an it were like he'd been waitin a long time for sumwun to talk to but that dint make no sense to her. Talked to fellas all day long but his voice wavered like he were startin a story he dint quite know the beginnin of.

How long you been with me now?

I dunno boss. Long time?

You can drop the boss out here. Must be a coupla years at least. Hard keepin track of it all now. You know why I brought you out here?

She held her tin tight, feelin the heat through the thin metal.
Me letters?

Part that. But more else. Got a job for ya. Bigger than a job, more a reason, unnerstand?

No.

Good girl. Truthll set ya free. You know why we are where we are?
Here?

The System, why it is where it is?
I dunno.

The plain answer is water. But I reckon you woulda figgered that on yer own. Around here theres moren enough deepdown water, clean they reckon, for us an for the others. Further out though, its dry for more miles than youll live to travel. Dint use to be that way. Used to be more like you, comin in from off the flats, but the water dried up or went bad an not so many any more. Those that went out lookin further dint come back. Nah the reason we're here is fellas came here runnin an found water. Moren they could keep a hold of, soaks an rockholes for all. Not only that they found leavebehinds of them that came before. The roadmakers, the builders, the diggers. There was stuff out here, out on the plains, buried out in them Glows an plenny of other places. It were here an ready for this to grow up, for them fearful fools to build their fence an call it a System. Ya need to ken that good. The knowin of evrythin is the histery of that thing. You wanna be a healer, you learn the histery of healin, unnerstand? That water an that stuff from the longago, thats why we're here.

11

Before

I dunno what hes up to, but I aint expectin to see you again.

He was silent as ever but if it were possible his hands was cacklin. The Watch stood silent behind him, eyes facin the sand, lookin like they was doin their job for once. Makin it look good for the show. She dint tell Karra it were her idea. That itd come to her in her sleep an hadnt left her mind till she voiced it quiet an scared to the boss. Said he'd been expectin it and asked did she wanna go see where she come from. She dint know where that was. Nuthin out there no more anyway, woulda been stripped soon as she were gone, werent even a dip in the ground no more she reckoned. Nah, she'd got the walkin in her bones though, in her feet themselves. The boss knew, she wanted to know where she were in the world and to do it alone. An here she were, outside the walls. She had a swag, sum water, a blade. Figgered on two nights outside, maybe longer dependin on what she ran into. Was supposed be in sight of the walls the whole time but that dint mean much with the type of jokers that was watchin it. Outside the circle you was outside the safety. Werent much that came close or this far inside the Boundaries but it were still the wild.

Before ya go, anythin you wanna tell me? Where you an the boss been goin? Whatcher doin outside? Might not get another chance to come clean. Gunna be a cold night.

He were near smilin. She aint never seen him look close.

Boss just teachin me the letters. Makin tea.

Karras face closed up. *Fuck ya then ya dont wanna talk. You make it back youll be singin, mark me.*

Im speakin truth. Just me letters.

Karra dint see her hands, were half turned, waitin for her to go. She dipped her head at him an then turned her back on the System, lookin East across the great flats and seein the haze of the hills on the horizon. She reckoned that might be the direction she'd been brought in from, but the trip across the sand long ago was gettin dim, like her memory of her mum an brother, faded with time an heat. She thought she mighta been in the System a long time but the Old Man seemed to have lost track. She were taller, she knew that much. Karra dint need to stoop to slap her no more. She looked back at the wall, the Watch were holdin up the small gate an Karra turned, his eyes meetin hers an then he was gone. He looked older, that were certain. Sposed she must too. The wall were higher, it were gettin bigger near evry day it seemed. The scrape of metal on metal as they slid the bolts in place an the heavy thump of the sleepers barrin it from the inside. She only noticed now she were locked out that the shadow of the wall were cast long on the sand. From the outside it looked higher an even though she could see easily into the towers she werent sure they could see her too well. The sky above was grey streaked with white, high up, catchin the late sun, an the temperature was fallin. She moved her swag so it sat high on her back an started trekkin away from the wall, the sounds of the System fadin quick. Half a mile out onto the sand and she knew she were already twice as far as she meant to go but her feet just kept carryin her an she knew if she dint stop em she'd never turn around. What was stoppin her? Nuthin much she sposed. She wanted to walk the circle though, that were why she were out here. Maybe after that she'd just keep walkin.

Her courage left her when it started to get real dark. She crept back towards the wall, yard by yard until she could see the watchfires a couple of hundred spans distant. The noise of the place dint reach her though an that were the strangest of all. The shouts an whistles an cries of folk were just gone an there werent nuthin out on the sand makin any kinda noise at all. Her own footsteps had been loud in her ears as she started workin her way round the edge. Here an there were little piles of bones an drifts of rubbish. Sum peeps just threw their shit straight up an over an the wind took it where it pleased. The wall was battered in places, like things had crashed into the big sheets of iron, but as far as she could see it were whole. Sleepers stuck up here an there where they was buildin new towers and the watch-fires burned like specks above the wire and glass that dotted the top. The wall were covered in tags too, scavs an passersby scratchin their names into it along with strange drawings. Tall creatures with big round faces, snakes an things thatd come outta the dark of sum histery. Big patches were covered in pitch. Protection against rust, or fillin in holes. She knew the Watch walked bits of it on the daily, checkin up. Her eyes were good in the low light, took her a while to realise since it werent never true dark in the System. She could see the sand near as clear as though it were bright moonlight though there werent moren a sliver hangin in the sky. She knew enough to know it werent like that for Karra an the boss. The Watch neither by the look of it. She sat herself down on the cold sand and rolled out her swag, stickin the knife the boss had given her tip down in the soft ground. Her stomach had settled down an she pulled her coat around her tighter, wonderin just what she were doin out there.

★

The howlin woke her in the cold hours before dawn. She reached for the knife, fumblin, knockin it over and then scrabblin out of her coat for it, layin chin to the sand like a snake on top of her bedroll. The noises were deep, almost a moan, an the hairs on her arms stood on end an in a blink her palms were slicked with sweat. They werent dingoes, or roos fightin or beasts in rut or anythin she'd heard before. They sounded fulla pain, like sumthin was wounded, an as she lay there listenin she caught her breath an took stock. At least a few kays from the door an noway anywun was openin it in a hurry, even if she got there. She looked across to her left at the wall. She'd bedded down in between watchfires anyway. She were worse than alone, she were alone an stupid. She closed her eyes a long moment an then opened them again, the remains of starlight seemin to soak in an then it were like day for her, the wall comin clear. She sniffed the air, catchin a drift of sumthin rank, sumthin dead or rotten an then came another of them awful moans, closer than before. She'd slept with her coat done up an left her canvas moccasins on, a small blessin at least. She switched the fightin knife to her left hand, tuckin coat into strides an started to snake across the sand on her belly, eyes swingin wun way an the other. Left to the wall an then right an round, sweepin out to the endless desert an then back in close.

12

Block looked at her. Finally here she were. Vexed an gritty. Her eyes, usually dark, were rimmed with ashy circles an she hadnt cleaned the charcoal proper off her teeth from when she'd been underground. The rest of her face was streaked with the grease-paint she wore in the dark an she looked like sumthin sumwun had dug up. He couldnt help the shiver across his shoulders. Skinny too, skinnier than usual. Still, she'd come off days on the sand an she were never proper with it when she come back to the light. Took her a while to get her head straight after the Glows. Had the stink of the Boundaries on her, the taint of the deep dark. His boys din wanna stand too close to her an he couldnt right blame them.

Orphan.

Block.

He flicked his head, tellin his lads to leave em alone an when theyd dropped the curtain to his back room he motioned for her to sit down on the locker in front of his desk. She sat with a sway and let her breath out and he saw she were hurt in sum way, but not bad.

Wheres yer ship?

Yeah good to see ya too.

She reached into her satchel an took out four shiny brass talls. .303 by the looks of em. He whistled low an held out his cupped hands and she carefully dropped them in wun by wun.

Were they dry?

As dust. Theyre good.

Nuthin else?

No guns, an no more of them neither.

Never is. Books?

Nuthin.

Maps?

Nuthin.

He sat back in his chair, eyes still glued to the bullets, the lamplight makin em glow like gold.

Salright. Ya done good gettin these. Wun day yer gunna find me a gun, I know it. Thesell come in handy I reckon. You eaten?

Yeah, enough.

He opened a drawer in his desk and put the bullets carefully out of sight. She caught a glimpse of red wax and brass, shotgun shells maybe, sum blades, razor wire. Blocks stash. Smaller than evrywun reckoned but that dint matter. Better they thought he was stacked to the teeth. She dint know why he cared about em so much. Not many took em as trade moren curiosities. He looked up at her as he closed the drawer.

If ya don't mind I'll fix ya up later. Usual price, however ya want it. You gunna tell me what happened to the ship? And what you was doin out there?

I was scavvin, Im a scav. Thats what I do.

You went too far out dintcha. Nuthin out there but Ghosts. You run into em again?

Maybe. But havent I found sum good stuff down them holes? Plenny of it you took off my hands.

I never seen it.

Dunno why ya pay for it then.

Feel sorry for ya.

It were their old game an theyd played it plenny of times. Dint change the prices none.

What happened to yer head?

She reached up and touched the lump fore she could stop herself. Howd he even seen it. Eyes front, back and side of his bludy head. She still wasnt feelin right but evry second the Wide Open Road stayed out there was another chance for sumwun or sumthin to come across it. She may as well tell him, werent nowun gunna believe it anyway.

Reckoner.

Block snorted.

Yeah, best save them stories for the yungens. Im not worried if yer clumsy, no shame in it. Wheres the Open Road?

Alright. Shes down a Spiral. Out Arkoola way, deep Glows. Further than I ever been. Stowed safe but I gotta go get her, an quick.

She took a deep breath.

They followed me up, I was down deeper than I ever went before an thats where I found them bullets. Ghosts was swarmin over it though, it were a big Spiral, bigger than I ever seen before an it went deeper too. Started gettin warm down there an you know, well you know how I get. I was near to findin sumthin big, mebbe sumthin real big.

Blocks eyes were shinin an he were leanin over the desk, waitin for whatever it were.

Got rumbled though an hadta get bluesky quick. They dint see me proper until I was nearlight, they dint know how deep Id gone. I ditched em in the dark an got out but I hadta leave her behind, stowed her down there. Too many scavs out there now, can't leave her in the open no more. I can find her again though, no worries, just gotta get back out.

How ya gunna do that?

She looked at him, hope an fear fightin for space. *Figgered you might run out the Taipan, send wun of the lads with me. Seven, eight days on the sand at most, providin all goes well.*

53

Block shook his head. *Shes not in order. Needs repairs, a week to find what we need at least. Evrywun else is out on the sand, days out an not turnin around any time soon. Besides, whatta ya promisin me? What do ya reckons out there, what makes it worth me while?*

Ya got them talls I just gave ya for starters. There's sumthin big though. Dunno what but I was seein shapes, feelin the colours. The Ghosts was strange too, they was organised, they wasnt wild like they sumtimes is. If you cant help, then I gotta wager for it in the Circle. Gotta get back out there quick, before they find her.

Block sat back, his fingers steepled, chair creakin as he leaned. Now it was her turn to look at him, speculatin, wonderin where he were gunna fall. Finally he spoke.

Its a big ask. Theyre gunna bet big for a trip like that. I know a few lads might take ya though. Fresh faces, dont know no better. Whatta ya wagerin?

She held up her hands. Looked at the spot where her little finger used to be. *Skin or scav. Whatever theyll take. Whatever you'll give me.*

He looked across the desk at her a long time an she wondered just what he were thinkin. Eventually he let his breath out an stood up, his palms flat on the battered wood top. *Better come with ya then.*

13

Before

She were a fucken idiot. An what were the boss thinkin? Karra sat in the dark of the study, puzzlin on what was goin on. Just to send her walkin out like that. Spent all this time raisin her up, all that time in the back rooms teachin her, showin her the books. Their bluddy walks. His face soured. Feedin her, waterin her. An now she were gone, just like that. A smirk spread across his face. The boss never explained much an there were plenny of weird shit that went on but he'd just thrown his little Orphan to the dingoes. The wild dogs an dust knew what else out there was gunna tear her to pieces. He dint know why he gave a shit, had been wishin the like for a while hisself. Just dint make no sense though for the boss to send her. He'd thought the old fella was goin soft but maybe it were just soft in the head. He dint know but he dint like the look of it neither. Evry time the Orphan was in there with the Old Man he made her tell him what it was they was doin and she told him they was countin, they was tryna lern letters or else the boss was fillin her head with stories about the old times. Maybe the boss just wanted sumthin to raise up. Karra worked his butchered mouth and spat. Werent right. Made for a real strange look and peeps was always gunna chatter. He dipped the quill an started back on the ledger, the boss were gone into the Centre for sum trade, dint care to share it with Karra. He hawked up a reddish ball of phlegm, tinted by the everlovin dust, an spat it onto the floor.

14

Before

She smelled it again before she saw it. The stink of carrion, brought back all kindsa bad blud. She caught movement out on the edges of her vision next an she lay dead still against the ground, wishin it would eat her up. Whatever it were, it were sumthin outta the West. Sumthin outta the deadlands, the old huntin grounds that vanished fellas like sandstorms. It were so black it seemed to drink light from all around it an she knew that even if fellas had been watchin from the wall this thing woulda been invisible. It were only her strange eyes that were lettin her see it an she were still figgerin out just how they worked. It slouched this way an that, swingin a mouth or head she couldnt make out against the blunt shape of it. She could hear it now too, testin the wind. It were blowin the wrong way for her, the beast probly already had a good gust of her, an she werent goin nowhere. Her hands was slippy but she held tight onto the knife, pullin herself up silent onto wun knee as the thing got closer, swayin its head, searchin for a scent. Without warnin it lifted its head up high an she could see its jaw, the height of the thing, at least as high as she were at the shoulder, maybe more. It raised up even higher an let out another wun of them terrible moans an from sumwhere way behind her she heard an answer. There were a pair of em, whatever it were. The wun in front of her sniffed the air again an she knew it had her scent, might be it dint know exactly where she were though yet. She tightened her grip on the greasy knife again an got ready to move.

15

You done fucked up fella. You know the rules, you cant step inta the circle without spitten yerself and ya sure as shit cant save this wun if she fucks up.

Block idly wound the twine that led into his pocket around his finger and looked up at the lads in the circle. *I dint know there was no rules in this place and I got this funny idea that if there was, Id be the wun maken em.*

He looked over at the girl. Did she know what he was doin out here? What he was riskin bein out here himself? This was the kinda shit he left behind a long time ago and yet here he was, out here with the cutters in a circle full of cando men just waitin to solve all his problems for him. He hadta let her spit if she wanted to bargain and whatever the boys decided was the wager, well that was it. After that, he'd just see how things panned out. It werent the worst spot he'd found himself in but countin six boys around him and probably three serious if it came to it, it could end up pretty bad. Enough to spoil his good mood. Reputation was only gunna carry him so far. People passed in both directions round the hook but nowun was lookin too close at the little crowd. These things happened but nowun wanted to get too involved with the borrowers unless they really had to. The lads had shifted a bit at his last words but they was thinkin he was on the geeup. That it were all part of the hype, all part of the circle. Best to let em keep thinkin that he sposed. No harm yet. He hadnt seen the girl singsong in a while though and that was a worry. Rust came slow on the metal but quick on the tongue out here. It were all up in the air. It mighta been a while but it all felt real familiar to the Block, like comin along a track he'd walked a whole lotta times before. He settled in, restin back and waitin for the circle to start.

★

She looked at Block, leanin like he were ready to go to sleep. It were only her knowin him well enough that she saw how tight the string were wound on his finger. His eyes was nearly closed but she knew he werent missin a trick. The cando men, cando boys more like, he'd gathered was circled up, teeth bared like dogs. They was sniffin for a fight, lookin for her to drop a gaze, but she'd been in the circle plenny and before sum of thesed ever heard of it by the looks of their whole hands an clear faces.

Girl, girl, girl, you gunna get kilt in the circle.

The spiteful chant was startin but she cut into em quick not lettin em get their blud up.

By you fucken yungens? By you pups that aint dogs an never will be? Got sorrow for you fucken pups, got sighs an sand an morrows I aint never thought to see the sunup.

She spat on the ground at their feet. Saw a ghost of a smile on Blocks face. His eyes still mostly closed. The lads in front of her grinned even harder. Their first stepped right into her grill, his breath stank of smoke and empty stomach an she knew where he were from. Could see the colours in him, see the fears that choked him up when he werent frontin hard an even as he wrapped his mouth around a verse she could feel she had words he dint an that he knew it too. She spat fierce at him, cuttin him.

You see this, pup? Ash on my teeth, thats hunger. Nuthin in my belly, you nuthin but yungens, gunna feed on yer tongues, and dust take ya under. Heart? Wheres ya heart? I'll take yer heart. Eat yer heart. Come from out the deep dark. Weak pups aint never seen what I seen, piss on yerselves, ya ever been where I been. Come with, come out the Glows with me, fucken cowards you aint never seen the walls from the sand, aint seen heart, aint got heart, aint seen dark.

She spat on the ground again, an the eyes opposite was scatterin, she were talkin about the sand, places theyd never been. They could come hard about the System but there werent nuthin theyd seen in here thatd come close to all her years out there sleepin in hulks, walkin through dead towns an dodgin Ghosts an beasts from the Glows an out the West. Come to that she were out of the narrows, from the Stacks, the back alleys an tyres an these candos come up in the Centre of the System such as it were. She let herself smile an she werent lookin at Block no more, dint care if he were there or not. This were her circle an she were singin it, spittin it fierce. The smiles on the lads faces was long gone and she were all teeth like wun of them dustborn dogs that loped the Boundaries.

★

She hadnt lost it, an she were smart he'd give her that anyday. Werent many who could stare down six lads and speak on em in the circle until they called it. She'd gone words for words with em till it were done an they'd kept their blades in their pockets an their tongues in their mouths. She were cocky but she werent stupid. Now they found themselves owin her stead of the other way round. Funny how things could flip like that in the circle. He walked out of the hook an up the cut, trailin her, chit in her hand an a promise of a ride from the lads. They was true, he'd say that for them. A wager was a wager an if they dint stick to that theyd have him to worry about first an the rest of the cornerboys an scavs not long after. Dint never pay to welch in the System. He watched the Orphans back and then she turned an threw him half a smile over her shoulder, her boots kickin up red dust in the arvo sun.

16

Before

It were like it werent even a touch dark no more. Whatever was goin on with her eyes had sorted itself good an she could see clear as day, maybe better. She could pick out detail in the thing, saw the yellowed tuskbone arced up from its jaw, the bristles an dark blud-matted fur as it huffed the night air again. She could smell it again, the rankness. Had the stink of blind corpses on it, blud an bone of the fresh dead. That werent a bad thing she figgered. Things what had full bellies was always less likely to tangle. Its grim little eyes dint seem to see much but it had her scent an it came closer, tastin the air with its snout, an she slowly unfolded herself from the ground, keepin the knife held in front. The beast were taller than her at the shoulder now it were close, an she couldnt right pick out what it were, even up close. She reckoned she knew whatd made the dings in the System wall though. She felt sumthin behind her an felt warm breath on her hand, a warm wet nose. She stayed dead still an the thing in front of her stepped to her on cleft hoof, part razorback maybe, she werent even sure. The wun behind her swung into view, even bigger than the first, an she were eye to eye with em both, the smell of death an murder waftin off em like sumthin burning. Teeth of stained ivory an blud. They was outta the West, she were certain. These were them things they talked about in the circles, the reason nowun never went that direction, the reason the sun went down that way. Evry day these things an others like em swallowed up the light only to cough it back up the next mornin. They huffed their snouts over her an sum feelin came back into her arms, the blade still held out stiff. The smaller of em got more curious an she felt the nip of teeth on her hand. She jerked it back sharp.

No!

They both started an she saw the big wun lower its head, droppin them tusks right down to where her guts was gunna come spillin from. She forced herself to take a slow breath and said it clear again.

No. Yer not takin no bites outta me. Im from here an yer not killin me tonight. Yer gunna back up an keep goin where yer goin.

They seemed to listen, small ears flickin and the big wun raised its head back up a little, weighin her up in its ancient black eyes. She looked back at it, not lettin go, her hand fixin to squeeze her pissy little blade in half. Werent gunna be any good if they came at her, small mercy it were gunna be over quick. They seemed to take sum quiet communion, sumthin passed between em an they snuffed at her again, markin her in their strange animal minds an then they both picked up hoof an circled her slow. She turned gentle with them, followin them as they walked round her twice, nose to tail, watchin her close. She stayed stuck to ground an then they took off slow, castin glances back at her as they headed westward, down track an gully, between the bluegrey scrub an towards the hills that was standin out to her even in the black of the night. She watched em until they was just specks an let her breath out in a great shout. Her eyes filled with water an she dint know why. Her heart had seemed stopped an now it were smashin at her ribs. She looked to the System an saw the fires of the Watch. Never seemed further away but she were glad they were there. She let her legs fold under her an sat crosslegged in the cold sand.

*

When the sun rose proper she could still see sum of their tracks in the dust but then the wind came up an they were gone. She mighta imagined it but for the nip on her hand an the feelin like her heart was still gunna curl up an pack it in. The wall stayed on her left an she walked the circuit, dust coloured as the light went stark an the breath got took from her lungs in the heat of the day. A North wind blew, an then changed to gusts outta the West an she could smell the carrion of the beasts comin over long miles an still strikin her in the gut. She was gunna live through the day an the night, she knew it now, was gunna sit again in the Old Mans house an sweep the floors and count the stones an boil up the billy. She had eyes that could see in the deep night an had the pig mark on her. Werent nowun gunna believe her. Dint matter. She was out here breathin an they was in there chokin. She thought of Karra. That bald bastard werent gunna be too happy to see her. She still couldnt figger why the old fella had let her come out an walk the loop but sumthin was comin clear in her, sum kinda idea takin shape like a stranger walkin clean out of a dust storm. Outline shaping out the wall of red dust an fierce wind. So high it touched the top of the sky an came crashin back down on them like she dint know what. She was lernin, that was what she was doing. She was findin out the method an the murder of the sand. Orphan or not, she was takin her own shape. Left foot, right foot, she trekked the circuit, swung the cradle an walked the loop. She were outside the wall an all her own. She took in a breath that scorched her inside. Left foot, right foot.

17

Before

Look around Orphan. You know about Spirals dontcha, them big holes out there? An the country where they are, them round here call the Glows. Real flat country. No proper hills but theres sumthin else missin out here too. Ya know what it is? Me forgettin you lived out here a while dintcha? Birds is missin an the scrub, dunno if you can tell but it aint quite right. I been places where the stands of trees are so thick ya cant see the sky. Up North its a whole different country. Its been scorched an ya may as well cut yer own throat as drink the water but theres trees up there thatve figgered a way to thrive an theys growin. Monsters up that way too, dragons an such, but where was we? Birds. Yeah I know ya see em time to time but for a place with so much water there oughta be more around the System. I reckon its cos they can feel sumthin bad happened out here. The birds is a sign Orphan an if ya stop seein em altogether youll know yer gettin close. Close to what? Dont rush me yungen, all in good time.

18

Down the Glowholes it was real dark. Like not even a smile gunna show in them holes unless you had a little sumthin special like she did. Her legs ached. Them boys had been cool for the game right up until she'd told em the truth about how far out she were goin. Noway nohow an not even fear of the Block was gettin em further than seven sails into the sand. To the dusk thats how far theyd took her on their beatup lump of a skiff. Never tried nuthin funny on in the dark though, kept a tidy camp an hands to themselves. Wished her well an gave her sum extra water for the walk. Nah she'd worry about that when she got back. Theyd all been keepin their plans close an she couldnt blame em too much for bein afraid. It were bad country. No country for halfway crooks. Most scavs stopped long before here an even though she knew places where there were water it came hot from below an strange things grew an ate from the springs. Things that dint look like they come from anyplace she'd seen in the wild. The Ghosts drew pictures on the spiral walls of beasts that dint look like nuthin she'd hunted or ate. She knew they was sum of the great monsters that come from the deep, or used to, leastaways she hoped.

Quiet down in the dark though. Took moren a lamp for most fellas to get around and the funny thing was it started out real cold once you got outta the sun but it got warmer and warmer the deeper ya went. Plenny of guesses about that wun. Sum of the old wuns what had their funny ideas said you was gettin close to old Nick the badman. That he was down deep there roastin all the badfellas on the end of a stick. She dint believe nunna that shit. Them old fellas had sum real strange ideas talkin about a god with three heads and couldnt never be kilt or sum shit like that. Sounded real strange. She dint know why she started thinkin of that. Maybe just goin back into the dark made her leery but at the same time there was a tiny speck inside her that felt like it was comin home. Down deep in the dark she could close her eyes and see with her breath and her ears and it was better, quieter sumtimes, than bein up on top with all the babble round the System, all the noise. Down here nuthin but holes headin in all directions and the stuff what was left behind when it all went to shit. She closed her eyes and sat down in the cool dirt. There was prolly too much light here for it to work proper but she was gunna sit and breathe it all in until her eyes got used to it and she could see with evry little bit of herself. She sat and breathed and she felt the cool come on her and when she opened her eyes again she dint know how much time had gone by but her eyes could see far and clear in all directions and her ears picked up the clicks and whistles of the Ghosts, doin whatever it was they done down here all day and night. She felt the old anger come up inside her when she thought of Jon and her mum but today she dint have time to sit with that. It was like Block was sittin here with her even though he was all the way back in the System holdin shit down.

You get in and you get the Wide Open Road and you get out. You unnerstand? That aint no question, you bring that ship back. Unnerstand? You grab that ship and you take her out in the sun and you open up them sails and you dont stop for nuthin. No iron, no gold, no tools, no nuthin. Bring it home, Orphan. Unnerstand.

He spat into the dust. Now the others was gone he was the only wun what ever called her that. She dint mind. It were true werent it? Never hurt to know what you was. She'd had a funny feelin she wouldnt see none of the Reckoner on her trip out through the flatlands this time. Straight out, straight back, wide open road. Well, half of that was true right now. She only need follow her ears and eyes and all the rest and she'd dig out the ship and be back on the wind before they knew she was there. She walked on down the tunnel, followin the twists and turns and leanin back against the gentle slope. It was round here sumwhere. She could hear them funny sounds sum of the Ghosts made but they was far off. She knew plenny of folk back at the System whod be shittin themselves just bein anywhere near the Glows but it dint sit real heavy with her for sum reason. Even if they coped with the Glows and the dark and the cool and all the other strange things there werent nowun too happy to know about the Ghosts. Half of the bluds back there thought the Ghosts was made up or they was happy to pretend. Yeah true enough there werent many whod be alright to know they spoke sum kinda funny language that travelled in the dark real good. Moved like spiders in the murk, screeched an whistled an called, wrapped in odd bits of scrap and leather that looked like they was clothed but wasnt. They was wild but she knew they werent beasts. They was people she guessed. Or had been. Sum moren others. She couldnt explain that she dint get the terrors. Not that she werent afraid of em but she just dint mind the idea that they was out there too. Evrythin had to be sumwhere and they was here. And she was here. And sumwhere down this fucken hole was her ship. She backtracked a little, stayin close to the walls. Her eyes had gone fulldark now and it was like she was in a bright lit room. Hadta keep that wun close back at the System, dint want nowun knowin she had the brighteyes like sum outthedark thing. She veered into a side tunnel, tastin the air and gettin nuthin but cool metal. It smelled of neglect down here, long years of things quietly turnin to nuthin. She took her charcoal from her ruck an blacked her teeth again, feelin the ash in her mouth, tastin the fire. She felt it turn to paste an spat the rest gentle into her hand before wipin it on her face. Evrythin slow, evrythin quiet. She knew. There was doors built into the walls evry forty paces on the step, sum of em busted open but she'd been through most of em when she was down here last and it were only the wuns down deeper she hadnt had time to get to. She'd been down here scavvin an doin the Old Mans business. Searchin for them secrets. Ways to make things right. She'd got more of the healer in him than he ever knew. Funny how she still thoughta the old bloke like that. Like an old man. Missed him she sposed. How long had it been? Them times outside the walls, all that talkin he'd done over brew after brew musta sunk in real deep and how long was it he been kilt? Too long she reckoned. An last time she'd been down here she'd gone too deep and too close and them Ghosts had known she was down here. She'd led em a mad chase all the way up top and out into the light where they dint like goin too much. Why had she taken the fucken ship down there? She knew it were because there was other scavs. Karras lads was often out the same tracks, pickin over the same piles. She'd had more than wun tussle with his boys over a brightnshiny. Sum she won sum she lost. But most of em was afraid, she knew. They was out here on Karras sayso and if they could get outta goin deep they always did. She dint know none who went as deep as her so they wasnt gunna get anywhere near the ship. Only problem was that neither was she if she dint keep her head on a swivel. Stay frosty. Like them fucken cando men was always sayin.

She went deeper, takin first a door an then along a metal walkway and down a staircase quiet and careful. She dint know what they made this wun outta but it had lasted. She dint remember no staircase from last time but she was havin them funny feelings

like when she could hear the water runnin deep below and see a
sound or taste a place. She dint quite know what it was but sumthin
was pullin her deeper. The Ghost noises had stopped too. That was
either real good or real bad dependin on how you was feelin in any
given moment. Passin all these doors was breakin her scav heart.
Who knew what was behind em? The locks had rusted through a
long time ago, all it took was a little push. She kept walkin down,
on the balls of her feet, arms out to the side, trailin a palm along
the wall, feelin her heart speed up. She took a door off the staircase and came into a collapsed hallway with just a single door
stuck into the wall. She took a step forwards and gave it a shove,
it swung back on a hinge that squealed a complaint. She hissed the
air out of her lungs and dropped into a crouch, listenin with her
mouth half open. The hinge was still in her ears. She waited. Still
nuthin, the Ghosts was quiet. What was this place? She clocked the
room, the long low benches, the chairs on three legs or rusted an
rotted down, keeled over like theyd seen a gust of wind but no wind
ever blew down here. Under a cover of thick dust was cups and
plates and other things she seen in the System now and then. She
remembered the shapes and what they were for. They used to eat
off em back in the day an instead of plastic bottles they had cups to
drink outta, what they washed in other water. And the other water
was good to drink but they chucked it out, chucked it on the ground
like it werent nuthin. All them stories from the old fella bout that
world that used to be. She dint know what to believe about them
old times. She moved silent through the room, it was bigger than
she first reckoned, with a long low bench along the wall and things
what looked like other things she'd only ever seen in the old boss's
place. Whatd he call em? Taps. They was taps, and once upon a
time water just come out of em like magic. Bullshit it did. She kept
low, stalkin through the room on the front of her feet, grey dust an
rotted cloth swirlin around her. She came to the end of the room an
looked back, markin the door, an then peered close at a big board

on the wall stuck with paper and all kindsa weird things. Her heart picked up an she felt a rush in her blud that she knew from times past it were best not to ignore. The board was sumthin, she could feel it. It looked alien but she also knew exactly what it were, she'd seen sumthin like it before. Lucky she had them brighteyes. She reached out and touched a bit of paper and her finger went right through it. She tried to pinch an edge between her fingers and the whole sheet went to dust. She tried another an it draped over her fingers like cobwebs an then vanished. Behind the paper though there was sumthin shiny. She banged her fist real gentle against the board and it rained paper and ash and dust down on her. A grey shower made outta all them things that dint matter no more. Behind the paper was another big thing stuck on the board but this wun was kinda shiny and stuck together better. It looked real old but sumhow it had stayed in wun piece. She looked closer in the dark. It had sum kinda lines and circles and numbers. They was all different colours and real small among the numbers was sum words. This were why she was here, she knew it. She peered at the thing, a thought startin slow in the base of her neck an creepin higher. The letters an numbers was hard to read cos it had been a long while since she done her lernin but there was sum words she knew real good on account of havin read em over and over evry day for a long time and she realised she was lookin at wun of em. It was like her heart stopped a little and she could see where she was from outside herself. She saw she was in a room down a deep spiral and she dint know where her ship was. She was in a room with only wun door and it was real far behind her and in her minds eye she saw a Ghost comin down that staircase like a spider in the dark towards her only way out. It was like it all stopped, like she was lookin over her own shoulder and she finally knew what it was that she was seein. It were her own end. She heard the door behind her as the hinge squealed again. Yeah she knew what she was lookin at but it was comin too late. That shiny thing on the board was a map, an the word she knew was Maralinga.

19

Before

Whats he gone off to do?

He's gone to do his business an you an me get to stay here an watch the place. Unnerstand? An the old fella wants evrythin clean and shinin by the time he come back.

Karra, what does the boss do?

Karra looked puzzled, his hands falterin where normal he were full of answers, even to questions ya werent askin.

Aint noneayours. If yer too fucken stupid to see what he's doin each day Im not the wun to tell ya Orphan.

She waited. She knew he couldnt know sumthin an not show that he knew it.

The old fellas a bank, that means he holds worth for fellas an gives it out on tick. An he tells them admen an cando men what they wanna hear. Tells em when the sandstorms is comin an the like. You seen him mixin up the poultices and powders, he's a healerman. Spends most his time worryin about all them old times though far as I can figger.

Karras hands drifted a little like they did when his thoughts was wanderin an that strange look come over his face.

Got sum secrets he does. He dont get enough from the fellas what come here to pay for me an you an all this around. Aint a place in the System has what we got in here, old stuff and paper an books and all them learnins. Not cheap. I seen them books, I can read the numbers, it dont fall even. Sumthin out there I reckon.

He looked down at the Orphan like he realised his hands was still conversin an then reached out snakequick an clipped her around the ear. She dint flinch, never did. She knew what he was thinkin, that there was sumthin wrong with her. Said it out loud often enough an in front of the boss too. She seen it comin an decided not to move. Same as it ever was. He werent never gunna know that though.

I know what yer doin Orphan.

He spat on the ground.

Yer skivin. Askin me these bludy stupid questions so ya can shirk yer chores. I dint blow in on the last fucken breeze. Get in there an get sweepin, that place better be spotless by the time the boss gets back ya hear.

He dint wait for any kinda reply, just turned on his heel an headed inside. She watched him go an then went out the back to get the broom. Sumthin werent all right about Karra, he were gettin all wound up about sumthin an for once she reckoned it werent about her. Truth told an she'd never show him but he were puttin her on edge. Nuthin for it but to get the broom though. Werent nuthin that couldnt be fixed with hard work an cleanin.

20

Before

Orphan this place we in now was part of sum real bad business if I aint wrong, a bad thing let out into the world. We livin now in the bad dreams of them times. Thats all I know. Far as I can tell sumwhere round here, an the System were a part of it, the first System I mean, they let a beast into the world. This thing were a mara, a totem they called it an it moved in the wind an in smoke an in fire an in light. It were great an small an it could turn the sand to glass an scoop out great handfuls of earth an bring a storm in an instant that might last a life. It were shapeless an invisible an it took yer life when it pleased an not before. I do mean to scare ya Orphan, if I can.

This thing got loosed out here an it wormed an skulked into the dust an the earth an the water an evrythin that crawled, walked or flew. Them in the long before that set it loose they knew theyd done a bad thing. Why? Why indeed Orphan, it might be I don't right know but I got me ideas. We'll talk about the why another time, Im fixin ya in on the what for now, just pay attention. Them fellas who let this thing out they tried to put it back, not realisin theyd poisoned themselves. They gathered the dust, the broken rocks, the glass, whatever they could find that carried the mark of their totem an hid it, tryna make things right, or at least secret. Settin this creature loose were a bad thing and they dint want nowun to know the kind of murder they was workin up. They took all them things the beast had touched and they hid em. Sumwhere out to the West, dont know where. Its a big story Orphan an I know Im droppin ya right in the middle of it. Plenny of this dont make sense to me, I only got bits an pieces of the old times to guide me. Sumthin ya need to know though. I need ya for sumthin yungen. Im not just teachin you cos I like the sound of me own voice. I want ya to find the leavins of this beast an I want ya to make sure they stay gone. You with your clever eyes and your little speck of Ghost blud in the black and brown an blue, you gunna need all them brains and memories. You unnerstand? Ya get why Im tellin ya this?

21

Block werent happy. It was well past sunset on the fortnight and she werent back. The boys she schooled in the circle swore they took her out there just like they promised else they wouldnta come back and told him so but they only ever said they was gunna take her out. They wasnt riskin gettin stuck out there, they just come straight back, and honest, he couldnt blame em none. You dint wanna be out there hangin about when the dark came down. He dint know how the Orphan made it back them nights across the sand last time but he reckoned she'd seen a thing or two. Them boys was back a day and he thought she'da been no moren another wun later than em accountin for time to find and rig the ship. The winds were good, she dint have no excuse. Sumthin werent right but there werent nuthin he could do about it now. He werent goin out there and it werent right to send none of his boys if he werent gunna risk it himself. Plenny of other things to worry about. Around him in the big shed the boys was lightin the lamps in between coughs and sum of em was dicin and cipherin and playin crosses. Few of em was lookin mighty thirsty, he'd haveta have a word an make sure they was gettin their water and tucker. He knew sum of em liked a smoke but if they was gunna be out of it all day evryday he was gunna haveta speak on it. Already sum kinda sick goin through the old drunks, couple of em fallin off evry day or so. He made a rough headcount, a few missin he reckoned. Sum of em was out scavvin and transactin per the usual. It was all in the game, all that hustlin, but it was strange quiet and he was wonderin if it were real or just on accounta his thoughts bein out there in the Glow an the Spirals with that bluddy girl. He dreamed up her face in his mind, dust caught in her brow an them sharp eyes seekin out the line. He hoped it were moren a wish he was seeing, hoped he was catchin sum realness, dint come to him often any more though. There were noise from outside, trouble he couldnt make out with sum of the fellas stood on the door. The yungens scattered through the shed was stoppin their verses and lookin up and Block raised himself outta his chair and made his way through the sleepers and the woke, his fingers twinin round and round the string that led into his pocket. He could see em now, three fellas hoodied up an as he come close their faces come out the shade. Two of Karras lads stood front on to Gus and Cutter and that bald bastard Karra were at the door himself, cocky as he liked. Block remembered when he werent the feared fella he were now though. He remembered when Karra was countin numbers for the Old Man though Karra done a lot to make that time far gone. Still doin a lotta countin, just a diffrent kind he sposed. The bald head looked up as Block shouldered through his yungens, Karras gaze lookin down at the string in Blocks hands. Yeah take a look ya bastard, you know where it goes. Block was holdin himself in but it werent no trouble. Plenny of practice these days. Karras eyes was like a brown snake, gave ya fucken nuthin.

Where is she?

The hands was direct. Real odd for him what moved his fingers like vipers.

Who?

Wun more time Ill ask ya.

77

You aint had no business with her a long time and ya sure as shit dont now. Dunno why you come down here, aint you council now? Or whatever yer callin yerself.

Its for her own good I wanna see her. You gunna tell me where she is?

Her own good huh. I dunno where she is and thats the truth. You wouldnt know nuthin about that.

He had to tread careful. Had to push back but not too hard. Not yet.

I got word she been treatin with Ghosts. She needs warnin. You know what we gunna do we find out she been near em. She carry that taint already comin from where she come from, we cant have nunna that.

You aint got word bout nuthin else itd be moren you and a few snakes down here right now. I aint seen her in a real long time.

Block moved in close so their chests was almost touchin and his hands was hidden from all but the bald bastard. Wun of Karras lads dropped his hand inside his coat an Block knew he were treadin real treacherous sand. Karra dint step back though, give him his coldbluded dues and plenny that woulda shifted bein that close to the Block.

I remember when you wasnt what you is now. I remember when you had a boss and you and that girl was just things what belonged to the Old Man. And you prolly remember me when I wasnt what I is now too, the difference tween you and me though is I aint tryna forget. Why dontcha do what yer sposed to an look after them whats sick. Moren more each day.

Karras eyes never moved off Blocks hands as he signed and then he flicked his own wrists in reply.

Old Mans been gone a long time now. You said it. Im the healerman now. Im the fella that feeds this place an Im the fella that keeps them walls up. That's what I am. You can forget the rest. You tell your little mate. She been called out. You tell her. We speakin her name and she gunna come in.

Karra stepped back finally and Block knew that nowun was gettin cut up right now but the weight of the hook blade felt real good right then, restin against his leg. The bald bastard turned on his heel and his fellas followed, leavin eyes on Block until they was well away. Block looked around and realised he was surrounded by twenty yungens, sum with hands in pockets, lads and lasses with hard faces and sum curious looks. He hadta stop hisself crackin a smile. Good kids, look at em.

Yez done good dintcha. Had me back.

They nodded all solemn like. Too much histery tween him and Karra to be borin these yungens with tonight. Not sure he wanted to tell it either, went back a real long way with that snake. It werent done though, nuthin more certain.

Yez done good. That bald bastard jus looken for sumwun he aint gunna find.

The yungens drifted back to their eatin and talkin. Block moved back through em keepin it all held down. Pattin em on the shoulders, tellin em they dun good. Well, they had hadnt they? Nowun got hype and started sumthin they couldnt finish. Where the fuck was that orphan? Always maken trouble. He pushed past the curtain that sectioned off his corner of the shed. Piled with leaves of paper an books fallin apart. Paper turnin right to dirt, he'd read it usedta come from trees. What a world. He sat down heavy on a stool an took the hook outta his pocket. He looked at the dirt floor and the lamplight on the blade. Where the fuck was that orphan?

22

Before

Ever since she come back from her loop thingsd been different. She was less trouble than she'd ever been an Karra werent sure if he liked it or it made him wanna flog her even harder. That mark on her hand. The way she'd looked when the boss took the knife back off her an the look in her eyes that was half scared an half lookin at sum place that werent nowhere near. She'd come back alive though. Baked from the heat an dust in evry crack but she'd stumbled her way back to the gate an the disbelievin Watch had called him down to walk her in. She was sleepin now, the boss readin his papers in the front room like he did near evry night. Seemed real tired for sum reason. The heatd gone outta the day an he were pacin the yard, halfway between the house an the stable, sun droppin fast an a chill creepin in. Yeah he werent real sure how to talk to the boss. Few days ago he'd been real certain but now he werent sure it mattered what the boss was tellin the girl. Her just an orphan kid and before her circuit he'd thought she prolly wouldnt last more than another year or two even if things went good. Werent so certain now. Talk was water was gettin short in the System. Talk was moren more Ghosts was gettin found inside the boundaries, moren more was goin missin. Not many yungens bein found outside an the wuns inside blind or dyin, sick if they was lucky. True or not Karra dint like the talk. The boss dealt in all kindsa trade, makin sense of old things, tellin people what was wrong with em, tellin em what was gunna happen next. All kindsa old stuff that smacked of the sand and bone and dust. He were a fearsum bloke, the boss, and Karra had felt the lash from him before. But surely he'd wanna know that people was talkin about that orphan. He'd gotta want to know that sum fellas was sayin he took in a kid with bad blud, a little wun what come from out the Boundaries and a mother with the taint of the Glows on her. It werent doin his reputation no good with sum of the fellas that collected down at the hook. There werent no solid boss of the System but plenny had tried. Best could be said the Old Man was feared so he was left most alone and even the real bad wuns knew that the boss could heal em if they got snakebit or heatbit. But there werent nuthin solid and Karra were afraid. Afraid that the Orphan was makin the Old Man weak. Afraid that the girl was gunna get em both staked out in the sand.

23

Dark

Reckoner.

My name is yours.

Yer name is ours. Reckoner, Walker, Ranger, Digger, Bludman, all them names.
I hear em.

*Them up above been comin deep, been comin dark an diggin in them old
things. They gunna taint the soaks an scorch the hills. Old time come round
again. We callin em to dust an you to reckon it.*

I hear it.

Will ya reckon?

I will.

Blud on it then.

24

A score of years. Musta been near enough but that was wun thing he never thought too much about countin. Maybe not twenny, coulda been ten. Time were the only thing he dint keep proper track of. Dint make no fucken difference anyway. He'd had his chance with the Orphan. Yeah he'd told the Block as much and hadnt that little piss stain come up. Not so far as Karra hisself but enough to make trouble if he wanted to. It werent good enough. He was gunna take care of the Orphan and then it was the Blocks turn, be damned to his rep. Karra sat high up, wun of the few dwellins with more than wun level built over the tarmac cross. Usedta be more on top of it sum fellas said. Dint matter, he were high enough. He'd made the council scrounge him up a table with drawers that worked an a flat alum top. Made sure they knew he was boss. Turned it into a room that looked a bit like what the boss used to have and the walls was crowded with books what he couldnt read but he knew how ya made a fella afraid just with signs. This were power. This was keepin things that dint have no real purpose. People scared of ya an what ya might know was no bad thing. This was what the System had been missin all them long years, sumwun to say what was up and what was down. Now he were head of the council.

Yeah plenny had tried to make a mark but werent nowun so smart as Karra, nor as ready to make a mess. No man inside as ready to spill blud an weigh it proper after. He'd cleaned up after others his whole life, he werent afraid of mess. Mess werent nuthin that couldnt be cleared up with sum effort and sum workin the arms. Countin werent no trouble for him neither, not like it were for sum of the fucken dregs hangin around. He got strong when he hadta. All them peeps needed was water an food an a little bit of the other an they lay down. Well he could sort that out couldnt he. Knew how it worked. Couldnt speak in the circle but made it so he never needed to. Karra banged his cup on the alum desktop and wun of his blokes came over with sum clear wine and gave him another cup. He dint have the clear wine much, made yer brain soft, just look at the old drunks on the drag, but tonight, after steppin to the Block like that he fancied he needed hisself a drink. All them things that nowun knew. Carryin the weight of secrets all them years. Only him and the fucken Orphan and maybe Block knew about them dark times and soon enough it would only be him and itd all be safe. Whatd he been thinkin all these years, that they was just gunna forget? He'd always been too soft on the Orphan. Look where that had got the Old Man. Werent nuthin but dust and ashes by now he guessed. Gone back to the earth. Karra touched his right hand to the ugly mesh of scars on the back of his left. Took a long time to learn to use that hand again after the boss had him lashed. Took a long time afore he werent stumblin and stutterin when he tried to speak the hands. Look where they both was now though. Wun in the ground and wun sittin on top of this shitheap. He banged his cup on the table again. More clear wine, it was all that was gunna settle him tonight.

25

Thank dust for the brighteyes. Thank dust for it all. She crouched at the back of the room with the map stuffed into her waistband an her palms sinkin into the soft grey dust on the floor. She could smell the Ghost and taste the stink of it. Been underground its whole longshort life she reckoned. She couldnt smell no hint of sun that ever touched it, it was all rotten and dank like the rags of the old men that just pissed where they lay. She couldnt see it from where she was but the eyes and nose and ears were blendin for her an it were like she could see the picture in her head. It had her scent she knew, she probly dint smell so good herself and she needed to move around it an get close to that door. Hadta get that map out inta the sun. Maralinga. It were like she were a yungen again. She hadnt ever thought to see that word again. Been lookin a long time but never dreamed nuthin was gunna come of it. Werent gunna do nowun no good though if she ended up gutted and fed on down in this hole. She could feel the curiosity comin off the Ghost but she dint dare raise her head above the countertop she hid behind. No tellin what itd do. She edged along, slidin her feet silent through the dust and all a sudden she dint know where it was. She stopped dead still, stopped her breath and heart and got nuthin. Slow, she turned her head up over her shoulder and came nose to nose with a pale face and big black eyes that seemed to cover half its head. She couldnt help herself and screamed, shuvvin herself back away from it and knockin over a table. The thing leaped back, makin a shriek of its own and clutchin the side of its head. She caught a glimpse of sharp teeth in a kinda grin of pain and she was up, rollin to her feet and dodgin between tables and chairs, knockin cups akimbo as she sprinted. It were like her brighteyes was flickin on and off with the beat of her heart and she could hear it behind her skitterin on the floor with its nails. She turned as she hit the doorway, draggin it closed after her and feelin the weight of the Ghost hit just as it shut. It gave another wun of them shrieks that she was sure was callin evry dustforsaken thing that lived under the earth to come and open her up. The bar on the outside of the door started to pull down and she wedged her arm into the gap, jammin it closed against the pressure, sure her arm was gunna break. The weight released as the thing flung itself wild against the door again and she wondered just how long it had been sittin down here rustin and just how long it was gunna hold. She knew she dint have much time and she could feel the map scrunchin an if it hadnt been coated with sum kinda plastic she knew it woulda been in a million pieces. She felt the Ghost back away from the door and start pacin the room and she grabbed the bit of pipe that was jagged stickin out from the wall runnin down the door frame. It was thin and greenish and looked soft as sand but it might give her a few seconds, specially if the thing in there still thought it was trapped. It had gone real quiet. She bent the bit of pipe over and wedged it into the bar holdin the door closed next to her arm that was throbbin with pain. Deep breath, nuthin for it. She let go the door and started sprintin back up the staircase, hands checkin all the time her precious cargo was still with her.

★

Up and round she went, vision flickin in and out and all her senses lookin behind and upwards, all around. Waitin to turn a corner and run into a pack of em, wunderin if this was her end, just when she was gettin started too. Before she even hadda chance to find out what the map meant, before she hadda chance to see Block again. She burst outta the stairwell at the top of the main tunnel and started poundin dust, dogleg followed corner until she were facin what she thought was close to the way out. Sumhow she was holdin sumthin an she saw her hand was clenchin the map fit to crush it and as she crossed a wide open space she saw a familiar lookin hole leadin into a big space filled with them massive old monsters from the old days, giant hulks what musta rolled on their four big wheels under sum other power than wind but what she dint know. Ferfucksake. She stopped and breathed hard before hookin left into the great room with the wheeled beasts, slowin to a walk. Her blud was poundin in her ears and evrythin was shakin but she couldnt hear nuthin comin after her right that second and that were a real good thing. She dint know how much further she coulda run or how good she could fight with a blade in wun hand and the precious paper in the other. She kneeled in the dark, drawin her bayonet and swingin the ruck she carried round to the front, carefully rollin the map up as best she could with wun hand and stuffin it inside. She slung the ruck over on her back and walked into the dark, her bright-eyes showin the way clear. She walked past monster after monster, their giant shapes towerin over her in the dark, the smell of cold metal comin off em in blue grey waves she could see in the air. Theyd been painted yellow back in the old times, she could see flecks of it on em, but theyd slowly shed that skin like snakes and now they was their true colour, waitin for sum magic to wake em so they could feed again. She knew she were in the right place now. Between two of em she spied a tarp that covered a shape made of angles and she walked between the sleepin creatures an pulled it aside. The Wide Open Road looked back at her, a loose collection of spars an threads, sittin on three wheels, name scratched on the frame, sail furled up tight. She stowed the tarp and picked up the anchor rope and wrapped it round her chest. She tied a loose knot and then leaned forwards an unclipped the brake. She turned back towards the main tunnel and started walking, towin the sand yacht behind her, its wheels makin no sound.

26

Before

The lash come down hard but she werent gunna cry. She could hear Karra pacin behind her but her hands was tied down. She'd had three, was gettin two more she knew about and maybe more. His hand grabbed a hank of her hair and pulled her face up so she could see his hand.

Too clever girl. You gettin too clever. Ya been here a long time now and me the fool takin ya in, keepin ya fed and alive. What a fool.

He dropped her head and walked behind her and she heard the whistle as he brought the catonine down on her. It were just the little wun, thanks for small mercies, but the ends was bound in knots just like the biggun and she could feel the blud run outta the split skin and wrap its warm finger round her ribcage before spatterin in the dust. She grit her teeth, caught her breath. Number four.

The hand in her hair again, jerkin her chin up savage.

You know what I done for you? What I done for him? For years I kept them fellas off him, and me and you. I been tellin evrywun you wasnt nuthin but a cur, that the boss just kept you round like a dog. You kiddin yerself, if they knew how much he was favourin sum trash from the flats, sum dirty Ghost Orphan what shoulda died out there and theyda come in here and slit us all up the belly. Shoulda just put you out for good an let dogs take your bludy heart.

It were like the pain was happenin to sumwun else. What was she even gettin the lash for? He'd asked her to get the dust outta the boss's readin room but there werent no gettin the dust outta this place. This place was made of dust and back into dust it was gunna go. The white roads, the cross, the tower, all of it. Her mind drifted to her mum an Jon an it were like she were dreamin. She remembered Jon teachin her names for the hulks that were close to their home. Them three that sat close together round the old empty water tank they named Yalata, after the faded letters painted on the drum. There were the big burned wun an the other what once had been white. Jon showed her the letters spellin out its name OTA an the specks of paint left on the underneath showin what colour itd been before storm after storm had stripped it back. She could see em clear in her head an near enough feel Jons hand still holdin hers, pullin her up inside the cabin when she were too small to climb. The cat came down again and it were over. Karra pulled her shift down over her back and the feel of the cloth touchin the welts was worse than the whipd been. She took her breath in sharp but she still werent gunna cry. His hands unhooked hers an then they was on her shoulders, makin her sit on the stump she'd been reachin over. He came round and stood in front of her, his hands slow and deliberate.

Next time I ask you to clean the dust outta the room you gunna do it proper.

She nodded, watchin his hands with her head half down. She dint want him to see her eyes.

All that filth out there wants to come in here and kill the boss and kill me and kill you. Yer too thick to get your head around it but me keepin you in line and makin sure peeps know the boss aint payin you too much nevermind is the only thing tween us an the dirt. They see us weak they gunna come in here and take it all. Theys afeard of the boss, he got his rep the hard way but time passes and fellas get forgetful. Start seein weakness where there aint none.

She nodded again.

Fuck off with ya then. Dunno why I waste my time splainin to ya.

She got to her feet, takin little breaths and took slow steps towards the shed. He clapped and she looked back.

Not that way. Get in there and get ridda that dust you left in there.

★

She turned and went back into the house, stripes of blud comin through the back of her rags. He stood watchin her go. Dint know what to make of her. No cryin but then she never had, not even the day they took her off the block and brought her here. Still thought there might be sumthin broken in her head, sumthin not all there. The boss was due back in two days from his trip out inta the desert. Out there tendin the land he always said. Talkin to the dust. The Old Man of the mountain. Karra shook his head. He dint know what the Old Man did out there but he was always headin out on his trips and commin back with all kindsa boxes and bits and pieces. Never short of gold neither, the boss. Nah, Karra reckoned sumwhere out there was a vein of it deep in the red dirt and he knew wun thing real good. It werent gunna be the girl what found it for the old fella, it were gunna be him. Karra looked around and sure he werent bein watched he reached his fingers in his mouth and touched the dusty tips to the stump of his tongue. Sum days he could still feel it in there and hadta check it werent come back. He spat on the ground. Fucken animals out there, stupid Orphan dint know nuthin about it.

27

She could hear the Ghosts callin for her blud. They howled like desert dogs sum of em and they had her scent. She leaned as far forwards as she could against the rope, up the incline against the weight of the Open Road. It werent heavy but right now it felt like she was draggin a bag of rocks up the steepest hill she could find an evry coupla seconds she hadta check her tailfeathers and make sure none of em was comin up on her. They could be real quiet when they needed and she werent gunna let em sneak up. She tightened her grip on the bayonet. Up ahead she could see a faint easin of the darkness and she knew she werent moren a few hundred metres from bein out in that beautiful desert sun where them Ghosts werent real keen to go. She picked up her feet and did her best to step faster, roundin the gentle curve and seein the big maw of the world open up in her vision. She had her eyes so fixed on the light that she dint notice a creature sittin with his back to the wall until she were almost level with it and thank the dust the tunnel were real wide and she had plenny of space between her and the shape. She leaped away, a rush in her blud, blade up an dropped low, hand still tight on the rope tied to the Open Road. Her breath was comin hard an she could hear Ghosts in the near distance comin closer. It were him she saw, it were him from the gully, the fella that had hit her with a rock. It were him what had left her sum water and disappeared. It were the Reckoner. His face were covered with the same wrap of cloth and his felt hat was pulled down low. He looked like he mighta been sleepin but out from under the brim was curious eyes colour of water over stone, watchin her drag the ship. He uncoiled himself from the ground real sudden and she dropped the knot from around her waist and kicked the wheelbrake, lockin it in place. She had her long knife up an facin but he dint have nuthin in his hands, just come closer like he done in the gully but keepin his gut clear of her steel. From down in the belly of the spiral was a storm of howlin and she could hear the hammerin of their feet on the ground, echoin up from below, soundin like she'd stirred up sum hell down there.

Go.

His voice were a flat scrape, and she couldnt help her self but shiver. She was facin him square, blade out and no more than a step away from him but there was sumthin comin off him that made her guts into water. He was givin her a fear she aint never felt before, not in all the times she diced in the cipher or dodged Ghosts in the dark.

Go.

Sure and if he wanted to bleed her out he'd had his chances and hadnt took em. She hadta trust he werent gunna do it now. She turned her back on him and all the fire and water in her belly mixed together and she picked up the rope, unlocked the wheels an charged the slope, not lookin back, ears fulla the sound of the Ghosts, howlin like animals and people mixed and sumhow more terrible for bein both at the same time. Out she ran, out and out, draggin her ship behind, past the metal floor, past the faded black an yellow stripes, past the lockers, past the empty rooms and long-smashed glass. The leavebehinds that the young of the flats carved into trinkets an charms. The terror gave her legs. Out inta the wind and the sun, her eyes painin as they adjusted back to the glare, out inta the scorchin desert that hated her nearly as much as the Ghosts but at least she had her ship.

She kept runnin as the ground levelled out, puttin space between herself and the entrance, not knowin if sum of em had the masks that let em walk out in the day. Not knowin if she were safe. She put a hundred maybe a hundred an fifty metres between herself and the dark hole of the entrance and then she caught her heavin breath and looked back, unfurlin the sail of the Wide Open Road as she did. The Reckoner were nowhere to be seen but just in the shade of the overhang she could spy four Ghosts, their white bodies reflectin back at her, makin em look like blind spiders what had learned to stand up, two nose in the dirt and the other two hunched over, lookin out at her. She peered close and saw that wun of em had what looked like a mask and as she watched it started fast, lopin towards her. Her heart was still poundin from the run but she kicked the brake off and swung the sail round to catch the wind. The Wide Open Road creaked forwards slow and the thing kept gainin ground, no moren a hundred metres distant and she could see its long white fingers endin in yellowed clawnails. She stuck her foot off the sandship and started pushin hard, catchin the breeze, and when she looked forwards she near shat herself, headin straight for a great boulder that hadta have been put there by Old Nick the badman hisself. She dragged the tiller left, lookin back and comin near face to face with the mask of the Ghost. It swung an arm for her but she musta paid her dues down there in the dark and a gust caught the mainsail an dragged her clear by a few feet. She looked forwards and saw the way open up, good flat saltland with nuthin biggern the spinifex and red marbles, a white spear of concrete runnin deep through it. She turned again and saw the Ghost droppin back, couldnt keep that pace up for long. Behind it she could still see the maw, and like specks, the others standin stiller than any creatures ever did. She thought of the Reckoner an she felt the terror on her again. Were like her mind was runnin away from the picture at the same time she put distance tween herself and him. She couldnt keep his face in her head and she was already forgettin what he looked like. Just that voice like a nail on rusted sheet metal. She turned her gaze back to the frozen dunes and felt the wind on her face. Pullin up her dust mask she kicked back around and pointed her nose towards the System. She werent home by a long stretch. She were out a perilous long way, pendin on the breeze an her fortune. How longd she been down that Glowhole anyway? Not moren a few hours she'da thought but the sun were higher than it shoulda been. Not the first time she'd thought the hours flowed different down below. Time were sticky down there, pulled an parted like them old roads meldin to boots in the midday sun. She dint know what was goin on but nuthin for it but to head to the System. The map was in her pack and Block was gunna wanna see her.

28

Before

What happened to ya?

She turned at the question. It was that yung fella she always saw when she was down the market. A coupla years older than her which she sposed made him eleven or twelve. He was always nickin shit or runnin from sumwun. Tall and skinny with dark eyes an curly black hair cut tight.

What happened to yer back? That old bastard bin givin ya the lash?

He was always watchin her. Werent too many yungens around so it caught her notice when he had his band around. Like the little kids in the System got caught up in his web or sumthin.

Whats yer name?

Whats yours?

She was done bein talked at. He smirked at her.

They call me the Block.

That cos yer thick?

His smirk grew. She turned her back on him and kept walkin ahead, ignorin him as he fell in step next to her.

Wanna job?

I got a job.

Come work with me and the rest of us.

Come work for ya, ya mean.

Only wun word different.

The last thing she needed was more lashes and the boss still werent back for another day. No tellin what Karra would do if he decided she'd took too long with the supplies. She rounded on the boy followin her, comin up to his chest height and havin to look up to meet his eyes.

It dont matter what happened to my back. I stuffed up and I got beat. But I dont wanna get beat again when I get back to my boss so just piss off an let me be. I got work to do.

Yeah alright. Block raised his palms. *I seen you ya know. I seen you the day you come in. Seen you traded.*

She stepped right to him an the look on her face made him take half a step back fore he could help himself. He kept his hands up, speakin calm an quick.

No shame in it. Plenny traded roun here. You aint the first wun I seen that bald bastard take off the block but you the only wun I aint seen him drop a week later at the pits.

You talk a lot dontcha?

Just sayin yungens dont last long here. Specially not them traded an specially not them that cross paths with that bald fella. Hes a bad wun, but I reckon you already know that. It aint gunna be like that though when I got sumthin to say bout it. You seen my peeps around, I know you have. Get enough of us together aint gunna be no more yungens n kin paid for. All brothers an sisters lookin out. Its gunna go hard on them wanna trade skin an bone, unnerstand?

She spat on the ground, lookin at him flat.

Unnerstand you talk too much. Unnerstand you're gunna get me lashed again.

She turned her back on him, makin her way among the shacks, bitin her lip and feelin her clothes rub this way and that on the open sores. Karra had poured sum oil in em to stop infection but they throbbed, just kept beatin away with her heart. She looked back and watched Block talkin to another kid, eyes bright and serious. Prolly givin that kid the same story. She put her head down and set to rememberin Karras orders.

29

Before

The System aint a place Id wish on ya, Orphan, but I walked a long ways as a yungen an far as I can tell its the only place that got new life breakin through. The only place I seen with this much clear water, the only place I seen people gathered all together like they once was an the only place I ever seen kids, sick as they are. When I was a yungen it were cold, Orphan. Cold all the time. Ya prolly cant imagine that but I come outta mountain country to the East an I wandered a long ways in me youth. I hear em call me the Old Man of the mountain in there an they aint know I nicked that name from sum that come a long time before me. When I came up there was still sum honest soil to be found an I still had a line to me family but the yearsve marched on Orphan an I been huntin the lair of the beast since them times. They knew, Orphan, they had stories of this place even back then. Called it all kinda things an it were all part of the Nullaba. The Nullaba were a crossroad, unnerstand? It were a place to hide things, a place to make things disappear. Nullaba means disappear in them old tongues. Its a place marked not by whats there but by whats missin. An thats where our beast comes from, thats where it dug its holes an sank its nests into the sand. All that steel an copper an concrete ya find hidden out there in the bush, those are the tracks we gotta follow. Shape of the beast? A story for another time, Orphan. We'll get to it.

30

On the run in she couldnt help herself, kept checkin behind herself for days like that spidery white Ghost was gunna be doggin her tracks. Slept blade up, ragmouthed like she'd learned nuthin at all, expectin each sunset to be her last but it were like the land held its breath an let her go. She werent sure the dust an the scrub wasnt playin with her. Still blacked her mouth as the sun went down. Any chance she had she figgered. She couldnt shake the look of the Ghost out of her head. She bunked early, like she were makin it last. In the shade cast by sum of the last eucalyptus she took a moment of quiet but evry time it got still she could hear the creatures workin in the dirt below, the endless diggin of the mites and ants and the crawlin of the fat grubs. Made her think of the old bloke. She an himd come out here for the commune, for the meet with the soil and the trees and the creatures. She werent sure where it got him. She sailed the last day on broken black top, littered with hulks picked clean, she had names for sum of em, names for the bones inside, names for their colours. The heat baked off em an even with their familiar sandblasted hides they looked like they was sumthin magic, things not from where she were from. Sumthin that werent never gunna be put right an on its way again. The System came up faster than the sun dropped and the Watch saw the dust plume long before she got close to the gate. Helped em that it was still daylight. She pulled the Wide Open Road in a big loopin arc, bringin her broadside on to the walls and pullin the sail in an lettin her coast to a stop in front of the Watch house. The Watchman were the same young kid but he werent leanin on his pike this time. This time it were pointed at her chest and it werent waverin nearly enough for her liking.

You. You again. Yer the Orphan int ya?

There were plenny more but she dint see no point denyin it. She nodded. The kid took a step back but kept the pike up and pointed dead at her.

The councils askin for ya. Been lookin for ya.

She nodded again. She knew who was callin themselves council these days. Yeah, Old Man been gone a long time, that was for sure. The kid rummaged in the sack he had slung over his back and pulled out a pair of rusted metal bracelets strung together with a bit of plastic rope. He chucked em at her and they fell in the sand.

Put em on.

She looked at the metal loops lyin in the dust and then down at her hands.

They aint gunna fit.

Dont matter, orders is orders.

She looked past the end of the pike and into the eyes of the kid. Not a whole lotta imagination there. Prolly wouldnt even see her move when she stepped past his big clumsy weapon but then again maybe he had just enough imagination to skewer her if she tried. This sorta thing was more Blocks game she reckoned. She bent down and slipped the bracelets over her hands, holdin em up to the kid. There werent no way to tighten em up and they hung loose around her scrawny wrists. She could slip her hands out with no more than a thought but the fact she had em on seemed to please him.

Lets go.

Not leavin me ship out here.

We'll bring it in.

Nowt to be done she figgered. The kid flicked his head towards the door an then stepped through, bangin the pike on the frame. She followed, a sposed prisoner, but he'd shouldered arms and was barely lookin at her now. Far as his mind went he'd done his duty real good. A pair of blokes from the inside wall was workin on openin the big door, hopefully to drag the Open Road inside an she reckoned that were as good as it was gettin for now. Wun of Blocks yungens was prolly already on his way back to him with news that she'd showed up and she had to hope he'd collect the ship and stow it sumwhere safe. Plenny of people around anyway, plenny of witnesses and when the Block set his mind to findin sumthin you dint really wanna be the wun holdin, or the wun holdin him up.

Come on then.

The kid gestured to her and started up the first ring road towards where the council sat.

You run into the Reckoner or sumthin out there?

She looked hard at the kid but his face were dumb. Just a story to him.

Come over all sour you have. Look like you seen a Ghost or sumthin. Not yer day is it.

He smirked at his own cleverness but she dint say nuthin. Seen a Ghost. Real fucken funny.

Dont worry, yer ships safe, they probly just wanna have a yarn to ya. Them yarns dont always go easy though. You should think real hard about who yer seen mixin with.

She finally spoke.

Been eatin scraps what fell off the big fellas table have ya? Set yer ears to catchin idle chatter. You know, out there, sum of them big Ghosts wear ears strung round their necks. Ten, a dozen, maybe. Them ears dont hear nuthin no more.

She were makin it up but the kids face closed an he dint say anythin else. Just set his nose towards the centre, where Karra sat up in his rooms tryna pretend he were the Old Man. Only both of them knew he weren't a shadow of the Old Man and she wondered for not the first time whether sum of the bad blud they carried was wun day gunna come to the light and whether or not today was gunna be the day.

31

Before

Karra knew the boss werent happy but for sum reason the old fella hadnt said nuthin. He dint know how long that were gunna last but the look on the Old Mans face when he saw them stripes the girl was wearin had been sumthin terrible. The waitin was worse than coppin a floggin straight away. The old fella had quizzed the girl but Karra had been listenin an she aint said nuthin past she earned em and she was gunna do better next time. At least she had the sense to keep her mouth from flappin but there were no mistakin whod put the cat on her an if he had to answer for it Karra reckoned she'd had it comin a long time. She'd been takin her chances with all that time book lernin and her chores gettin left till last and not dun proper. He sat in the annex, countin the profits from the days sales of scrap and the tithes dropped off from sum of them what sat on the council and them what had been healed by tinctures or hands of the boss. There were plenny to count, and Karra entered the numbers and the weights of gold in the big ledger, takin note to do it real careful. He had his head down, scribin neat when he heard the scuffin footsteps of the boss and looked up to see the Old Man come in the room.

You put the cat on the Orphan?

Karra put down the quill. *Yeah boss. Sumthin wrong?*

The boss switched to the hands. *What for?*

She was daydreamin, not pullin her weight. Werent the first time neither boss, hadta bring her in line.

That Orphan belongs to me. Unnerstand? Same way you do? You wanna damage sumthin that belongs to me that means you owe me.

Karra felt the fear. This werent the boss he'd seen much in the last two or so years. This were the old boss. The wun what swung the catonine his self, the wun what had bought Karra from his old master. The boss was speakin with the hands again.

How long you been here Karra?

Maybe ten years.

An how many times I flogged ya?

Four times boss.

An do ya recall what ya done to earn it?

Karra dropped his eyes. He dint like the way this was goin but he let his hands answer the boss.

Wun was wine, two was hoardin, three was that dead yungen I were too hard on and the last was breakin wun of the old books.

And it were years ago that we was done with the cat, werent it?

Karra nodded.

But ya done it again dint ya, ya took liberties and ya laid hands on that Orphan. I dont believe she done nuthin to deserve it and her a yungen still. You well know the lash can kill em young as that and after all the lernin I been given her, all the work I been puttin in to make sure she's ready yer just gunna flog her cos ya think Im favourin her? Aint I dun right by you these years?

There was a long silence and Karra felt the blud rushin in his ears.

Go get the cat, Karra. Lets get this dun so you wont forget.

The boss turned his back and looked out through the window, lookin out an up at the stars and Karras hand almost without thinkin took the quill. In the low light he crossed the room slow and steady and still all without thinkin, the blud loud in his ears, crashin like the sound of faroff thunder he grabbed the Old Mans face from behind and stuck the quill into the side of his neck, again and again and again. The boss tried to turn but Karra stayed behind him, not wantin to see the eyes, not wantin to see the work of his hands and the hot blud that was coverin em. The boss dint make no proper sound but sum wet noises deep in his throat and Karra kept jammin the quill in until the end snapped off an he was left holdin the broken stick. The old fella slipped to his knees real slow and come to rest, forehead against the sill, blud hittin the frame, drippin out inta the yard and back inside all over the dusty floor. He stood there lookin down at the boss, seein how thin and grey the hair was on top and how the skin come through lookin like old leather. He felt madness on him, like he aint done what he just done. Like it werent real and he werent standin here lookin down at the boss. Karra dropped the broken quill and stepped back from where the boss kneeled. The smell of blud was in the air like hot iron and it were makin him sick. Whatd he done? What the fuckd he done?

32

Before

Theyd come to a different place than they usually had their parlays. The old fella took em East first an then South a ways by the sun an to a soak she aint never seen before. It dropped down off the floor of the flats into a little gully an it were cooler an shaded though there was no trees. He cast around a while an then sat, tellin her to dig so she dug an there was sweet water where the ground had looked dry. They made a brew an the Old Man took a smoke an then they sat a while in silence. She watched the old fella an then she lost her focus, mind driftin to her mum an how it felt to sleep next to her an the smell of her an the breath of her. Her hair smelled of dust an sweat but it were sweet an she could almost catch it again. The old fella coughed an she were back in the soak an she reckoned it were the smell of the sweet water thatd caught her. She blinked her eyes careful, not lookin at the old bloke, lissenin to him hack an clear his throat.

We come sumwhere new today Orphan. Want ya ta start rememberin these kinda places and what they feel like. Might be they save yer life wun day an it might be what I tell ya saves sumwun elses life too. You remember

107

the beast? You remember the light an the heat an the fire. Took many fellas to their rest Orphan. Not just here but evrywhere. I reckon its the thing that happened to all things. I been in places to the east, great fallen bridges an rivers run dry. Dammed with the bones of dead men an cattle. I seen towers fallen on each other an fires that mighta been burnin for a lifetime. Smoke in the air so thick ya cant never approach. But this beast is a many-shaped thing. This beast got other signs. Ya cant see it but it can creep in the water and the air and the animals then sooner or later it gets in you and then your chest burns and yer eyes bleed and yer hair falls out and yer too weak to stand and it dont care if yer the boss or a beggar, yer done for. Thats me terror. Anythin but that. An I got sumthin for ya that gotta be spoke. Not much to give ya in the way of lernins but I got a name for ya to remember, lissen well. A place. A place called Maralinga, hear me? Ken it good.

33

Do ya know why I had ya brung here?

She shook her head.

Still not a big wun for talkin are ya? Still got them stripes on ya back?

They stood, just the two of em in Karras version of the old fellas readin room. He sat, leanin forwards, bunkered behind the desk, cup and bottle of clear wine within reach and she could smell it comin off him so strong she could see it.

What ya been doin out there in the desert? Still chasin the old fellas leavins?

Just scavvin.

Karras throat worked and sum sounds what passed for a laugh hacked their way past his stump. *Just scavvin. I heard tell you been out there treatin with Ghosts. How I know you aint had sumthin to do with all that darkness way back when. How I know the old fella dint tell you where all his treasure was an it were you what had him all laced up?*

The stink of clear wine was washin over her and his eyes was spinnin round, not focussin on her proper.

You know I was sleepin. I never even seen them Ghosts.

His eyes got real sharp for a second and he studied her close. *Yeah, you was sleepin wasnt ya. But that dont mean you werent responsible.*

His hate was washin off him like the stink of the wine.

Long time ago, just a kid back then.

He snorted. *Just a kid now. What I wanna know is where and what ya been scavvin? My fellas on the gate said ya come back without yer ship and lookin all beat and woozy and now ya come back in bold as brass after bein gone a long while, a real long while, back out across the flatland like it aint nuthin to head out inta the Glows. You still doin his work? He tell ya where all that gold he kept visitin was? That what ya doin out there? Sum boys round the hook told me they took ya way out into the Glow fields, way out near the big Spirals. Arkoola way they said. Thats bad country, yer long past the Boundaries there. Whats a skinny orphan like you want out there? Nuthin but dust and sand and Glows . . . and Ghosts. You bringin Ghosts with ya? That what ya did way back when? Always had the taint on ya. First day you was bought, and you was bought cheap, mind, cos ya had the stink of them Glows on ya. I know what happened to ya out there way back when. I asked em later, them scavs what brought ya in. They kilt yer mum and yer brother, werent but a few bones to be found, the Ghosts et em clean.*

She could feel the flush creepin up her chest, her heart bangin on her breast but she knew too there werent nuthin showin on her face. As was, breathe slow. There werent no nice way outta this wun. She kept her chin tucked and her eyes on his hands, not lookin at his face while he rambled on, his fingers slurrin and driftin all over the place.

They kilt em and et em then they come again and kilt the old fella and yev been twice orphaned but yer still goin out there, still scavvin. Still lookin for sumthin I reckon and I reckon I know what it is.

She breathed deep fore she spoke. Makin sure her hands was steady. *It aint the old fellas gold Karra, I swear to ya. I got no use for more gold than what can feed me and keep my ship rollin. He dint never speak about no gold or nuthin like that to me.*

He leaned back an it were a long time fore his hands moved again.

Ya know what Orphan, I think I might even believe ya. But theres sumthin that you aint tellin. Yer mate the Block, the wun what fancies hisself sum kinda big fella down there in the rubbish heaps don't mind gold. He got plenny of use for it and he got plenny of use for you.

She thought of tellin him the truth but she knew what it was gunna sound like. It were gunna sound like there were a pile of treasure so deep the old fella made up a real big story of death and poison and old times to make sure nowun was ever gunna go near it. Karra could read and scribe enough to know that the old fella musta hadda a stash of old stuff sumwhere but she reckoned that secret an whatever loot he had died with him and that werent nowuns fault. Well mayhap it were sumwuns fault but she dint wanna start thinkin things in here that might come up in her eyes. Clear wine or no clear wine Karra were a brownsnake and ya treaded real light around them an preferable not at all.

It aint like that Karra.

Yeah and you can call me boss in here Orphan, I was always boss to you an dont forget it.

OK boss.

Get the fuck outta here then. Im gunna send sumwun to come get ya again, were not done here. Theres sumthin yer not tellin.

Im just scavvin.

Fuck off, go on, get outta here.

★

He watched her go and then banged on the desk hard. A lad came into the room with a bottle of clear wine and made to pour sum in his cup but Karra held up his hand. He looked at the skinny yungen in front of him, a few dark threads on his chin an stickin out the top of his tunic, near enough a kid but eyes like pits. Heard tell he were hard at it, come up scrappin an scavvin spite his years. Who knew where he come from? The hungry wuns was the easiest to own. Dint even know half the fellas that was on the council these days. The more Ghost stories got told, the more fellas feared the bludy Reckoner comin for em in the night, the more was flockin to him, askin for directions. The rush to pay tribute an get answers was moren the ledger could handle sum days.

Cull aint it? Lissen good then Cull. Follow the girl. Unnerstand me? Get hold of a ship and keep it ready to go. I wanna know what she does inside and if she heads out inta the Glows I want ya followin yunnerstand? Shes goin out again an this time I dont want no fucken stories from them whipped cornerboys about too far an too deep. You follow her wherever she goes.

The yungfella nodded.

And get this fucken shit outta here.

He gestured at the bottle. Cull took the bottle, the door closed and Karra were alone again. The stink of clear wine was over-powerin and his skin was stingin a little where he'd splashed it on his clothes. The bit he'd dripped on the floor was doin its job pretty good too, the whole place smelled like it were the den of a fella whose brain was mush or soon to be that way. Better to let the Orphan an her mate think that he reckoned, better to let her reckon he was fadin. He'd learned a few things from the old fella. Whatever they thought, it were real for them. He was gunna get the Old Mans stash, he was gunna clean up this pile of shit and then he were gunna sit right on top of it, there werent gunna be no Block or no other piss stain creepin in the dark an plottin on him. Them that couldnt be bought was takin dust naps, all of em. Dint know why it werent already done.

34

Before

He picked up the quill from the floor and then reached around the boss's hot and slippy neck till he found the brokenoff nib. He pulled it out and threw it in the stove all together, watchin the stick burn and the soft copper blacken up in the flames. The boss was still kneelin against the sill so he took him down and laid him on his back on the floor. Dust but there was a lotta blud seepin inta the dirt and he found his self angry at the Orphan all of a sudden. If she hadda cleaned this floor proper he wouldnt be in this shit right now. Maybe if he kilt her and said she gone mad and kilt the Old Man and him just a loyal fella kilt the girl tryna save his boss. But who was gunna believe sum tiny scrap of an orphan got her blud up and kilt the Old Man. Nah, it was gunna look like old Karra finally done what he looked like he was gunna do in his dark moments and then they was gunna cut him up and feed him to the dogs. Or worse yet theyd stake him out near the Glows in the sun and let the Ghosts et him as the sun went down. He shivered. Nah, what he'd gotta do is rouse the girl, then the alarm. There were rumours flyin round all the time that Ghosts was inside the walls an takin fellas from their sleep. The Reckoner walked among em they said, looked same as anywun but he werent human, he was a creature out the deep dark. Enough was frightened witless of the terrors that it were wun thing on Karras side. If he could get the girl to say what she thought she heard or seen it were gunna be alright. In fact, if he were real smart an could remember his scribin, it might end up real alright. As long as the two of em had the same story the old fellas customers and bondmen was gunna believe it. They might have their susses about Karra but they was gunna believe whatever the Orphan said. Reckoned she were too simple for any kinda nonsense. That was it. Get them on tellin the same story, singin the same song and maybe Karra could make all this shit work out real well for hisself and down the track he could take care of the Orphan. Commotion first though. He reached down into the Old Mans blud and got more of it all over his hands.

35

Just like she expected the Wide Open Road was gone from the gate. She hoped it were Blocks lads that had grabbed it. Coupla fellas hackin an coughin in the glow from the wall, dint look like they had enough sense about em to be nickin shit. Even as she watched, wun of em dropped down to his his knees, sum kinda gunk dribblin out his mouth an then pitched forwards into the sand, breathin heavy. Nah, werent nowun in sight with the chops to take the ship though it dint mean it never happened. She werent sure what she'd just seen at Karras place but it looked like he'd gone the soak. Battlin with sum troubles was the bald bastard. She and him dint see each other much these days and it been a long time since he'd put her out and told her whatever he owed the Old Man was done and dusted and she was on her own.

She came round the hook, road stretchin in two directions, wun to the Block and hopefully her ship and the other to the tyre stacks and a place where she could rest a little. Outta sight of the System she'd stowed the map in wun of the hollow spars on her ship so there was no quiet studyin to be done yet, no real reason for her to head back through the towers other than the fierce ache in her head an a wishin for just a little time to sit on what she'd found an think it through. She needed to see them words again in clear light of day an have sumwun else read em too. Whyd she got the feelin there was a big weight pressin down? She hadnt seen Karra for a long time an that werent no accident on her part. She could feel reckonin comin an the stranger in the Glows was throwin her. She shoulda been dead twice over out there. Had she really found directions? Found sumthin the old fella had been lookin for as long as she'd known him an longer? She dint know what had happened down the Glowhole neither, still felt like there was time missin from her memories and each time she tried to drag the Reckoner back into focus his eyes and face slipped further away. She turned down the dusty street, headin towards the Block, finally havin the time to be wunderin about Maralinga. Her feet was unsteady an she struggled to keep her chin up as she walked. Felt sumthin stalkin, huntin her again like she were on the sand but when she checked her tail there weren't nowun trailin her, just the System crowdin her same as it ever was. Thinkin of the old fella, she wished he were here to see the map with her, help her make sense of it, set her mind at rest that she done good. She'd snuck another look out when she was stashin it in the ship but her head was scrambled and the rush was still on her and not only were it shakin too hard to see proper she couldnt make sense of the lines and even though she worked on her letters when she could summa the words was too long or too strange for her to wrap herself around just yet. Yeah, Block was the fella she needed to see. Aside from her and Karra he were the only wun she knew what knew his letters near as good as the Old Man. Knew em a sight better than her and Karra in fact. Leanin on the Block, just like old times.

36

Before

The alarm were raised. It were a night like none in the System ever seen, leastaways not since the whole place was just a few sticks and scraps drawn into a circle out in the dust to ward off the night and old Nick the badman. Nun of them old souls left to remember. Ghosts, Ghosts in the System was the word. They kilt the Old Man, the old bloke what done the healin and the seein. There was Ghosts walkin in the night, mayhap the Reckoner himself sum was sayin, and theyd hadda shot at the Old Mans chattels too but theyd not got to neither of em. It were a strange tale but it rung true and nowun knew exactly what it was the Old Man had been into but chances were it werent nuthin good. Werent the first time him an the Reckoner was mentioned in the same breath. The cando men was out with fire and steel, rakin the circles, checkin the unders as much as they dared, goin through the rubbish pile and they old tyre towers like theyd never been gone through before. Karra were the old blokes head of house an he'd seen em come an was out sortin em. They needed sum kinda counsel and sum of the old fellas and the wuns what been around a while was sittin in their

117

own kinda cipher workin it out an Karra sat with em. The fire carriers was in the Stacks an the unders flushin em through. Ghosts in the system, Reckoner done come, and all them tales what had been brewin for years out there on the sand come home to roost at once and the panic were on em all. Sum was for headin out to the Glows and killin as many as they could afore they got kilt themselves and others was talkin about uppin sticks, was thinkin maybe itd be safer, there was rumours of great walls out there too high for Ghosts to climb. What about the unders sumwun countered and round and round it went and ciphers breakin out here and there, no sense to be had outta any of em.

★

When the sun come up it broke on the body of the old fella, bein sent onwards as they sat. Soon he'd be on the burn pits, werent many ever escaped that these days, save them castouts that got the old justice an was left to die outside. The Orphan crouched there silent, just watchin fellas comin an goin, sayin their piece over the figure layin out on the table, the floor still specked with rust brown and the sill dripped and sprayed where theyd come up on him. The Old Mans face dint look like he were restin, not like sum of the others was sayin. His eyes was part open an dust had already settled on the creases in his face. Nah he werent restin, never had. Not while he still had worries clawin at him from out the long ago. Them worries he'd gifted to her, dust rest him. Might be the only fella in the world cared for her, lyin on the table. She felt a keen come up in her chest like a wound openin but she choked it inta a cough an sat still so nowun looked her way.

★

Karra had the old fellas papers out and peeps was comin and goin, askin Karra just what he'd seen, and how many and where he reckoned theyd gone and the old feel of the System was ebbin in like the dust bein tracked through. That a bloke werent nuthin but what he could do with his hands, his guts an his head and they were treatin Karra less like cattle belongin to the old fella and more and more like the wun what was gunna take his place. Things moved fast an slow in the System, sumtimes all at once she noticed. Karra had them papers out and they sat like marks of what was an what he might be and the more advice he doled out while he sat over the body of the boss the more evrywun started to see that this might be the way it was gunna be. Could he heal? My word he could, trained by the best. There werent a whole lotta gold layin round, not really and werent it better to have the Orphan stay here and follow the trade. Could he do the seein? Yeah and sure enough he could make up a pretty story if he couldnt. Plus he'd faced off them Ghosts and kept the Orphan safe. The day wore on and deep in his bludy bandages Karra was flickin his hands this way and that and offerin advice that werent especially asked for but it were a head that spoke fair clear and werent too many of them to be heard. All along the Orphan sat quiet, still not cryin, never cryin, just watchin the body of the Old Man through the smoke blowin in and maybe just maybe quietly wonderin if things hadnt come up real good for the bald bastard. Dint matter no way or another though. It was what it was and on the table laid her second mother dead.

37

Before

Its time you knew sumthin about me Orphan what nowun else knows. Yer letters is good enough and ya know yer way around the old maps and poultices and ya can count nearly as good as Karra an him the best numberman in the System. Wun day theres gunna be a reckonin for me cos dust knows I aint lived a clean life all the way through. I read that wun meself a long time ago. How long? A promise from the old times it was. I gotta make sure that all them useful things I collected my whole long life aint get lost and that all them pages I collected and stashed and stored dont become so much dust. I got enough readins here ya couldnt read em all if ya had a whole life free to do nuthin else. I been teachin ya so ya can help this place in the end and find that bad thing out the long ago but I been teachin ya too so that yer might pass this on yerself wunday if it dont happen to be yer lot. But theres sumthin that nowun knows and nowun should ever while I live and maybe not een after. I dont mean to give it to ya too straight Orphan but ya werent the first yungen I ever had in the house. I had Karra bring others off the block, boys an girls. Before that, before I had Karra there was others still but none of em made it to be grown.. You was the first wun that lived an the first one that took to the lernins. I came to a realisin too, after a while, that the System bein what it is, aint no place for a girl child. But thats why you gotta be a girl child from the start and stay that way. Yer dont even know what Im talkin about do ya? What do they call me out there? The old fella, the Old Man. The Old Man of the Mountains if they feelin kind. None of em even know why they call me that and they done forgot if they ever knew. I aint tellin ya for props that I was a bad bloke. I dint use my knowins for good all the time Orphan but in the end the promises I made to the wuns before me held me fast and I got meself back into line and did what I said Id do. I carried the weight. Still carryin. Just a ramblin old fella but yer a good wun, yer keep listenin dontcha. Siftin my words like all that muck just waitin for sum gold in there. Heres the thing Orphan, the System aint no place for a woman. Not now and not back then but sooner or later things gotta change. Theres a reason I cant be nuthin but the old fella but you gunna come up in a diffrent time. They shoulda been callin me the Old Woman of the Mountains all these years, ya unnerstand Orphan?

38

Before

She stood outside the gate of the house, facin Karra square, framed in the iron he'd set up quick smart once the dust had settled on the Old Man.

Yer out, time for ya to figger things out on yer own. Keep yer clothes and dont say I never gave ya nuthin. I dont got the time to be watchin ya and makin sure yer cleanin up proper these days. Got me own things to worry about, get me own help, dont need no leavebehinds from the Old Man. You been eatin off this plate alltoo many years for my likin.

Been a while comin this day she reckoned. Hadda place to go, stacked with readins she'd taken out bit by bit over time. She werent stupid. And for all he reckoned he was carryin on what the old fella done he dint really care for them things. She'd been cleanin this long year gone, doin his numbers for him and wonderin just when and what was gunna fall on her. Plenny a long night she'd stayed awake in the shelter. Got ridda anythin that mighta given him suspicions about the old fella too. There werent nuthin back there, no maps nor else that gave away the old fella not bein an old fella at all. Body burned, an just ash on the wind. She'd cleaned for her life the year past she reckoned. The floor, the shed, the bits of the house what Karra had taken over though he still tripped up an called em the Old Mans rooms bout half the time. Werent hardly no dust inside but she still wore another set of stripes from the cat across her shoulders. Cleaned and cleaned. Cleaned the stove too, funny thing about that. She tapped her hand against her pocket and felt the little charred bit of metal there. Kept it hidden since she found it. Looked for all the world like the old fella mighta chucked a quill on the stove fore the Ghosts come but that dint make too much sense and followin them thoughts all the way to the end werent nowhere she wanted to go while she was still in reach of the bald bastard. Orphans, even lucky wuns like her what stayed alive moren a little while, dint have no friends. She werent forgettin. Like or not, he was lettin her go alive and she were grateful for that.

Go on, piss off then. Dont hang about here starin at me.

She turned her back, half expectin sumthin to come at her but she heard the rusted hinges squeak and the scrape of the latch and then she was standin on the track. Across from her was fresh shacks set up, shoved on top of them what come before an made outta the fresh scav that was getting brung in all the time. Stalls an cando men sellin bits an pieces. More evry day. She looked at the peeps cookin an buildin an then turned away from em, pattin the burned quill in her pocket an movin not slow nor fast down the cut.

★

Inside Karra stood starin at the corrugated metal awhile. He werent a bad fella, dun the right thing in the end. Had plans all year to make sure she were stitched up tight but in the end he reckoned she dint know nuthin an it were more hassle than it were worth. He'd woken her outta sleep hadnt he? She'd looked terrified an at the mention of Ghosts it were like she could see em right there. That look on her face evrytime she'd heard the word had gone a long way to helpin evrywun believe theyd been there. And werent it fear of them Ghosts that made the council seem like a real good idea? Now the Orphan hadta go, but Karrad done right by her and nowun in the System or on the council could say different. He stared nowhere for a minute more an then turned away from the closed gate, the Old Mans place to himself.

39

Block heard tell of her comin long before she reached his shed. The kids was out weavin around the tyre stacks and he'd even sent a few of his harder heads into the narrows just in case she'd shown her face there. He'd a lad watchin Karras place and the moment she'd gone in the kid had passed the message and tagged another wun to keep watchin. Block dint want to think about what mighta gone down if she hadnt come out. He'd had her ship picked up from the gate and stowed it out back in the hangar. And here she was, comin up the track days late by his reckonin, walkin like she were born to weariness. He stood outside the doorway, sippin water and all the kids sittin back inside, not knowin quite what to make of the girl. She nodded to him as she came close and then at his bottle. He gave it to her.

Finish it off.

She ducked her head again in thanks and then gulped what was left.

Dry.
You know it.
You see Karra?
Yeah.

125

Better come inside.

You got the Open Road?

Out back with the Taipan.

Gotta get sumthin from her. And thanks.

Block dint say nuthin, just jerked his thumb towards the back and went inside. She stepped over a sleepin dog and past a few of Blocks lads. They raised her a watchful glance but dint say nuthin and she went on through an found the ship stowed near as neat and careful as she woulda done herself. Next to it Blocks ship the Taipan sat under a tarp, itself covered with just a light coat of dust, an she bet if she raised the tarp this time she'd find it wrapped an oiled an ready to roll. She unscrewed wun of the spars that ran the length of the Open Roads deck and took out the long, inchthick tube. She shook it out onto the ground and the map slid halfway out. This was the prize. This were the thing she'd been lookin for for a real long time and here it was, just sittin in her hand, not quite real.

She kept it all tight in her fist and went through, back into the Blocks big shed. There were a lotta yungens around she noticed, lotta kids lookin watchful and maybe a little nervous. A few blades close to hand an she bet others she couldnt see. They watched her pass out the back where Block was sittin at his little desk, all spread out with papers and books and leaves of ledgers. All good fellas and bad come to paper an dust she reckoned. Couldnt escape it in the end. All the books writ long ago and the voices of all them dead peoples was echoin down past all the catastrophe and landin right here in the System. They never saw that comin she reckoned.

Expectin trouble?

Block looked up, looked at her hard an then shook his head no. *Never hurts to be ready Orphan, thought I taught ya that.*

Yeah ya did.

Whatcha got there?

126

A map I reckon.

Block looked at what she was holdin an then back up at her. His eyes was sharp an she could see him cravin the knowins she was holdin. She aint seen but three maps the whole time she'd been in the System. The Old Man had wun an Block two but they all had big gaps in the desert all faded red dust and blank like the System werent nowhere, like it never existed, even back in the old times.

A map of what?

I think I found it Block. I think I found what the old fella was wantin me to find, the thing he was worryin about all them years.

She couldnt keep the spark out her voice and he looked funny at her, like he never seen her care about a thing like she was weighin this paper.

Easy, Orphan. That Old Man worried about plenny of things from what I remember.

This were the big wun. I think this were the reason he come here in the first place. Cant nowun remember a time without him but I reckon thats just cos he was fearsum old. I reckon he come here lookin for this map or wun like it. Theres things on it he was fixed on, things he'd been lookin for a long time.

Block stayed quiet a long time.

Can ya read it?

Yeah. Most of it. But I reckon I need yer help.

Block smiled. *Yeah and ya always did, dint ya?*

He got up and came round next to her, smellin of sweat and paper like always. He moved a pile of books outta the way and she carefully unrolled the map out across his desk, weighin down the corners. It looked worse the wear from its trip in the spar, an for bein dragged up in her fist from the deep dark. Across the top in black letters was SURVEY TOPOGRAPHY and SATELLITE and a bunch of other words that dint make no sense but down in the middle was lines like the fingerprint of the land. She knew enough from all them years spent learnin with the old fella to know that they was cliffs and gullies and the closer the lines was together the sharper the climb. Lookin down on it was a magic feelin like bein a bird she reckoned. The whole desert laid out in front of her but of course this map were from the old times and there werent no marker for the System. Instead there was a red circle what read, she took it slow, Mount Painter Group Subsidiary Test Mines. That, she reckoned, were wun of the Glowholes she'd been down. She knew they was called mines in the old but that dint make no sense to her. They was Spirals an cuts, Glows an the deep. That were sumwhere round where she figgered she'd run from the Ghosts and the Reckoner, two times now. She'd been near ten days travellin East which meant the System was sumwhere in the middle between Maralinga an where she'd been. She dragged her finger back across the map and made a dent where she reckoned the System might be if she was guessin the distance and scale right. Her finger sat right near a big word that was scuffed an broke with a pin hole torn through the plastic an paper. She could make out the letters COMMONW an her mouth made the shape. It were familiar again but nuthin came clear in her memories. She looked again at the colours and the little specks of blue dotted around.

Reckon they was water?

Block nodded.

She kept her eyes combin the map, seein all them words familiar from the readins of the old fella and them black an yellow circles she'd seen plenny of out on the flats an deep in the Spirals. They meant poison, she knew, the three black wedges an three yellow in the circle. The circle of six, marks of the old. More words she half knew, Emu Field, Taranaki, Ooldea. There was tracks too she'd come across the ruins of em on her scavvin, rails of sandpitted iron, broke up by generations of scavs, an old roads made outta a pale white stone mixed with concrete that were real crumbly in most places but ran deepern she could dig. Now an then she could see theyd been good an flat an perfect for sailin. From overhead they ran all over, this way and that and clean off the edges of the square. On evry other map she ever seen them spots was always plain white nuthin. But here she had it all laid out. She wished the old fella were here to tell her she done good but when she thought about it honest she dint think that sounded much like summin he would say anyway. It were always about the next lesson with that wun. Fuck she missed him sumtimes. Missed her. She let herself hold that word in her for a moment an the old pain caught her by surprise. Block were nose to the map like he couldnt get close enough to all the lernins and knowins that was flowin out the paper. After a long time he looked up an she saw the fire in his eyes an the wild grin that dint come out real often. Looked like he were a kid again, down the hook. It chilled her a bit.

This is a new wun, Orphan. I seen maps before but this wun is missin sum places I know of an its got fresh wuns on there that I aint seen before. You got any idea what it means? What all these places are?

It were a real long story and she werent sure the Block had time for it. Couldnt do nuthin now but take a chance though she reckoned. She put a dirty fingernail on the spot marked Maralinga.

You already know about the circles of six. I told you what the old bloke told me. Three black, three yellow. The poison. Mark of the beast.

Block nodded.

This is all or most of em I think. This is the Glows or like on wun map, all connected, an they was all connected back then too, flat top linkin the big wuns, sealed tracks to others an sum of em nuthin at all. Dunno how they ever got in an out, bad country, cant sail, too steep. The Old Man used to say we had wings. Wun or two fellas makin their own way over the ranges can get through but it aint easy an I dunno how they ever dug so deep. I seen sum strange things in there, they aint settled places, they got rumblins in em, the ground complains if ya stay too long. The water come out the ground hot an I seen plants I never seen no place else. I scavved sum alright stuff out there, sum of its in yer locker I reckon, sum of them small shells. Mostaways though its picked clean or it werent never much to begin with, too far out out, too wild. Thats why they buried their secrets out there. You know that thing I been lookin for.

The thing you never wanna talk about but you been kinda talkin about as long as I known ya.

This is that thing. That place. Maralinga.

An it aint worth nuthin.

Nuthin an evrythin. The old fella told me it were a bad beast. Done a lot of killin back in them bad times fore they put it in the ground. It's gotta stay buried. Gotta make sure.

Block never did need much time to think but he took a hot minute to look up from the map an look at her. *I reckon yer right about the circles of six an all of em bein connected. Makes good sense to me an it seems like this might be yer place. But if all thats true why in the fuck you wanna go pokin around in it, Orphan?*

Gotta see whats out there or I reckon the killin aint done.

Block took a long time fore he spoke. *I seen summa these names before in me readins. Read stories about summa these things. Stories about what fellas done.*

He looked at her sharp.

Stories, Orphan. Tellins like they brung fire on themselves. Tellins like maybe summa this place we in now is part of that place. Called this place the Section, maybe. Told tellins like them that scorched the earth is them same wuns what found the water and dug the unders an started the Stacks. Tellins like them that done them things is our forebears.

40

Dark

Reckoner.
Im here.
Your brothers an sisters spoke on you.
I know it.
Why do you not reckon?
I will.
You know yer not the first.
I know it.
It was done before.
An will be done after.
Then reckon.

41

He was losin count of em. Were it ten? Twenny? He dint know what were strikin em down and his talents as a healer werent much tested these days. He'd taught what he knew to a bunch of fellas on the council and he dint lay hands on peeps no more. Too busy keepin the council in check an figgerin out new ways to keep all them mouths fed. The great huntin parties he'd marshalled was bringin in moren ever but it never seemed enough to keep the whingin council from his door. These sick wuns was takin up his time an sumthin about it bothered him moren he cared it to. Folk died in the System of not enough food or not enough water and he knew enough to recognise peeps whatd been eatin poison things and the whites of their eyes all yellowed and their teeth fallin outta their heads. Seen infections an flyblown fellas with the cloudeye an them with bugs an worms in em an them with fingers an toes gone rotten. Plenny of them goin round, special the clear wine drinkers. Seen snakebite, an heatstroke, an wounds from teeth an blade but this were summin else an he couldnt exactly figger what. It struck an old bell in his mind that were sumhow tied in with the old fella but whatever lesson he'd learned or overheard werent comin back easy, if at all. He paced around his office, crackin his fingers.

Real strange. They was weak, sum of em couldnt take food and their teeth was all loose in their gums. Yungens was takin it hardest. Werent no more than a day or two twixt them comin in an cartin their brokenlimbed bodies to the burn. Most was comin in on the West border as well, the councilmen sat out there was raisin hell as best they could. Lookin to him for answers but he aint got none yet. Too much time spent thinkin about that bluddy orphan he reckoned. She'd gone straight to the Block just like he expected and his lads was keepin watch on her there. She aint moved, just gone in there and stayed in there. Good riddance to her, and good riddance to that fucken sneakthief Block and the old fella too while he was cursin. Karra dint have no time right now to be worryin about what she was up to, he got real hassles like if them sick wuns turned into more he was gunna have a problem. Thered be a line out his door of cando men and all the other dregs and hangers on what come with em demandin to know what the council was doin to look after em. But, what if the Orphan had finally found sumthin? Sum vein out there in the Glow. He'd had his boys out lookin for who knew how long? Theyd been comin in for years with scare tales an worthless shit they dug from the oldtime, tryna tell him it were gold or the like. The last lot bringin him earth believe or not. Handfuls of dirt an sayin it come from a special place unnerground. Where was the good stuff? Where was the precious metal? Had enough of em. Had sent scavs to the winds for years an years and never found no great haul. The last of them lyin dogs he'd sent searchin a month ago was staked out, could tell their stories to the beasts an the Ghosts. Bring their shit to sum other fool. Their bones was clean by now, singin songs to the moon. He aint never seen nuthin of the Old Mans treasure in spite of years searchin an more readin. Tryna make sense of the old world an always comin up short. Now the Orphan come back lookin all suss and if he'd learned wun thing, it werent no accident when his path crossed sumwun else. Saved his life a few times that feelin, werent no such thing as coincidence. Werent no such animal in the System. It were all there in front of him, he knew it. The Orphan and the gold and Block, they was all connected sumhow but it werent comin clear just yet. It were odd times like this where he was hatin the Old Man but a little part was wishin he were here to ask. Karra banished the thought. That ship been sailed a long time. He paced back an forth, tryin not to let his eye catch all them books he couldnt proper understand.

42

Before

Ya know how you can see sounds and taste the places ya been? Ya know how words got colours? Not evrywuns like that. In fact, I aint never seen nowun like that. Ya gotta keep all them things on ya chest ya hear? Dust, its been a long time since I come up and dust knows I probly aint seen sum of the trouble yer gunna but indulge an old fella, sorry, an old dam like me, we can say that out here, just these once and twice, feels nice that ya know, I gotta tell ya girl.

They sat in the shade of a gum and the old fella, or old dam as she liked out here, was brewin sum leaves. They was near a days sail from the System, further than they usually went. Took the Old Mans ship that were stowed most of the year. Karra was mindin the station, dust knew what that meant but the bossd seen fit to get em out here. Seemed to think it were important evry few months to head out and check on the old places. Here and there was paintins, marks and leave behinds from long before any kinda bad times and the boss liked to point em out.

Yer cant go tellin nowun what ya can see or special how ya can see it. You got that speck of sumthin else about ya like yer the next thing comin

Orphan. Peeps gunna get real afeard of ya if they start realisin just how different ya might actually be. Ah yer a good wun Orphan, just I can feel sumthin big comin past the Boundaries and I dunno how much longer Im gunna be around. Im gettin terrible old ya see, even older than I was all them years ago and I werent young then. Even back then I were a bad dam, a kinda bad fella ya know. I got the blud of lots of blokes on me hands over the years, an most of em prolly deserved it wun way or the other but who out here dont sumtimes? Plenny still livin that mighta earned a dust nap too. But I came out that mountain country I told ya about an I walked the East roads and seen them burned cities an I spent years off the roads avoidin them what prowled an hunted until most of em saw each others end and I seen sum terrible reckonings out there an sum I put on fellas meself. An then the fella what spilled the blud walked West an West an West an then I come here. I became a healer and it werent a bad way for me to put a few things right what I put bad, even if the balancin of the books was only ever in me head. I do go on dont I, an you a patient wun, gunna serve ya good Orphan, mark me.

43

Block were preppin to ship and there werent much she could do about it. She couldnt pretend she werent glad to be havin him out on the sand again with her but she knew there was sumthin she hadnt been full upfront about. He were mutterin like he were complainin and she could tell a part of it were real enough what with Karra and his fellas gettin bolder near evry day and the Ghost stories gettin worse and worse. Sum of Blocks fellas had come down sick too an word was gettin around that there were plenny more out there, hunkered down an weak. The boys on the mornin water run came back sayin there werent nowun around an they dint even have to scrap down at the wells. Sumthin werent right an she dint put it past Karra to be workin up sum kinda scare to make himself king, sum kinda fresh terror that were gunna make him even stronger. Nah, she reckoned the best place for Block were here but there werent much what could stop him though once his course was set. He'd fellas he could trust enough to keep it held down. Theyd been inta the books all night and she'd spilled mosta what the old fellad told her about the long ago. Sum of it were surprisin to him but more than a little were things he'd read about or lerned or had his own daydreamins about and by the time most of the talkin was done she had herself a blud settin his heart to travel alongside her. Only thing was he dint know bout the Reckoner and even now, only a while or so on she had to touch the back of her head where she'd healed up to make sure that it werent all sum kinda fever dream that she'd fallen into out there on the flatland.

Yer sure about this?

Block turned from his rummagin and gave her a hard look. *Dont ask me again Orphan. If yer goin out there to see about the Old Mans business Im gunna come with ya. Aint nowun handier with a blade round here save maybe you an I dont reckon you can suss this wun on yer own. Aint nuthin personal, this is gunna be my System and I gotta look after my peoples. Set the course Orphan and Ill be there and ready.*

Yeah he were solid Block were. Hadda plan, an that was more than most.

Alright then. We're headin West, to Maralinga. Gunna be Ghost country all the way, plenny of em out there these days, seemin like moren ever. We gunna be on the sand awhile, ya sure yer game?

Fucken cheek of ya Orphan. Told ya, just get us on the right line and Ill see ya there.

He smirked at her as he stuffed sum hard tack into his ruck and went back to his packing. She'd seen him dip into the locked chest an run his fingers through the ransom of brass and wax in there but he'd dropped the lid back down emptyhanded an she'd been glad. She looked down for the hundredth time at the map that was layin out over the desk. It were a pretty thing an each time she looked at it she still got that flyin over evrythin feeling. Werent no way she knew though but through dust.

44

Before

The System were changin, Block could feel it all around him. Them council fellas was takin over and them weak admen was scrapin an bendin to get summa the gold and food an protection they was promisin. Aint nowun but Karra ever seen them Ghosts what kilt the old healerman but the thought of em was bad enough and all over the System fellas goin missin and the cry of Ghost ringin out, an peeps bled out in their beds an it seemed like evry other day a scav werent comin back. Out there on the sand you could nearenough navigate by the bones of them what hadnt made it. There were no denyin the Ghosts was real and gettin more bold. Just sum happy luck that it all fit real nice with the bald bastards plans. Moren more of em was movin into the cinder digs an towers that sat astride the concrete cross in the middle of the System. The girl what had worked for the Old Man was missin too. Sum of his lads had seen her headin inta the tyre towers and rubbish heaps weeks before and nowun seen her since.

Block were scoutin, he'd enough young fellas an lasses standin with him now that it were time they had a place to gather an lay their heads an if anywun was askin they was just bandin together strong to stand against the Ghosts an fucken slavers. Block were layin plans he dint hope to never see the end of. Placin yungens here an there, workin em into the trades. Coupla cando men an he were sorry for em but it were gunna pay wun day. It were a hard game but there it were. Couldnt tell evrywun evrythin, hadta keep the long game movin on. Whatd them books say? Chess an checkers an all them good things. Yeah he got a soft heart for sum things gone he reckoned. Bigger worries on his mind now though. Needed digs for his lads. The rubbish heaps was too dangerous he reckoned, too many blind corners and places where a fella could get all filled in. Besides, them what lived there werent gunna take too kindly to him declarin himself lorda the dump. Nah, the Stacks was gunna be on his side when they saw he meant em no harm. He'd heard the rumours about them what lived there an he werent bothered so long as they wanted to live along with him an his. What he wanted was a place that were right out in the open, close to the Centre as he could find, sumwhere where what he was doin could carry on in plain sight. An what exactly was he doin? He'd puzzled on that wun for a long time but he figgered the answer he gave himself years ago was probly still right. He was gunna sit atop this pile and all his fellas with him and that were that. Make his own safe, close the blocks, and then send peeps out lookin for others. He'd read enough leaves an broken books to be near certain there was others out there, not just the nomads an scavs that roamed the flats an beyond. Was strange there werent never no messengers but itd been a long time from what he could figger. Maybe there was another System just past where the furthest Boundary rider stopped. It kept him up nights dreamin of that. If that werent true, what else was there? He moved though the late arvo crowds like handfulla sand just slippin and weavin through em, movin with the sweet science he'd been lernin from the papers, slip, jab, weave. Yeah them papers, and evry now and then a book, was what set him apart an he knew it. All these fools an followers dint realise ya dint need to make evry mistake yerself. Plenny fellas made em before ya an the good wuns writ it all down just to save ya the trouble. The sun was droppin an he realised he was in the shadows of the Stacks, he'd come out wanderin all the way on the West edge, hardly realisin where he was. Bludy daydreamin again. He hooked towards the centre an stopped up short, spyin a girl child an then coppin a better look. It were the Orphan, he were sure. Her hair was cut jagged and shorter but she were still the same knockkneed skinny kid he'd seen dragged in that day and sold to the Old Man. She was lopin with sum kinda bag slung over her shoulders, movin fast towards a narrow entrance to the heaps. There were sum kinda commotion and he saw her duck down real quick and reappear on the wrong side of a table, fingers flyin, snatchin up sumthin an then vanishin again. He was gunna have to be quick if he wanted to catch her but lucky quick were a speciality. He struck out, duckin and divin between fellas and just as she were slippin between two shacks he put his hand out an latched onto her shoulder. Stead a turnin she shrugged down and a real strong hand grabbed his wrist and pulled him off balance so he fell in the dust facedown. He'd got his arms out but he lay there a sec, more surprised than winded and he felt her step over him and the same hand thatd dropped him pulled his head up. Block werent waitin too much longer to see where this was goin and he bucked upwards, buttin his head up between her legs and then rollin fast to his feet, half out with the hook as he come to his feet. He came up facin her, a drawn bayonet half as tall as her wavin in his face, the point strayin from face to balls.

Ill fucken gut ya stay away. Open you up, back it up, back up.

She was hissin an spittin like a snake. He dint let his grip on the hook go loose but he let his face relax like he was soothin wun of the camels the scavs used, dropped his voice real low like he were talkin to a wild thing. *Just wanna know if ya want sumthin to eat? Place to stay? Nuthin else.*

He saw her size him up fore she spoke, blade steady.

I can sort meself.

Yeah I can see that. How long since the bald bastard put ya out?

Nunofyours.

Fair enough. But you aint used to this place. You come from the Glows straight to the oldfella and I can see ya dont know much about survivin in the System. You got lucky with them things ya nicked, I saw ya pinchin food and yer lucky there was a ruckus goin on or sum of them cando men woulda had yer hand or yer tongue.

She sniffed an spat, sizin him up.

That ruckus werent no accident.

He looked at her sharp, seein her fresh.

Not bad then, if yer bein true.

What was yer name again, Block werent it?

Yeah thats what they call me. Reckon you could use a little work with yer sticker though.

He gestured at the end of the bayonet that had started to drop. It came up again when he pointed at it and he made his voice calm an slow. *I aint here ta hurt ya. I aint even here ta hustle ya Orphan. Like I told ya last time Im puttin together a crew for whatever storms comin and I reckon youd fit right in with us.*

She kept the blade up an stared at him a real long time till he werent sure she'd heard him speak or what.

Dont go in much for fellas, or crews. Just wanna live on. Got sumthin to do, unnerstand.

Block thought about that. *What about we do a trade then? Yer carryin that big knife round with ya and the best thing thats gunna happen from what I seen is that ya dont get stuck with yer own shiv. Mebbe I can teach ya ta move with it and how to make sure the pointy end is always pointin at the fella ya dont like and so it never ends up facin the wrong way. I can teach ya a few tricks on howta live out here an get by in the System. Special since things are changin on account a your old mate.*

He cracked a smile to show he was half jokin but only half. She made him wait a real long time fore she spoke.

I wanna ship. I wanna scav.

His eyes widened an he dint speak for a bit.

Yer serious intya? Yer dead serious?

As the lash.

He whistled low. *Why? Why you wanna go out there?*

Nunofyours. Dontcha want them things Ill find though?

I might. But where you reckon Im gunna get a ship?

She shrugged. *Take wun. Make wun. No nevermind. But Ill trade ya them things I bring back for yer help.*

Not sure I trust ya. How do I know yer any kind of scav? Might take a ship an be gone.

I dint come askin you for nuthin.

Ya dint didja. Alright. Gunna need time to see about a ship. Dunno how long but I reckon I might be able to get wun together. Meantime why dont you get to scavvin if thats what yer keen on. I want them old things an if ya want me help yer gunna bring em to me. You dont gotta be part of my crew neither but ya come runnin when I call a favour. Whaddaya say Orphan? We got a deal then? Ship for trade. Nuthin to lose I reckon.

That bald bastard aint my mate.

Yeah I know, I figgered that wun all on me lonesum when he chucked ya out. So whaddaya reckon?

I reckon Ill come find ya.

She dropped the blade finally and slipped it back inta the scabbard what was nearly draggin on the ground. It looked funny till ya saw the look in her eye when she handled it.

See ya round Block.

She threw it over her shoulder and headed on down the alley till she slipped tween a gap in the wall to the side and were gone in the long shadows. Block stood watchin the spot where she disappeared and then shrugged to hisself. Strange kid he reckoned, sumthin not all there about that wun but same could be said of near evrywun he come across. Kept runnin across his path. Hadta remember though, were only the Block what he could rely on, only the Block gunna keep him alive.

45

Dark

Reckoner.

Blud.

You speak it, but it aint done.

It will be.

Reckon. Scorch them from the sand. Gather a clutch of yer brothers an be gone about our reckonin.

I will.

The olders favoured ya. Yer brothers favoured ya. Let it be done or spill yer own blud an let a reckoner come again.

I will.

You know the truth of it. Theys tainted the soak. Theys opened the hollow and pit. They carryin it with them now. Time growin short till old time come again.

46

Out on the sand there werent no excuses. Werent no hidin nuthin from each other, they shat and pissed an ate and slept next to each other. Cept she still aint mentioned the Reckoner to him and she dint know why. Well that was sorta a lie, she'd told him once but she dint want to tell him cos the Reckoner werent nuthin but the Ghost of all Ghosts and a scare tale what Karra used to tell her late at night in the shed to terrify her. Werent a kid that come up in the System in the last ten years that dint know tales of the Reckoner and there werent a wun of em that kept believin once they got growed. An Block, Block were more growed than most, special when it came to night terrors. Right now there werent no tellin anywho, they was in their ships, maybe thirty spans apart, enough to stay safe, ridin the same wind West. The sund come up quick behind em now but when theyd snuck outta Blocks place and left Cutter an Gus lookin after the rest of em itd been a dark moonless night in the System. Jus perfect for what they was doin in fact. Wet work Block called it but she dint know how he come about that kinda name, were nuthin but dry as far as she could tell. She'd led him out by the Silent Gates, them old tunnels in the rubbish heaps by the Stacks that sumwund dug way back when, an most of em had collapsed. Were only her an a few of the old wuns from the Stacks what remembered em these days and Karras blokcsd never sussed em out. Coupla Blocks lads had dragged the ships out through the East gate fore settin short sail an meetin em up. Best they could do considerin, werent a perfect plan but best they could hope for was Karra wouldnt figger she'd gone for at least a coupla hours, maybe more and if dust was smilin on em he'd never even realise that Blockd gone at all. It were good to be back out on the plains though strange to be travellin the opposite direction to where she most often scavved and into the badlands where nowun ever headed. She guessed she knew why now, maybe sumthin to them old superstitions. It were hard to fathom that the old fellad never found the place but lookin around at the wide open space jus dotted here and there with tree and spinifex she figgered there were room enough to hide near anythin out here. That were probly why they come all the way out here to begin with, figgered theyd stash their secrets and their poison way out yonder where nowund ever think to look. Seemed like itd worked pretty good too. She had to keep remindin herself that there werent no System out here when them oldtime fellas had come out here to spread their shit on the wind. Back then this were jus a hole in the map, like them other maps in the System she'd known. Block was tackin left to avoid a gully up ahead an she dragged the sail over, pullin the wheels on their smooth bearings across the givin sand and into a new line, sittin near in the tracks of the Taipan. Block looked over his shoulder and threw her back a wave an she grinned. Near enough to as happy as she'd ever been she reckoned. Were real strange. Out here chasin down sumthin the old bloked been lookin for her whole life an now she were the wun what was gunna find it. She wondered if it were gunna look like sumthin bad, like if she could tell just by smellin it, like would it have a bad taste or a bad colour goin with it? Was the water gunna have a bad sound what sat in the breeze, waitin to poison evrythin? She dint know but there were sumthin about the clear air and seein Block leadin em out that made her glad for a minute. She skipped the Wide Open Road a few spans over again and pulled forwards, the patched fabric of the sail snappin as it took the pressure. Real good wind too she reckoned, got lucky there, dust was with em for now but dint she know how quick that could change. She caught a gust and it sent the Wide Open Road ahead of the Taipan an she glanced over at Block an saw him grinnin as he stared ahead, keepin his eye on safe passage like a good sailor. Like he never forgot a lesson given or taught. The sun were full up now an soon enough theyd stow em in the heat of the day an set up canopy for an hour or so, take a break in the heat, maybe hunt if there was anythin out here that dint need too much chasin. They was headin into badlands but how far did the poison spread? Was the animals out here full of it? Maybe theyd just stick to the tack, bully and water theyd brought from home. She dint know. Were a new world out here now. She kept her nose aimed West, the dust trail from the two ships stretchin back before it vanished in the breeze.

47

Before

She were a natural he reckoned. Had sum kinda extra sense what made her quick an strong an real hard to surprise. She were far an away the quickest lerner he'd ever seen. He was comin to lean on her more than he reckoned was good but part of him dint care too much. The System had changed alright but not quite in the way he'd figgered when the council started lookin after the protection as they called it. Things was tighter in sum ways but a whole heap looser in others, an things what mighta cost ya yer hand or yer tongue back in the day was gettin settled moren more often with gold. Block weren real sure how he felt about that. He dint miss usin the blade on the regular but the ciphers wasnt happnin quite as often an that meant sum real fat, slow fellas was risin to the top of the pile. Yeah it helped a whole lot to be lean an quick but these days it werent the only way to the top an he dint know right how to behave sumtimes when he come up against sum of these council fellas with deep pockets. Bein loyal, that were sumthin Block unnerstood. Bein sharp and bein hungry an fightin for yerself. He knew all about that. An so did the Orphan. But evry moon now fellas paid their tithes to the new council to keep em safe from the Ghost attacks inside the walls what still happened nowanthen. Paid fellas to man the walls an gate. It were the new way an spite there bein more food goin round an more hunters an more scavs he dint know that he liked it. Funny how all roads led to the baldman too.

The Orphan had started headin out the Glow ways as well an he werent right sure how to take that. Month before she come back banged up an bleedin out the chest, sumthin collapsed on her when she was down deep an she'd been crushed under it a while. She come back with a handfulla small brass an paper though, turned it over to him, made her sum an then settled for another month while she healed up in the Stacks. Checked in on her skiff he was buildin. Liked to look at it. Told him to keep his eyes open for bearings an spars an fabric that werent rotted an he had to check his smile at her cheek. Plenny of peeps come tradin favours with the Block an he done as she asked an spent what she left with him on wrought iron an greased axles. She was callin it the Wide Open Road she reckoned, after sumthin she dug up in a spiral. Liked the way it sounded she said. He shook his head thinkin of her. Werent exactly chuffed with himself how often he caught himself doin same. Was what it was though. Mighta known her since she were a littlun but couldnt never keep nowun alive forever, dint need old readins to teach himself that.

48

I read wun time that that up there, all them stars together, is called a galaxy an a milky way.

Like milk like from a camel?

Yeah, ya can kinda see that it looks like spilled milk all swirled over the sky.

I reckon you got a real good imagination Orphan.

I reckon you aint got none then. We're sittin under the milky way tonight, whether you unnerstand it or not.

She looked over at him an saw his shoulders shakin as he laughed real quiet.

Yer a fucken shit Block.

Yeah, I know. It does kinda look like spilled milk but I reckon them old fellas what named it spent too much time on the clear wine.

I read too that all them stars is actually places like this, like theres lands out there an other places to live.

I seen a few things like that meself, Orphan. Never sure whats true or not.

It were in wun of the old fellas books but it was only half there. All them old pages ripped out or turned to dust so I couldnt figger what happened next, just I reckon they was reachin higher than what we do now.

Gets ya in a funny mood bein out here dont it. I reckon I never heard ya speak so much as what yev dun in the last few days. Yer sure yer alright? Nun of that poison got to ya?

Yer a funny wun.

Im real. You was gone a long time out at the Glows. Stayed longer than what I reckon it shoulda took an ya come back lookin like ya seen trouble. Moren usual.

She stared up at the stars, just thinkin an lettin his words settle.

I seen a Ghost or two out there but that aint it. I seen Ghosts before but mayhap never this close.

So what happened out there? Ya come back with the Open Road an ya come back with a map. A map like I aint never seen before. How deep did ya go an what Glow was ya in, a freshie? Dust, Orphan, ya takin risks out there like I never seen an I been scavvin with ya moren once.

I seen sum real strange things this time Block. I seen Ghosts workin together in a diffrent way. I seen a fella out there what looked Ghost but maybe wasnt.

She paused. Afraid he were gunna think she'd lost it. Were shook, or worse, mad.

I think I seen the Reckoner out there Block, or summin what looked powerful like it.

49

Before

He'd been waitin a long time but Karra was makin his move. The Orphand been out the house now mebbe a year an he knew that whatever else, he were clear of killin the boss. All them council fellas what he'd scared and cajoled was all comin into line an he reckoned the time were right. His boys was out there now in the night, sum boys what liked gold an clear wine moren anythin else and after it were all done he'd bring em in anyway an make sure they knew real good that there was no talkin about any of it. Dead men dint tell no tales anyway he figgered an what was good enough for the boss was good enough for any of them deadbeat cando men he had workin for him. Tonight he was gunna make sure the council was real important an stayed that way a real long time. An on top of that council was gunna be a bloke what had lived through them Ghosts twice over, a healerman what knew his letters an his numbers, never mind it were only half true but round these parts he were a man of lernin an if he healed wun outta two that came his way well that were wun more than woulda lived without him. Yeah, he done set this wun up real good an in the mornin when they found the bodies of them unlucky wuns what hadnt survived them Ghosts in the night there were gunna be a vote, no cipherin, that were for the dark ages an Karra were gunna end up right where he belonged. Had his eye on the tower that sat right off the cross, near the Centre of the rings. Were well past time to be gettin out of the Old Mans place, too many rememberins, too much of his own blud spilled an he couldnt stand lookin at things what he once cleaned gettin all tarnished. He were done with this place. Gunna trade the title for gold once all this were done, dint have no doubt that the work of this night was gunna set him up proper.

50

Before

She woke with a hand over her mouth an she started up, starin into
the Blocks eyes, his blade held over her throat. Her guts turned to
water but she kicked an bit his hand deep, tastin blud as she made
for her long knife but he dint make a sound. Sumthin in his look
stilled her an she stopped strugglin, seein the fearwhite in his eyes.
He kept his hand over her mouth an shook his head fore flickin his
eyes left. She crept her hand to her knife an slipped it wunhanded
from the sheath, holdin it out an to the side, point restin hard on
his ribs so he knew it were there.

He shook his head an moved his eyes left again an she heard
the heavy sound of sumthin animal not too distant. The Block
nodded slow when he saw her hear it an took his hand off her
mouth real slow.

Beast.

He said silent.

Ghost mebbe.

She nodded an dropped the blade away from his body. He took
his weight off her silent an they lay under the stowed sail side by

side, listenin as the sounds faded, got louder, faded again. She kept her blade handy an they lay that way until the sky started wakin. She fought it but she slept again.

★

Cold tack for breakfast an the Block had run bandage around his hand where she'd sunk her teeth in but he dint say nuthin about it.

They packed the ship quiet an took a walk out into the bluebush. She saw em first, heavy tracks, three or four walkin on two legs, wun on four. She circled the marks, seein em fade onto harder ground, broken stone an bush hops stickin through the cracks like dry blud. They sat a long time an eventually the Block stood up an stretched his arms over his head.

Good they dint find us. Three we mighta been alright. Five I dont reckon.

Werent much to say about that. She walked back an started raisin the sail, a breeze pickin up as she did it like she'd called it into being. The Block whistled an cracked a smile.

Good fortune you are.

We'll see.

Look around Orphan. Yer breathin an were out here. Plenny in the ground for the takin. Much to learn, unnerstand?

Block smiled again. She shook her head. He were mad. Or proper happy. Which was worse.

Much to learn.

She dint answer and he helped her drag the ship through the rutted scrub an back to the bladestraight road runnin south. Much to learn were right. She were gunna teach him. No fires past the Boundaries to call evry murderous thing their way. Cold tack. Sharp blade. Rag mouth, black teeth. Choose yer shipmates careful. She'd spent her time wise, listenin by the camps of them scavs lucky enough to survive a run out.

Hit the Spirals in a day or two but we aint goin there this time, Orphan. Theres an old camp out here I aint picked clean an you might neverve

155

seen it. Yer after Spirals though aintcha? Wanna go dark dontcha? You got the spark in ya.

He dint know the half of it an that werent gettin told.

Yeah dont worry about it, tell me sum other time. We're gunna help each other, Orphan.

It were like he were readin her bludy thoughts sumtime. They wheeled the ship to the shoulder of the way an he kicked the brake off, the ship catchin breath straight away an pullin ahead slow. He swung aboard an she followed.

Hey Orphan, stop talkin so much, can barely hear meself think.

He flashed a smirk at her an she turned her head back to the road as they started sailin.

51

The West roads was if anythin better kept than any she'd ever sailed. Block dint seem to wanna speak on the Reckoner after she brung him up so she left him to his thoughts an kept her eyes on the gullies an ruts that might turn out to be shipbreakers if she dint keep frosty. She figgered the white concrete looked so fresh cos nowun in their right minds ever come out this way an if they did they dint never make the trip back. The scrub picked up a little, gettin higher than it ever seemed to get round the System an now an then she caught shapes out the corner of her eye that she knew wasnt nuthin ever made by the bush itself. No hulks though, she aint seen wun at all an that were a strange thing, special how as they specked the dunes in all kinda repair evry other direction she'd ever sailed.

Block kept his place starbd of her an the breeze was good so they stayed on it, sailin clean through the middle of the day, pushin themselves further an just sharin the odd glance. The rattle of the struts werent so loud they couldntve shouted to each other but she got the feelin he werent in a speakin mood an truth be told she werent neither. Evry bit further West they crept she felt sumthin growin in her chest an she noticed sumthin else as theyd tracked across the land. There werent no spoors, no tracks, no shit, no nuthin that mighta shown life. Still as the Boundaries was, an deep as she'd gone, she aint never felt a quiet like the wun they was in. All her senses tuned to the soil an the road an not a flutter, not a breath come to her. An them things they kept passin, the scrub like a wall twixt them an the past but evrywhere she looked she could see hidden back from the road the leave behinds of sumthin she dint unnerstand. Was Block seein it too? Slabs an blocks of sanded off stone an concrete. Steps an steel frames. Like thered been sum whole other town, a city maybe, an sumwund done a real bad job of wipin it from the earth.

She crested a rise, the Wide Open Road strainin as it hit the top of the hill an all of a sudden she saw a vast pale slab stretchin into the heat an a chill come over her an she knew they was in the right place, that they was on the right road. She slowed the ship an pulled next to the Taipan.

See that?

Block nodded.

Check it out?

Course.

Course. Bluddy Block. Could at least pretend to be shook.

They rolled down the hill at halfahead, dippin low so whatever it were dropped outta sight, an then they came to a track leadin off to the right that opened up into clear sky through the bush, sum kinda path still visible. They stepped off silent an pulled the ships slow through the long grass an for all Blocks sureness she knew they was both lookin at sumthin strange that neither of emd ever seen before. In front of em were dunes creepin in on the surface an she could see as they got closer it were a kind of rough pale grey road of some sort. Ringed with white concrete an a pale pink sand on the edges but massive, like no slab she'd ever seen, unbelievable big, an she knew there couldn't have ever been no buildin in the world with a footprint this big an she dint have no idea what she was lookin at.

They rolled towards it an she saw at the edge of the trees a collapsed shed, roof rusted through an what looked like a path across sum kind a built riverbed. What was left of the buildins walls was a dull green but whatever shelter itd once been it werent no more. She kicked the brake an stopped the ship an the quiet weighed in on her heavy like she were bein squeezed. The Block was stowin his ship an tied it off to a metal pole stickin out the ground at an angle an she did the same an together they walked over the little bridge. Itd fallen in the middle but the dry channel was only shallow an they stuck to its path an then they was across into the vastness of the cleared space. She turned to look back at the trees, markin the distance in case they needed to get into the scrub quick an she saw faded on the buildin sum kinda drawin of a roo. Just the shadow left but she knew it were a red roo in a pale circle. This were real oldtime stuff she knew an she an the Block were likeenough the first fellas to come this way in a real long time. Still werent no speck of life as far as she could feel for days in any direction. Signs the Old Woman had told her. Signs just like this.

We goin out there?

Block gestured to the huge open space in front of them.

Course.

He smiled an gave her the lead.

52

Before

Karra leaned over his desk, eyes bright lookin at the fat ledger in front of him an the weights of gold marked all neat an proper. Hadnt been but a handfulla years since he'd had blud on his hands an wunderin just how he was gunna keep his head. Now he were on top an instead of holdin a blade themselves peeps was happy to pay sum to Karra an let him sort it out. After all, werent he the bloke whatd survived them devils moren once an come out the other side strongern ever? He were startin to make this place his own too. Gettin readins an paper over from the old place and stackin it up, tellin fellas he were lernin all about the old times an how to keep them Ghosts at bay. Had decided he was gunna turn the Old Mans place into a way station for the auction blocks too, let the traders rest the camels out back. Drink their clear wine an put their boots all over that room what he'd once had to sweep an scrub. An here he sat just waitin on more gold to be delivered that he were gunna stash away. He cracked his fingers an looked around himself. A carpet on the floor. Lamps that was lit all day if he wanted. Glass in them windows an between him an the dark outside. The collectors was gunna be back soon enough an he could get to his ledgers again, strange enough the only thing he used to do that he still enjoyed. Sumthin real right an orderly bout them lines of numbers all addin up to the same thing no matter how many ways you looked at em. Sumthin real nice about that.

53

Before

Four days sail. He said he were gunna come for her if she was gone
longern ten. She aint never been so far out an her skin was crawlin
with a mix of fear an the feel of the wind. She were dressed in
boots, strides an a green canvas coat over a shirt, new glasses in her
pocket an the long blade slung at her side on a short lanyard. He'd
kitted her from his own store with a satch, scope and a wrap. Told
her to pay for it when she come back. Settle up with brass, wax or
paper was the word. She dint know why he were so keen on them
old bullets, she aint seen but wun rifle her whole life an itd been
broken, welded solid with rust an softened with a coupla hundred
years of neglect. She reckoned them thingsd vanished with the old
world an the art of makin em with it. She werent sure how they
worked anyway but from the scraps she'd pieced together out the
old fellas histery pages she had an idea that mighta been a good
thing. Not Block though, he were dead keen. Wanted all them
old things she could find, liked havin em around for sum reason
though she couldnt see the point. Long as he valued em high an
were ready to pay up though she dint care, happy to bring em in

for his war chest. War chest. Even that she dint unnerstand but his eyes glowed when he looked at it. She looked back at where she'd stowed the ship in the lee of a giant red marble. She was still steppin off the deck evry coupla hours an just lookin at the beautiful thing. The Wide Open Road. It were all hers an it worked. She'd taken it an run the loop a few times around the System but now, days from anywun else, camped in the spinifex an burned out bushes, it were like a real animal all its own. It bucked an caught the breeze an the spars creaked an bumped over ruts she aint even seen. First few days she waited for a wheel to come off an send her, neck broke, cartwheelin into the scrub, but the feard died down a little an she'd started to get used to the speed. Helped no end that she followed a flat, broken road through old abandoned farmland. She knew there was worse trails out there, had walked a few already. Now an then she saw rusted sheet metal half dug into the dust an she'd picked up a few pieces, seein it was once painted a dark green but scoured near clean by years of wind. She couldnt right figger what theyd been but they turned up now an then along the road. Not worth the scav on the way out, she was gunna see what she found further out an if she come up dry she might take another look. She knew rough where she were goin anyway. Had spent days hauntin the hooks where the traders an scavs et an drank an she'd picked up enough to know she were headin out Glow ways, maybe even past the Boundaries though where they was seemed to be different dependin on who ya listened to. She breathed in the hot mineral smell of the dust an looked again at her ship. She still had a ways to go she reckoned an the light was droppin fast.

★

It were bad timin but there were nuthin she could do about it. She hit the outer arm as the sun disappeared behind a range that were further again than she'd travelled already. She heeled the Wide Open Road takin in what she could from a distance, the deep cut into the land runnin down below ground level in a massive spiral scar. Open maws cut here an there runnin back outta sight into the walls an evrywhere she looked rustin chain fences fallen flat an sheet metal goin back to the earth. Were a giant nest of sorts she figgered, an like nuthin she'd ever seen. Them smalls she'd crept down when she first come out had seemed so deep an dark back then but now she saw they scarce earned the words. This thing were still as a stripped hulk. She anchored the Open Road a hundred yards back from the edge of the first ramp an crept through the scrub, slow an careful, the last few metres to the crest on her belly. Takin her time, no telltale puffs of dust comin up. The light were almost totally gone now but her eyes was makin up the difference. She laid flat on her chest an pulled up her scope, focussin on the entrance to the Glow hole near a mile distant, dug down into the desert floor. She scanned the rough terrain rememberin the scare tales the travellersd told about the Reckoner an all them things that went on in the dark but as the sun set and the dust turned true rust red it looked nearpeaceful. She felt her shoulders ease up an her breathin slow an the noise of things burrowin in the dirt an faroff bird call seemed soothin rather than fearful to her. Down in the middle of the helix nuthin was lookin like movin an propped on her elbows she soaked it in. She were goin in, she were goin all in an she could feel it risin up an only wun thing gunna settle her. She were goin dark in the dark. She slid her way back from the crest an set about stowin the Open Road proper, dint want nowun comin across it while she was under.

54

As they crossed the tarmac she could see it changed colour in places, like white stoned been mixed in with it, an it were rough, made for sum purpose she couldnt ken. The distance stretched and stretched an she could see a stand of trees an what looked like even more open space so she led em towards it, disbelievin as the first space opened up into another that was five, ten times bigger than the first. She walked through the pale gums an it took her breath. Her eyes seemed like they was playin tricks, stretchin a coupla miles distant. To her right was wide open, cleared of all trees, edged with scrub an washed out red dunes. On an on an Block standin next to her lost for words himself. She turned to him an his hand was up, shadin his eyes an starin at the strangeness. She followed his gaze an saw the shadow an shape of sumthin at the end of the surface, maybe two miles away an only visible cos it sat at the top of where the whole slab ramped up an hit bush again.

What is it?

Block shook his head. *Dunno. Its white. Maybe been burned. Lets give it a look.*

Sail?

Nah, lets walk. Nuthin livin out here. Whaddaya reckon?

Cant feel nuthin but us.

Block started walkin an they kept to the edge of the great track, that were how she were gunna think of it. Sum kinda animal fear stoppin em from gettin too far from cover but she did have an itch to run out into the wide middle of it just to see what it would be like. Werent hard to stop herself though an the ground itself was askin plenny of questions she dint have the answer for. Marked an smeared with black streaks an more of em as they got closer an closer to the weird thing at the end of the concrete.

Block were right, itd caught fire a long time ago but itd once been white an she saw it were sum kinda hulk mebbe but not no kind she'd ever seen before. Big scorched holes at the back an what looked like stubby wings to her. A sail stickin up above its tail with a mark on it. White letters on a faded blue circle. It were shaped like a bird if she stretched her imagination a bit. Tipped forwards, beak dug into the ground an scraps of metal an sum other kinda plastic were stuck under logs an fallen trees thatd been piled at the end of the tarmac. It were a big thing, plenny of metal on it she reckoned an well worth the scavvin. They walked around to the pointy bit what she reckoned was the front an she could see glass windows still intact, scorched black like fired got into it an hollowed it out from the inside.

What is it?

Block turned to her. *Its a ship. It were a ship.*

She looked at it again. *Truth? Dont look like no ship I ever seen.*

Look again Orphan. This a ship. A sky ship if I aint mistaken.

Yeah?

I reckon this is a ship that were built to sail in the sky. Id forgotten all about em, read it a long time ago. Dint never know if it were just fancy but this thing looks powerful like how it were told. A big white ship built for sky sailin. Them wings carried it. Fellas sailed inside.

She looked at the thing again. Tipped nosedown on a broken wheel an blacked out with fire on the inside. *What happened to it? To them fellas?*

Id say theyre still in there. This things partburned sumhow an it dont look like nowun come out of it. Might be sum good scav in there?

She felt a powerful chill on her like her body just remembered where they was. Like she just marked how far West theyd come. Block walked a few paces towards it, shieldin his eyes from the glare.

Maybe not though Orphan, maybe it aint what I think it is. I can stand to leave it be if you can. Its your show.

She looked up at the skyship. If she'd found summin like it out on the flats she'dve stripped it for evry screw an buried what she couldnt take for another trip. She looked all around, takin in the bush an this huge wide open space an the feelin she couldn't shake that she was bein watched, hunted by sumthin. *Leave it for now. Dunno how much further we gotta travel an this thing aint goin anywhere soon.*

She turned away from it, fightin her curiosity. Ship. Grave. Both mebbe. Whatever it were she dint need a cursed gift from them old times right now. Dint need nuthin slowin em down or fancy diggin up no bones less she really had to.

55

Dark

Wake yerself Reckoner.
Im woke.
Yer close intya. We can feel yer close.
Yeah, Im close.
Remember whats gotta be done. Remember that yer our blud an kin.
I know it.
Protect us, protect all of us. Yev reckoned for us, reckon again.
I know it.

56

Two days sail on from the skyship an the thought of it started to creep into her wakin thoughts. They made cold camp for the night an she guessed things was weighin heavy on the Block too cos he sat there chewin strips off his roo an just stared out into the night as the moon come up. Theyd sailed late to wring evry last bit outta the friendly wind an the stars was comin up faint against the dark blue. Cold now. She thought of them dead fellas in their ship. She were sure now they was still in there an she were double glad she'd not tried to scav nuthin from it. She snuck a glance at the Block an he was just starin at a spot in the dark. There were a lot more moon tonight than when theyd left an things was outlined in blue fore they faded to black. She followed his gaze.

Whats that out there? Sumthin movin.

His voiced dropped to a real quiet murmur. Not a whisper, he were too old a sneakthief for that. She looked out into the night where he was starin an felt all the little hairs raise up on her arms an on the back of her neck. Out there maybe a hundred paces distant was a fella sittin on his heels on the flat sand, facin em, just still as a stone. A ways behind him, sittin an standin just as quiet was four

Ghosts an she reckoned Block hadnt seen em. She looked over at him an he'd drawn knife long an hook blade short, silent as ash fallin an he were sittin there just waitin for a move.

Thats him Block. Thats the fella I seen on the sand, thats the Reckoner.

57

Before

Theyll try an tell ya Orphan that nuthin ever happens in the past but that aint the whole of it. Ya see, what happens to each of us gets remembered as best we can but it aint perfect. That means evrywuns gunna have a different view on any thing what happens. So far so good right, ya followin me? I know these is big words an maybe hard to follow but ya gotta try cos this is gunna stand ya right when things is gettin outta hand in yer head an yer vexed real bad. Evrywun reckons the past is finished an in a place like the System where its pure survivin the past is gunna seem sumtimes like it aint worth the rememberin. But if yer wun of the wuns what remembers Orphan then yer wun of the wuns that can change it with a thought. You can change what happened real easy Orphan, you can make new memories or change old wuns an you can work the rememberins inta stories an them stories is what makes ya world. You gotta be careful of the stories you tell other fellas but most careful with the stories you tell yaself. You can take sumthin real innocent an make it inta such a poison that itll run ya life an thats sumthin I been real guilty of from time to time but ya can also take poison an make it inta fresh water if needs be. Yer lookin at me all fulla knowin Orphan an it warms me. I want ya to remember what I said remember it real good. Water inta poison an vice versa. The past aint fixed Orphan, its all there for the changin and makin new.

58

It were only that she could see in the dark that she saw what was happenin. The Ghosts what sat further out started movin silent an slow, all of em standin upright an flowin round their little campsite. They kept their distance but she could see they was penned in good an still she dint move. Block just raised himself real quiet up on wun knee an she knew he'd spotted the others by now. The bloke out in the dark just sat there for a while, not movin for what seemed like an age an then he stood, advancin on em without makin so much as a sound. The walk she knew now, leanin on that left hip, carryin sumthin that sat under his coat. It were him alright. She'd looked at him for them days when she was runnin on foot back from the Glows an her memory was comin back now she were lookin at him again. She was rememberin him sittin against the wall of the big tunnel where she found the map an now she reckoned he knew exactly what they was doin out here. How longd that map been up on the wall? She dint have time for all the questions an she stood up, drawin her bayonet an wrappin the soft cosh she carried around her left fist. It sure looked like it were happenin. She turned her head to catch Block in the corner of her eye an he were movin fast. Were real still that wun, until he decided to go. The four Ghosts on the edge dint move, just sat like trees, watchin over things as Block met the fella midway out on the sand with a dull clasha metal and then they was apart again. The Reckoner had dropped his coat an she saw he carried a short parang an he were faster than Block with it. Blocks long knife an short hook were no easy meal though an as she sprinted to em across the sand she saw the Reckoner have to give a little under Blocks fury. She come upon them in the dark, seein em both clear an she swung to the side of the Reckoner, makin a short chop with her blade an swingin her fist at the side of his ribs while he was focussin on Block. He slipped her punch an her blade swung through clean air as he stepped back from both of em. His hat were gone an she saw his hair was a light colour an his dust cover still sat maskin his face. The eyes werent givin nuthin, they was just concentratin an too late she checked her tail for the other Ghosts but no, she were fine, they hadnt even moved to follow the fight. They just sat on the four points of the compass round she an Blocks campsite, seemin not even bothered that wun of their own was fightin for his life. She ducked a wild swing from the fella an saw that itd been just a play to open up Block. The Reckoner kicked dust up at his eyes but Blockd been in too many street scraps for that wun an he just blinked through it an grit his teeth. Her bayonet clashed with the parang with a bad scrapin noise an she knew she dint wanna land anythin front on where the heavy thickness of the machete would carry straight through the finer steel of her blade. The Reckoner were rollin his shoulders this way an that like he'd been practisin the sweet science all his life, feet movin together or not at all an Block was throwin hook an knife at him, just a blur. The sweat were startin to sting her eyes an she flat out dint know how anywun but she were even seein what was happenin in this dark. Nowund even landed a cut yet an her breath was comin ragged. Been a long time since she'd gone on this long, outta practice and the Reckoner dint even look like losin his temper an he were facin two of the best knives in the System.

But she'd took her mind off what she were doin for a sec, or maybe a drop of sweat was in her eye at the wrong moment an the parang slid down towards the hilt of the bayonet, catchin for a second in the guard an jarrin her wrist down. It were like the Reckoner were almost too good, like he werent expectin her to make a mistake cos for the first time his feet was a little off balance an Block swept across his face with the hook and grazed his forehead afore catchin on his dust wrap an draggin it off. It were only the work of half a second but Blocks hand were all fouled with the fabric an no time to unravel it. The Reckoner followed the parang blow down through her hilt, drivin her down to wun knee an then swung a backhand fist at Block, catchin a hook blade across his knuckles for his trouble but sendin Block offbalance and inta the sand. She dint wait for no second chances an ripped a vicious left hook up inta the Reckoners ribs, feelin sumthin give as she swept inside his reach an tried to drive the bayonet up inta his groin. He swung aside, droppin his shoulder inta her nose an her eyes filled with tears. When she could see clear again she had her own bayonet against her throat an his parang were outstretched at Block who stood on the balls of his feet, ready to go for broke. The Reckoners face wrap stretched out in the sand behind him an Blockd switched hands but he had both blades an was two up again. Her cosh was as good as useless an she could feel it wouldnt take much more pressure to open up the vein on the side of her neck. She looked at Block an saw the look in his eye. He took half a step back an as he did the Orphan threw herself backwards onto the sand an away from the blade at her throat. Block flung his long knife at her, flippin end over end in the dark an she followed the dull silver as it skimmed over her fallin an disappeared into the sand. The Reckoner, attention split as she fell werent prepared an Block, back as he were born to it with just the hook blade in his hand drove off the balls of his feet, divin at the Reckoner. It were so fast an so reckless that it seemed like it took him by surprise an he fell back, swingin the parang too late an only succeedin in clinchin Block close. Block reached round him, searchin for the cut to the spine that was gunna end this. They fell hard inta the sand an the Orphan snatched up Blocks long knife as they wrestled. Her bayonet had been spilled inta the sand when they fell an they was both scrabblin for advantage when she lined up her left hand again an swung at the Reckoner, only catchin him a glance but enough to send him off Block. He rolled away an got his feet an the rest of the Ghosts finally moved. Comin in close on em an she picked up the long knife an then she an the Block stood back to back, watchin the long, pale bodies curl an uncurl in the dark, endins in evry move they made.

Alright Orphan?

Yep.

She were short of breath an her eyes was waterin but they was glued to the Reckoner, holdin himself, blud leakin from round his hand but not lookin angry, jus the same blankness as ever was.

You ready?

Yep.

Ill take the Reckoner then, you look after them others.

Was he fucken serious? She could near enough hear a smile in his voice an not for the first time she reckoned the Block were mad. She dropped into stance an tried to catch her breath, fixin her grip on the bayonet. They werent comin though. She dint unnerstand but then she saw the Reckoner backin away, not takin his eyes off em an the murder of Ghosts picked up an backed away too, lookin over their shoulders as they moved. The Reckoner stayed at their centre an Block moved up quiet on her shoulder, watchin as they shadowed themselves into the dark, fadin beyond the reach of her eyes. She dint know what had just happened but they was still breathin an that werent nuthin she'd expected five minutes before. Block roused himself first.

We gotta move. They might come back.

She knew they wasnt gunna come back but she dint know why she were so certain.

What the fuck were that, Orphan?

That were him. That were the Reckoner.

No kiddin Orphan. But why int we dust? Five of em an just us.

She were shakin, hands all over the place. Eyes not workin an her knees was about to go on her. Dint trust her voice.

I . . . I dunno. You drew first an he hadda chance to open me up here an twice more besides. Mebbe he werent here for blud.

Whaddaya mean twice more besides? An what elsed he be here for?

I was tellin ya. I seen this fella before, on the flatlands an again out in the Glow a few days ago. Hes hadda chance or two to end me an he aint taken it. Mayhap hes tryin ta warn us off? End us? Mebbe they know where were goin? Either way yer right, lets move. Cant stay here no more.

59

Before

The insect sound was loud an under it she could hear more whispers of tunnellin an conversations deep beneath her feet. Itd taken half the night to walk down the spiral, careful as she did. She'd darked her teeth an wore the blud marks under her eyes. She smeared the blade of her bayonet with spit an ash like she'd been told an tied evrythin down, strapped tight to her chest an she were as ready as she were gunna be. The entrance were massive, coulda run twenny fellas in there side by side an stacked em ten high. She walked into it feelin like she were steppin into the mouth of sum great beast, the black an yellow stripes on roof, wall an floor lookin like teeth to her eyes. The air were cool an dark, not terrible different to the outside, an she kept close to the wall, draggin her left hand past it, feelin faint rumbles of shiftin ground an who knew what, feelin shudders thatd started so deep below as just shivers. Her eyes was startin to figger out there werent any extra starlight comin their way an they was brightenin up the gloom, showin her the greyedout shapes of doors an tunnels leadin off left an right, great machines an pipes runnin out of lockers an doorways, runnin out of sight down, ever down into the earth. Scattered bones on the passage floor, plastic helmets an torn fabric. Boots with the soles rotted out an maybe sum with the bits o fellas still in em. She could hear her breathin pickin up, against her will her heart picked up and the beat of it felt like it was sendin a message to evrythin on two legs or none that there was fresh meat, fresh blud, an it were bringin itself right to their doors. She near turned around, a hundred yards into her first proper Glow, near picked up feet an blazed back out. A second later she were glad she hadnt. The sound of beats was real now, an it were outside her. She dropped down, openin her ears the way the Old Woman had taught her, listenin with her throat an feelin their air move as it come towards her. She hurried forwards on her toes, seein a nook ahead an tuckin herself behind a rockfall, makin herself small. Out the dark come first a pantin like a pack of dingoes an long after she heard the slap of bare feet on packed dust. She knew it were four an they passed her without a look back, lopin up tall, four Ghosts joggin up towards the night sky, wrapped in scraps an rags an movin in perfect match with each other. She held her breath, not lettin it go until they was long gone. She were about to step back into the tunnel when sumthin made her stop, sum kinda flash of colour on the inside of her eyes like a warnin an she waited an extra sec an saw a long, tall shadow with long claws stalk past her hidin spot makin no more noise than a dust mote fallin in the dark. No patter of foot or claw, it marched like it never even touched the earth an she could see a masked face swingin this way an that an she felt a cold in her centre that made her wish to be gone. It were true Ghost alright an it werent even close to anythin she understood. She dint dare breathe an it flowed past her up the slope to the exit an she were glad she werent out there with that thing huntin her.

★

Twice more she waited, hidden by steel door an sheet metal as packs of Ghosts passed her in the dark headin up towards the surface but she never saw nuthin like the tall wun again. Most of em looked like they mighta once been human but that wun, that wund been more beast than anythin else. Sum kinda merge like she'd heard in the darkest tales, a thing not quite all animal an smart enough to hunt ya blind. Beast enough to open ya up like barbed wire across the belly. She dint realise until the third groupd passed her that she were sweatin an the air were warm like a mornin in the desert before the sun got fullhigh. In the rush of dodgin Ghosts she'd clean forgot what she were supposed to be doin. Hadnt checked a single locker, hadnt searched a single room. Sum kinda scav she were, carryin same out as she come in with. She figgered she were probably half a kay at least in the deep, wun way in, wun way out. She saw the outline of an empty doorway in the tunnel ahead an stopped sharp, listenin for any kinda noise. Far away were a low growl but she'd been hearin the same for a while an it never come closer. She moved slowly forwards an slipped into the doorway, findin herself in a small room cut into the tunnel wall. Inside was two low tables an them funny boxes sittin on them that she'd seen on the rubbish heaps at the system. They had glass in them, she knew. Sum of the grinders could make rough scopes outta the tubes inside but they dint fetch much an sure not worth the weight of draggin all the way back across the broken roads. She crouched down an opened the drawers. Nuthin. On the second table they was locked an she took it as a good sign, takin out her rasp an jemmy an wrappin them in felt before poppin the locks. Inside was a plastic lighter. She held it up. Long empty, she dint dare spark it. Itd kill her eyes for a few minutes, she werent that green not to figger that out. She reached in further an pulled out a waxed box, slidin open the top an seein the blunt heads of six small rounds in a circle clip. Treasure. Her palms sprung a sweat. She put them on the desktop an reached in further, pullin out a small plastic case. She flipped it open an dint

179

know what she were lookin at for a second. Teeth. They was teeth, tops an bottoms. She picked them outta the case an held them up. Never seen nuthin like it. She shook her head, puttin them back in their little container an droppin it in her coat. She looked into the drawer an saw a stain, sumthin in there once but whatever it were had rotted through the bottom. She stuck her hand underneath the desk an pushed on the bottom panel, her hand bustin right through the rot an soft metal. Hadnt needed to bust the lock. Stupid. Know better next time. She pocketed the rounds an stood, openin the cabinet against the wall. It were full of dust that once was paper. Behind wun of the square boxes was sumthin else though, a book, wrapped in a plastic bag that looked still sealed. She picked it up careful an tried soundin out the words on the front but they was faded an it dint mean nuthin to her. Blockd want it though, she knew. She'd hit good luck an no mistakes about it. Short of findin pure gold or sumthin the Old Womand want her to, it were a grand haul. She pocketed the book careful an had a last sweep about the room. Good enough, she werent there for a rest, just time enough to snatch sumthin up an get out. She'd come back longer next time, go deeper, see what other secrets the Glow had for her. She were gettin edgy though an once ya started seein Ghosts in shadows she knew it were time to go. The old blokes at the exchange had been certain on that like they dint agree on near nuthin else.

★

She took the climb real slow, knowin this time that the Ghosts might come from either direction but she dint see nuthin of em. The heat ebbed away as she climbed back up towards the surface an the sweat dried on her face an back, turnin to a chill in her coat by the time she saw the faint starlight in the distance at the tunnel mouth. It were another while spent watchin an edgin closer before she came out, huggin the edge of the wall an slippin into evry shadow she could find. Workin her way back up the spiral she heard howls on the wind an once she smelled Ghost close by, saw the red hunger of it as she looked towards the scent but she dint see nuthin with her eyes. She hit the top of the helix as the sun broke the range on the horizon an by the time she crawled under the deck of the Open Road and put her head down her eyes was closin of their own accord. She fell asleep with one hand on the shells an teeth in her pocket an the other on her blade.

60

They made camp again in the mean shade of sheoak an dead, dry mallee bones an the sun dropped fast on em. Cold order an she could see their tack was runnin low, that they aint had nuthin fresh for days an they wasnt likely to. She nursed her bruised knuckles an sharpened the long knife an watched Block do the same with both his shivs but he still wasnt much for talkin. Could see him scoutin the horizon evry few minutes, waitin for sum sign of them thatd come out of darkness but she was certain they werent comin. Theyd been movin a full day an they was shattered tired. Just enough left in her to quarter the plain but she knew she werent gunna see nuthin. They was gone. Whatever they wanted lost an forgotten. The Block aint wanted to talk an she couldnt blame him neither. All that scrappin, then sailin, then watchin. No proper camp. Twixt the two of em an all the days theyd spent on sand together there werent much for the sayin. They tied off the ships against the dead tree an wrapped themselves in the sails against the chill.

Storm comin up.

She could see the stain of it against the last dregs of light.

Yep. Stay close.

They sat next to each other aside the trunk an she were glad of the warmth comin off him. Ran hot did the Block. Not the first time theyd made this camp. They pulled their hoods down an wrapped themselves together an when the sand hit it were just the two of em in the whole world. Too noisy to talk an no light, just swappin breath an heat an tryna kip as best they could. She knew it werent gunna come though an then she felt him sleep an she was out too.

She woke still leanin on the Block, him still asleep an the wind died down a bit, quiet enough but she felt sumthin out there on the sand. She shifted an he dint stir an she rolled back her hood an felt the dust hit her face. She tied off her wrap an shielded her eyes, starin into the haze, tryna figger what she was seein when sumthin hit her out the dark, a shape trippin on her an she heard the Block yell out an the sound of another voice. The sand cleared a little an for a second she though the Ghosts was on em again, close quarters an it were gunna be vicious wet work an then she saw it were just wun fella. Just wun shape an it held a long blade to the Block whod been caught by bad luck an happenstance.

The sand whipped around in a whirly an more starlight crept through the cloud an she could see the shape of him better an it were just a yung fella, not moren a yungen maybe but she reckoned she knew the face from down the hooks an corners an that sumhow, wun of Karras ladsd been trackin em all this way. Musta been followin them for days an they aint seen nuthin. Fucken sleepers needed wakin, they was gettin woke now. Block had murder on his face but he were caught cold an the Orphan could see the yungen were twitchy an with good reason. Nowt but Ghosts and killers an bad blud out here, she could vouch.

Easy yungen. What is it ya want? Who are ya?

The kid dint answer, just kept blade to the Block an sized her up.

Ya dint mean to stumble on us didja? Just come on us out the storm, right? Maybe you can just go on yer way?

183

There were a moment she thought she saw him waver but sumthin, fear mebbe, straightened his back.

Empty yer food out. And yer water.

Alright.

She opened her satch an dropped the jerky an tack, watchin his eyes follow the scraps of food.

Wun of Karras lads are ya?

Block shifted as he spoke an the kid raised the knife, quick as anything, to his throat.

Dont fucken move. I know who ya are. I know youse.

The Orphan raised her palms up slow an steady. *Nowun needs to bleed tonight. Ya can take the tack an leave us, we aint gunna follow.*

Do what I like cant I.

The kid were tryna brass it but she could see the fear.

An there aint no way yer takin us both back. Yer ship must be around here sumwhere, right? Why dontcha just walk on back an take off. No harm.

Whatever yer doin out here yer too late. We already been this way. Aint nuthin. And yer fellas are already dead.

The blud drained outta Block's face. He shifted again an he got the knife point hard against his neck for the trouble. *Orphan, whats he look like to you?*

Looks scared. But he believes what hes sayin. Dontcha yungen?

Dont fucken yungen me, dog. All yer mates is bled out by now. We knew when ya left. Been trackin ya for days.

He were tauntin now an she figgered the more he talked the better her chances got. Her hands was out an free an she knew she could have the blade out fast enough if it come to it. Block were always cool for the game but he was lookin shook at what the yungen was saying. Were it true? Were Block's peeps in trouble? She were sizin him up the yungen when she caught a whiff of sumthin rank on the wind. Sumthin dead an halfforgotten. Raised up old memories. She hadnt smelled nuthin proper for days an the

184

shock of it, the stink were so strong she could see the greasy yellow colour of it in the night sky.

Orphan?

Block called her back.

Stop yer fucken talkin. Enough!

The wind had near died down completely an it were like the storm never happened. Evrythin comin clear an sharp to her in the starlight like itd been washed with dust. The smell though. It hit her memory like a slap. Far out in the dark she caught sumthin movin. She squinted an then turned her head to the side. Always saw brightest out the corners of her eyes. There were sumthin movin for sure, werent Ghost, sumthin else. Sumthin big, an the dead smell came to her on a little gust an she knew what she were seein spite herself.

I know you been told to keep yer eyes on me no matter what yungen but ya need to look over yer shoulder now.

Yer fucken mates is bled out an the baldmans got it now. Unnerstand.

Block's face was horror. She dint know if what the kid were sayin was true or not but she could see him geein up to shed blud an time went real slow for her.

Last time Im tellin ya, hunker down yungen, sumthins comin behind ya.

The hulkin shape were comin close now an the smell of death on it were crawlin up inside her head an gut an makin her even dizzier than she were already. Her eyes was playin up, beatin light an dark with her heart an the air around her seemed to pulse. The yungen was still lookin at her an she saw the beast come past the trunk of the tree an heard its breath for the first time. Block threw himself aside as the yungen half turned an she saw the kid's eyes go wide an he spun all the way around to face it. Werent no stoppin it now though an she were rooted to the ground like she'd come up from the unders. The tusks an teeth punched into his chest an carried him off his feet an she wanted to close her eyes but couldnt. Owed the debt of witness to the thing. It shook its head

185

careless an fierce an she felt blud lash across her cheek on her an the yungen aint even had time to cry out. She seen where the bone gone into his heart an she knew it were gunna be over quick an that were the only mercy he could ask for. The great boar stamped an huffed out a gust of putrid air an the smell of iron an shit an rot were all around her. Block rolled away from the blud an the boar started, tossed its head again, openin the yungen right up an pushin its blunt nose inside as they stood starin. It raised its head, lookin at em both square as the kid slumped to the ground, innards spillin in the dust an nuthin but surprise on his face as his breath rattled outta him.

She took the Blocks hand an looked at the beast, speakin as firm as she could.

Blud. Blud. Unnerstand?

Block were frozen, fingers like dead sticks in hers, but she knew the thingd heard her.

She closed her eyes this time an felt her knees buckle under her until she was sittin in the sand, the Block with her, both their heads bowed down while the beast done its grisly work. After a while she felt it come towards her an she opened her eyes to see it set down on the dust in front of em, sated. It raised its giant head up when it felt her gaze an looked at her with flat black eyes that had no end nor beginning. She felt sick to her gut but she knew her obligations.

Yer got me thanks.

The beast huffed at her an she hung her head down.

Wheres yer mate?

It dint seem to unnerstand. Just laid its muzzle back down on the cold dark sand. She put her arm around the Blocks shoulders an held onto him tight as they sat side by side.

61

She woke curled against the Block, stiff an cold just before dawn. It were a breeze that woke her an she sat up, seein a fine line of light in the east. She cast around in a panic but there were nuthin but two ships, the tree an the rest featureless sand. No beast an no body but the dust was stained with blud. It musta took its prize away in the dark, she could see sum draggin marks an tracks but they was already goin. Itd headed even further West an spite the journey they was on she dint wanna know what was that way she reckoned. She an the Block unfolded from each other an she saw sumthin real unfamiliar on his face an it took her a while to place that it were worry.

Reckon we might as well get a brew on.

He nodded, near to himself, lookin far away.

She tried again. *Figger things is as bad as they gunna get.*

What were that thing last night, Orphan?

She busied herself makin the fire, takin her time. *That were a beast I met a long time ago. I dunno why it come now. Aint seen it in years.*

She could see Block workin that thought over but it dint make no sense to her so who knew what root it were gunna take in him. After a while he came an sat by the smoke an he still werent lookin at her proper. Like he'd seen her real shape last night or sumthin an dint wanna look again too close. He were seein now, that she were sure of. Seein that there was bigger things at work, stranger things. The sun picked up an the first heat washed over em an she felt herself calmin spite the night an spite the blud they was sittin a stones throw from. Sumwhere close was that boys ship but she dint have no time to be lookin for it, nor for what were left of him, if there were anything.

Orphan, that yungen knew we was out here.

She nodded.

We dint get out clean like we hoped.

Seems not.

I gotta go back. Look after the yungens. If yer old boss's made his move I gotta be there. Im sorry Orphan. I gotta go.

She let her breath out slow an hurtful. Werent no changin it. But werent no maskin it neither.

I know.

62

She looked East where she could see the Taipan throwin up dust an she felt terrible alone. She were right out on the West edge of where the last familiar things was endin. Up this way, whether they knew the reason for it or not, fellas dint come. She knowed why now. She finished makin the Wide Open Road ready an stowed her gear tight. A wind was comin up and she were gunna need to take it while she could. At least another days sail, maybe day an a half until she would start to reach the place on the map an she dint even know exactly what she was lookin for. She dint think there was gunna be a nice sign sayin welcome to the darkest secret ya can think of. She boarded up an unfurled the sail, catchin a gust an draggin the wheels round, the light ship heelin over in the wind, little outriggers skimmin the top of the spinifex an cuttin through an around the stunted saltbush. The Open Road picked up speed an she stopped thinkin of anythin at all, just watchin the sand like she was huntin.

★

The high point of the sun came an went an as it crossed the top of the sky she got becalmed an had to step out an start draggin the ship. She tied on the harness an made sure she kept her water close. The cloth wrap that covered her face got tied into a shawl an she covered her mouth as little gusts in the wrong direction started throwin dust into her mouth. Her glasses kept mosta the grit out of her eyes but it were hard goin an in the heat of the high sun she was gettin terrible parched. The ground were just broken enough that she had to watch it evry step. Nuthin moved on the rocks, not a lizard bakin or a spider or nuthin. No birds, no water nearby, she couldnt taste nuthin in the air, not even the poison she thought she'd be feelin as she got close. Still, she reckoned she had plenny of distance still left to cover. Were strange to think that sumthin this far out could be powerful enough to mayhap reach the System but she suspected nuthin was out the reach of them dark magics of the old days. The wind come up even more against her an she hadta stop. Furlin the sail werent enough, she hadta take down the mast an stow evrythin in the containers strapped to the sideboards. She chopped the Open Road down to a metal frame sittin on wheels an then tilted her nose inta the wind again, headin West, ever West.

★

The sund seemed to come up real slow that mornin but she dint notice it goin down proper until it sped up, slippin down the horizon like it were bein pushed, an afore she knew it she had ten minutes light left an the best she could say was the wind had stopped again an it werent shovin her backwards at least. She stopped her walkin for a second an she could feel that her legs was buzzin, hummin like they was about to quit an warm like theyd been sittin fireside for a long time. She dint know how long itd been since her last sippa water but she were rationin it out an a dry throat werent nuthin new. She reckoned she'd be a fool to get caught parched an dehydrated though. Never live it down with Block if she made it back. She trekked on an the shadows got real long, fadin until they was nuthin and she were just puttin wun foot in front of the other in the dark. Too dangerous for most but she had them bright eyes what come in so handy down the Glows an she figgered evry step she took while she still had the energy were wun more she dint have to take tomorrow. The temperature dropped as quick as the light an where the harnessd been chafin away with sweat an heat was sharp turnin to a chill. She stopped an had a dig in the cargo net of the Open Road, draggin out a woven poncho that were lined with fur an droppin it over herself. She could feel her energy sappin away but now she'd been travellin all day it dint seem to make no difference if she were goin a bit further. She was just gunna go a bit more, just a little bit she reckoned, then she'd stop an give herself a rest, a sip of water an dig out sum of the good meat she'd salted an saved for her dinner. Might even get a brew on. She were just goin on a little more.

★

The Orphan woke up face down in the sand an she thrashed as she come to, but the harness checked her writhin an once she felt that the panic started droppin. What happened? She pushed herself up onto her knees, the desert stark an cold around her an all lit up on account of her eyes an the dirty moon what had shown up. She musta passed out she reckoned? Bludy idiot. Was fair game for any beast what come lookin jus lucky there werent nuthin besides her stupid enough to be out here she reckoned. She crawled back to the ship that were tethered to her on the slack line an with her had she shoved the brake down. Looked like she found her campsite for the night. She took off the harness real slow, all her muscles cryin out at her an the leather stuck in the grooves where itd cut into her. She hung it on the ship an then she sat on the ground next to it, near enough too tired for a fire an a brew but knowin how much her body was cryin out for food. She dug around in her kit, commin out with a lighter an sum tinder an after a minutes work she hadda little thing goin, burnin wun of them coal squares the admen sold back at the System an dug a shallow pit for it so the flame were invisible. Werent as clean as a proper fire but it were better than nuthin an at least she could get a brew on. She were too tired be diggin out much else but she took out her billy an sum hardtack an made herself a biscuit soup with sum water an chucked a handful of string biltong in there as well, makin sumthin warm at least. She werent gunna get a full fire tonight anyway, she were gunna sleep wrapped up under the Road like she done a plenny of times when she were scavvin. She took her time drinkin the beef tea an felt it drainin through her, the warmth makin her sleepy but she crawled careful round the ship, peggin out the anchors an makin sure there were nuthin to catch the wind if it come up durin the night. She checked the ropes an then checked em again, feelin Block an the Old Woman with her as she did it, both of em tellin her to do it right once instead a poor twice. Good fellas both of em. She were havin a bit of the delirium she knew it. Things was swimmin in her vision an as she crawled inta the poncho again an pulled the warm fur around her she hadda feelin like it were both all wrong an all right with the world. Like it dint matter really what she dun or was gunna do next, that it were gunna be alright an she knew that it were the poison talkin to her. She'd made less ground than she'd hoped but she still musta come a fair way an that meant she was prolly gettin pretty close to where she did an dint wanna be.

*

She were powerful tired but she woke durin the night a coupla times, hand to knife. Once she were dreamin of an army of Ghosts an they was just sittin there watchin her sleep. She come up searchin but there was nuthin but the cold wind out there, not a creature bringin any kinda warmth. This were waste, she knew it now. This were sum proper badlands an she knew that all her travellin in the Glows an all what she done werent no preparation for this place she were comin to. Things had happened out on this land that even the dust was tryna forget. There was ghosts of a different kind here an memories comin to her that sure dint belong in her head. She musta drifted cos she woke again with a start, this time dreamin of Block. She was seein him comin home to the System but there were sumthin wrong an it were all burnin. She seen a cloud risin up over the land an evrywhere it rained things was burnin, meltin, fadin to ash. The wind come with it too an there were a light an a heat like nuthin she'd ever saw. Dust knew she had moren a few reasons to hate that place but moren a part of her still called it home an she had the fear in her for Block an his fellas. Werent no tellin what Karra would do if he were on top an worse if he had his back up. She werent ready to see it burn an the dream put a powerful fear in her. She were a long way from evrythin but not in the normal way she were used to. Things was gettin real out here an she hadda lot to be thinkin on an not a whole lotta time to do it. She sucked in sum of the cold air, wonderin if she were drinkin in the poison itself an just zackly what it were she was lookin for. The fire had gone out long before an the tea she'd brewed were just a tiny speck of warm memory fightin against the dark an the cold. She'd sand in her mouth an she hadnt put a cloth in. Might not be a beast in cooee but there was more bad fellas out there than she knew so she took the rag from her pocket an chewed on it as she fell asleep.

★

She woke again as the sun was comin up but she were sleepin facin West an it just come on slow as a black turnin to blue an she left her head layin down, lookin out from under the struts of the ship, feelin good it were there an that she'd lasted the night. She dint wanna move anythin cos she knew what it was gunna feel like when she tried so she jus stayed there, watchin the fingers of dawn reach out an feelin the warm glow on the back of her wrap. Itd been a long dark night she reckoned an wun she were glad to see the end of. In the light she could see proper where she was an it looked like no place she'd seen in all her years of trekkin the sand. No more trees, just sand, but it were a different colour, paler than the red she knew, an darker brown in other places, near a burned colour like a stick that hadnt caught proper in the flames. Either side of her she could see big flat pads of concrete or sum kinda carved stone an she'd seen enough out on the flats to know they was the footprints of buildings made in the old times an long since vanished into dust an wind. Past them was great rocks here an there but they dint look like they was meant to be where they was an even though she could see the edges was rounded by time an sand they still looked like they was wounded, cracked an tossed there by sum great careless hand. She couldnt stay where she was, she knew that, even though it were powerful temptin to just huddle there under the ship for a bit longer. She could feel a breeze was gunna pick up an she knew from the map an her own rough reckonins that she couldnt be more than a day or two from the Maralinga place. Even though she carried a drawin of it with her the map were stuck in her head an when she closed her eyes she could see it clear as at Blocks table. She crawled out from under the deck, stiff an cold an still tired, an then she turned herself around sittin there so she was facin the sun comin up. It were a reckonin she knew now, it were a day where she were gunna find sumthin she'd been lookin for a real long time. It were a shame Block werent with her an it were a shame she dint have the Old Woman with her to see it too. Nuthin woulda made her warmer than knowin she were there with her showin her what to do next but she knew it were only proper that she was on her lonesum again. She was gunna lose count of all the times she figgered herself an orphan but that were near enough her name werent it? She hauled herself to her feet, knees crackin and bones grumblin at the poor treatment but she werent feelin quite so heavy right now. There were a great settlin comin an she were makin herself ready for whatever it were she were gunna find.

★

The wind were the only thing movin, besides the Wide Open Road, an she dint hardly have to steer her save around sum of them strange rocks that come up evry now an then. She'd checked the map twice to make real sure an she knew she were on a good course for where it said the place were. There was strange glitterin out there too like salt were crustin on the sand but when she went to take a look she found it hard an green an melted lookin. Sorta like the glass that she'd seen down sum of the better Glowholes an like scavs sumtimes dug outta the hulks that were buried or left rustin out on the plains, autos the old fella had called em once, funny name. Dint make no sense like so many of the things what she'd been told. Yeah an sure enough this were dead country, she saw bones out on the sand but she dint wanna go too close to em, dint wanna find out what kinda creature they was from, special if they was the same kinda creature she was. What had happened out here? There were a powerful bad feelin like the land aint forgot the treatment itd had an it werent healed an it werent ready to welcome nowun back to it yet, if ever. She were scannin the horizon an thought she saw sumthin. A few minutes more sailin she knew she was comin up on sum built thing, whatever it were, sumthin square what dint fit into the land. She stopped the Open Road an took out the scratched scope but it were near the same colour as the desert an she were still too far away to get much idea of what it was. Sum kinda marker an more than she'd seen in days of crossin pure dead nuthin without so much as the sense of water or anythin havin ever been alive out here. Nuthin for it now she reckoned, been a while comin.

63

Blockd seen smoke from miles off an he'd stowed the Taipan afore his dust announced him proper an he'd been walkin from there. The System were on the horizon, a glow comin off it he dint like much at all and what with the wind dyin itd taken days back across the sand, sum of it in harness an now he were comin up on the place in the dusk, which truth be werent a bad time if he had to be comin in unannounced but it were sure as dust a lot later than he woulda chosen for himself. As he come closer he could smell it. It were the taste of panic an burnin rubber like the tyre towers was goin up an he knew if they was burnin things was pretty bad. He dint know what Karra might be capable of but he reckoned it were the worst. Reckoned he'da done whatever he saw fit to run things. Block started comin real close an even against the blueblack sky he could see the smoke risin an the terrible thing were the quiet. He was plannin on goin in the Silent Gates if the Orphans friends was still keepin watch like theyd promised so he kept hisself hidden by the wadis an river-runs, movin quiet in the neardark. He came within a half mile of the walls an could see better now. The burnin he'd smelled seemed to be comin from well inside the loomin walls an the Stacks stood black an cold as they ever was, untouched by flame an silent. He snaked across the sand slow, smellin the smoke on the breeze an closer he got the surer he were that things was as bad as could be. The entrance theyd come outta was quiet an the Orphans mates was nowhere at all an he dint trust it in the end. Block shrugged his pack an took out the hook as he sat in the shadows of the stack, moren wun way in an out and he werent such an old bloke yet that he couldnt climb. It were a long fall though an itd been a while. He breathed a long breath an scanned the wall that sat distant either side of the black cliffs that stood over him. There dint seem to be no Watch set that he could see an that suited him just fine. It were the quiet though that were most unnervin, he dint think he was that late that evrywund be slaughtered but there was no tellin from where he stood.

*

He came down West of the burn pits after workin his way up the cracks an gaps in the wall. The rubber were petrified like stone and he'd hadta dig the hook in moren once for purchase as he climbed. Droppin deep in the rubbish the smell nearly felled him. Shit an rottin meat and he jus hoped it were mostly animals he was smellin. The smoke were thicker now that he were inside the System but he still couldnt see nuthin burnin an strange enough there werent nowun to be seen. He made his way in from the outer rings, not seein anywun, were like evrythin livin had been vanished all at wunce. He were near spooked but now an then there were a glow behind an he felt hisself bein watched from a whole lotta diffrent directions though he dint see a face nowhere. The place dint look destroyed neither but there were black smoke in the air, thick an stingin his eyes an it were comin from sumwhere near the centre he reckoned. He started hurryin along even faster, a tick in the back of his mind, a faint scratchin like a memory you was tryna forget or hopin not to haveta remember. He came round the hook an it all come clear, droppin like a weight but not so surprisin that he dint stick to the shadows. It were Blocks place an all them that was next to it that were burnin.

The place were surrounded by Karras fellas, them same fellas he'd seen a hundred times before an not paid too much nevermind. Standin free among em was a heavybuilt lad with candlesoot ink on both his arms, an it were Gus. Wun of the two Blockd left lookin after things. He'd done a real good job of lookin after them. Block could see a few fallen in the street, lads an lasses with pikes and parangs through em, sum still half alive an tryna get away but there werent nowhere to go. He knew now why there weren't nowun in the streets. Big bludlettin gettin done. Gus's mate Cutter was bein held by a coupla big lads an he was bleedin out the head far as Block could tell an fierce wounded through the chest by the way his shoulders was heavin. As Block watched Gus took up a long blade an walked up to Cutter an ran him through without so much as a byyourleave. They was friends too, Block knew em to be close knit, always hangin about, stayin close to each other. He'd figgered em good mates. Showed how much he knew. Gus wiped the blade on his strides an then took Cutter from the lads holdin him an set him down gentle on the sand. They was all lit by firelight comin through the front of the place an it was startin to burn up through the roof, spittin tongues of flame to the night sky. Even though the bile were risin in Blocks gullet the more he looked at his lads strewn in the dust he was thinkin clear about what musta gone down. Gusd waited till he were gone for sure, had waited long an patient like hed been taught an then told Karra the hourd come. Theyd figgered Block were only dangerous while he were here an it looked like theyd been right for the most part about that. Sum of his lads musta got away cos there werent enough laid out in the street an he were just hopin fierce there werent any trapped inside by the flames. Sumwhere out there in the dark hidin from smoke an Karras blokes was a handful of his yungens what had survived an before he did nuthin else he hadta find em an get em together an safe. Sumthin gotta be done he reckoned an it were fallin to him. Sumtimes the game werent chess or checkers or nuthin like that. Sumtimes the game was kill or get kilt an he were plenny good at that wun too.

64

Of all the things she were sure she werent gunna find it were big black letters sayin Maralinga an yet here she were, lookin at em. Maralinga Nuclear Test Site on a gate standin in the middle of nowhere an next to the letters a whole mess of numbers an the circle of six, three black, three yellow. She knew what they meant an she stood starin at it for a while, ship anchored, just takin it in an wonderin what it meant that her secret were sittin there three spans high, starin her in the face. Behind the gate the road stretched long into the distance, edged with low mallee scrub before it turned left into a stand of dead gums an vanished from sight. She left the ship where it was an walked around the gate, lookin at it both ways, sniffin the air comin from the West an gettin nuthin from it. There were no fence either side but she figgered there musta been wun time. It were dead. Not just dead but sterile, like itd never been livin but she knew from the Old Woman that werent the case. She looked at the gate itself an took the latch off its hook, swingin them big old doors wide an they moved awful good for sumthin that oughtntve seen no grease in dust knew how long. Maybe they was just built to last. She got that Ghost feelin on her an stopped an breathed openmouth, tryna taste what direction blud was gunna come but her senses werent what they shoulda been. Just a lotta dustforsaken nuthin an her own blud in her ears the only reminder all was not forgotten.

★

She dragged the Wide Open Road through an then set the sail along the white road. It were just a breeze, not much more than walkin but she were glad of it an it carried her past the low scrub, more an more of them flat concrete blocks out in the bush an around em rusted spars an corrugated iron. Burned glass an stands of poisonous bush tomatoes growin through the ruins. On corners of the road she could see crumbled concrete boxes an rusted iron drums an the further she travelled in the more an more leavebehinds started to creep in. Overtakin the scrub until she were back on a flatland, scarred orange earth stretchin evrywhichway, hills of pale green in the long distance an a scrub inches high fightin its way through in the odd hollow. The heat come up an started to bear on her but the wind stayed true an the ship rattled on, crossin junction after junction of smooth white road stretchin out in all directions an she knew she were on sum kinda grid, that these straight lines was laid down by them with no love of the land. Lines laid down by fellas what never had to walk em. Out the sand came poles like broken teeth an she could see from the deck of her ship there was sum that was fallen in between the wuns that was standin an they lay part buried, sand washed up on em an pullin em back to the earth. She could see strands of wire too, so old it were the colour of the ground but parts of it still wrapped in black plastic gone grey an she knew that she dint wanna scav a scrap of it no matter what it were. It were like travellin through the Boundaries cept there werent bodies staked out, it were a grave for all them things thatd come before. Like she'd wished it on herself the wind died halfway up a ridge an she were becalmed again. Might be more gusts on the crest, she dint know, but she stepped off the spars at a jog an then took up the rope again. No harness for now, she were still too battered from the long walk. She took the tension an started pullin her ship up the hill, heat droppin on her like a blanket.

65

Before

I never knew it but I dreamed it, Orphan. There were a heat. There were a light. An it were a light like you never seen an if ya did you werent never gunna see again. A cloud, miles high, earth turned to glass an a wind to strip the skin from ya, flay ya an turn ya ta ash where ya stood. Turn family to memories. Unnerstand Orphan? This is what yer facin. The warp an weft of the truth. I know my own end is comin soon but about summa them old times my knowin gets scarce. I dont know how it were dun an in the end I dont know why Im sorry Orphan. I know ya got a place in yer heart for me an I hope I aint led ya astray. I know Im gunna bleed out on this sand but after all that, about you I dont reckon I know nuthin. Thought I did but I was wrong. Thought you was gunna live through it all but now its all gone cloudy on me.

66

Dark

You showed quarter.

He dint say nuthin.

You showed quarter an you let them go. They had a recknin comin an you showed quarter. Why them when youve made blud peace with so many of them what come before?

It weren't a question that needed answerin. He kept his head low, waitin for them to make the decision. There were noises come out of them that sounded like sighs an gusts of wind an he knew they was speakin in a way he couldnt. In a way he werent built for, spite all the graces theyd shown him. Itd been stirrin up in him a long time but out on the sand he'd not been certain. In ways he aint never come across. He were always so sure, aint never had cause to hold his steel but this time. This time. He knew they was takin it all in. That to them he dint have no secrets. That he owed em his very life an the debt was to hold the old ways dear an do as they bid. Lest we forget the fallen. Still they spoke the sigh an whisper about him an he felt himself held by the thinnest web, just the faintest blessin on him, held in the palm of the rocks an dust an trees with just their favour keepin him breathin.

Reckoner.

Im here.

We favour you Reckoner. Even still.

He let his breath out slow an deliberate, not realisin he'd been holdin it.

Them from the upabove have already been an gone. Theyve been sectionway an no turnin back. They will taint the soaks an scorch whats left. Only wun way to make it right.

He saw himself from above an from below an he knew what was comin.

Reckoner reckoner reckoner.

They was chantin now an he felt the voice of his blud risin up in him. Givin him strength.

All of them. All of them. Reckon. Reckon. Reckon.

67

She were sweatin hard when she hit the crest an like she hoped there was a breeze, but it went forgotten as she looked down on the plain in front of her. Three, four miles distant was two great open sheds sittin in the middle of nuthiness. The roof on wun of em had collapsed but they stood stark on the plain an next to them was a long low buildin near enough the same colour as the dust what surrounded it. Another mile further was what looked like a great red earth pyramid an out on the plain there was a small grey speck that weren't nuthin natural. She kicked the brake on the Open Road an sat down on the deck, feelin the cold creep into her spite the sun an even with the gusts pushin past her it were quiet an she marvelled at the flatness of it, the anklehigh scrub an the colourless bleach of it all. Out either side of her she could see spikes set into the soil evry fifty paces or so an she walked out to look at the nearest. There were sum kinda sign fixed to it with what looked like a faded picture of a roo on it an sandblasted bits of letters she couldnt make out. The same thing evry fifty yards stretched off into the distance. Dint make no sense to her an she walked back to the ship an sat back on the spars. She stayed put a while, just watchin the plain below, not wantin to go closer but the changin wind made a choice for her an she skated the ship down the hill until she was close enough to the sheds an then she tied the ship off an gathered her things about her an started in on em. The sheds was just wide open an she could see the bones of em, sum rusted through an others collapsed with time, an in another life she might canvassed the ground for bolts an the like but not now. Whatever their secrets they werent givin up nunofem an their reason for bein was lost to more years than she reckoned she knew. Through their open walls she looked at the strange low buildin that musta been built later but not as good. It were pitted by a thousand dust storms an the roof looked like it were collapsed in sum places, no doubt rainin sand an dust inta the inside. Sumwun out here had saw fit to remember Maralinga an there were still sum kinda buildin out here standin to mark the place. Sum kinda lesson from the Old Woman nigglin in the back of her head an makin her pull up her scarf an wrap her mouth and pull her field glasses down over her eyes. The place looked like sumthin she mighta seen around the System but it were even more abandoned than the worst places in there an it carried sum kinda evil feelin with it she could taste on the back of her tongue, even through the mask. As she come closer she could see the door had fallen off a long time ago an it lay on the ground. Inside it looked mostly dark an her brighteyes dint seem to be workin too good while she stood on the edge of it so she screwed up the fear what were inside her an stepped across an into the hot dark buildin. It took a sec but her eyes sorted emselves out an she were in a long room filled with so much dust it looked like smoke in the air. Evry time a storm come it musta gone through the place. Little cases standin up evry few spans, drifts of red dirt against em an on the walls was sum kinda paintins an pictures what were stuck up high sumhow. She'd seen books with pictures before but these were bigger an when she looked close she could make out yellowed shapes an they looked like people. She walked slow an careful down the length of the room, tryin not to

205

kick too much dust into the air an she come to a stop in front of a picture that were in better nick than the others, sum kinda glass in front of it, frosted with cracks but good enough to look through. The picture was showin all kindsa fellas, jus lookin back at her from the wall. A lot of em had real sad eyes an sum of em had the milk eyes that sum of the old fellas back at the System had. She could tell sum of em was real sick an there was other fellas with em all wearin the same kinda clothes. She stood lookin at it a long time but it werent givin up none of its secrets. The picture next to it had what looked like words across the bottom but the air an storms an heat over the years hadnt been real kind to the paper an the letters was lost. She worked her way round, lookin in all the cases an where theyd been preserved there was pictures of fire an kids an pictures of the dust an pictures of hulks, an people was standin around wun of em an it looked like itd caught fire real good, it were black an parched an burned. There was pictures of folk that had that look like they was real important an there was pictures of peeps what looked like they dint think they was no better than dust. The Orphan knew them looks real good. She seen em her whole life. Dint make no sense though, she knew she was lookin at them old times the Old Woman was always bangin on about. Them perfect old times what she liked to dream about even when she was tellin the Orphan about all the bad things what got done. An here was sum moments what had survived and them old times looked a lot less than perfect. She made her way deeper inta the shed, tryna unnerstand the pictures she was seein but more often gettin stuck on what was goin on. Too much time had passed for her to figger out what exactly was happenin but over an over again she saw faces what looked terrible familiar. She thought them faces was part of her own time but it looked like they wasnt. Towards the back she stood over a wide case with the glass lid still in place an inside she saw sumthin familiar. It were another map of Maralinga but this wun were smaller an written on it was a spot readin you are here, next to them same words what were on the sign outside, Maralinga Memorial Site. Well, that were where she was. She circled the case, readin all the words she could find. There were points sayin blast site, safety area, observation post, vehicle test, unused test site, all kindsa words she hadta sound out an take her time gettin to know. She saw it upside down from the other side of the case an hadta walk slow around, the words what was real familiar again, words what she'd heard an maybe seen in sum of the Old Womans papers. It read Taranaki Waste Material Burial Pit. She unnerstood enough of that to know. Here were the real thing, the thing she come to find. It dint look like no more than a few miles away from where she were standin right now an she felt the weight again, the same wun what had dropped on her when she were down the Glows an seen the other map for the first time. She stood over the case, memorisin the landmarks an the land itself before she took her eyes away an looked at the back of the room. She were close to the end of the cases an she dint see nuthin important in the other wuns but at the back of the room near where the roof had caved in there were a cloth what run across the ceilin on sum kinda runner an it were drawn across, sealin off the end bit. She crossed the room an tugged gentle on the cloth. The runner musta been held together by pure rust, came crashin off the roof an onto the floor, raisin up such a thick cloud of dust that if she hadnt been wearin her wrap she mighta coughed herself to death. She jumped back, waitin for the dust to settle an she saw a fella loomin up at her out the back of the room an she went for her blade as fast as she ever had. Droppin into a crouch she held the bayonet out strong an steady but the fella din move, just stood there like a statue. She took another look through the dust that was still filterin down an she realised there werent no rise an fall, the fella werent a fella at all. It were a strange lookin thing standin up inside a glass case that had sumhow lived through whatever had happened to the buildin. She walked closer, not afraid anymore but still wary of the strangelookin thing. It were a pale yellow colour an sum kind of plastic or leather an it were in the shape of a person. Dint have a mark on it, were like itd never been touched, come fresh out the past without no blight on it. There were sum kinda sign on the bottom of the case etched in stained metal. She read it slow. Radiation Protection Suit Mk IV. She dint know what all that meant but she unnerstood protection real good. Whatever that thing in the case were it were sum kinda protection against whatever were out here. She stood in the filterin dust for a long time lookin at it. Did she trust it? Why else were it here. She felt the Old Woman close to her an she stepped back a pace reversin her grip on the bayonet in her hand an swingin it at the glass, raisin a hand to shield her face.

68

Block dint have much on him but a hook blade an a long knife an he dint fancy his chances real good against twenny or more of Karras blokes. It were typical o that snake to have all them fellas out there an Gus who was clear enough his man but the bald bastard himself werent nowhere to be seen. The fire were ragin fierce through the buildin now an Block could tell it were reachin all his precious leaves, all the papers an books he'd collected from the old times, all the voices of the dead was bein lost to the flames. He started movin closer, huggin the shadows like he were a Ghost hisself an afraid o the light. He had a cold killin anger on him now an there werent no comin back from this without sum blud spilled. Werent nun of Karra's lads watchin their backs save for the odd turn to banter with each other. Block were creepin past summa the bodies of his yungens an as he moved past em he caught the glassy reflection of light outta their flat eyes an he made his heart hard against the fear an kept slidin an slippin through the dark like he dint never know no diffrent. All them years of playin long cons an makin careful moves was fallin off him as he got closer an all he were thinkin about was bein a littlun again an seein that orphan goin up for sale down at the auction block. He'd been sold hisself down there once, picked up the name, all theyd called him for the first ten years of his life. Afore he'd up an gone an kept it to spite em. He were patient but sumtimes it dint pay to be patient. Sumtimes it paid to carry hate a long time an use it to keep ya goin an sumtimes come a time that ya had to let it out. The closer he was gettin to Karras lads the more he was feelin like the old, old Block an when he were ten spans from Gus an still in the shadows of the firelight he caught the whiff of grog on em an he knew they was cowards what couldnt do their wet work dry an that the odds was in his favour all of a sudden. He were about to draw the long knife and the hook blade an drop all cover when he heard a crack like a whip but far off an felt sumthin wasp past his head. He stopped in the shadows, both knives out an watched as the blokes in front of him looked around, confused. The came another whipcrack, and another, and another, an Block knew what was happenin, even if Karras lads dint. The rounds he'd saved up careful for moren ten years was cookin off an werent no tellin where they was goin. Block dropped to his stomach quick an the sound of bullets goin off turned into a fast tattoo an he heard the bigger thump of shotgun shells an .303 rounds punchin through the corrugated iron an wood of the building. Wun of Karras lads caught wun in the neck an dropped screamin an the others all had blade out, spinnin round, not knowin what was happenin. The buzzin got louder an bits of hot metal was ricochetin off tin an steel an out in the middle of the street the boys was finally twiggin that sumthin werent right an a few of em had dropped belly to the sand and had their hands over their ears. Gus werent so quick an wun slashed across his thigh an even in the firelight Block could see itd clipped sumthin serious an bright red blud bubbled up through his fingers as he dropped, cryin out to the dust. The noise an shoutin of the lads was startin to die down, just the odd pop of a .22 still fizzin around inside an Block reckoned his chances werent gunna get no better. He stood up an stepped clean outta the shadows, crossin the dusty street quick an kicked Gus's legs round so he were lookin straight at him. Before he could even cry out again, Blockd pushed the long knife straight between his ribs, puttin his weight on the hilt and leanin in so he was lookin right at him. Block spat in his face as his eyes opened up wide in horror an then dragged the hook blade across his throat to be sure of it. It hadnt taken moren two seconds an Karras fellas was still layin in the dust, a few caught by bullets but most just stunned, jaws dropped an knives stuck in their belts. Blockd been expectin sum kinda sharp fight on his hands but they was just lookin at him like he were a Ghost. He got a few steps back outta the group of em, farther than he reckoned he woulda an then Block were runnin, runnin hard through them back alleys with both blades still dark an drawn.

69

Karra were ragin fit to murder sumwun. To murder more sumwuns than he had already. Them fucken fools he'd sent to take care of Blocks boys had only managed to get a few of em which meant sumwhere out there was a mess of yungens fixin to spill his blud all over the System. An to top it all off them fucken idiots lit the place up an itd near enough exploded. What the fuckd the Block been keepin in there? Killed four of his blokes an put another two off their feet wounded. Wun was already infected an Karra knew there werent nuthin he could do for him but ease the way out. Add them fools to the hundred sick from out near the pits an he'd had cando men askin at his door two days straight what were wrong with em an he aint had much to tell em cept piss off. Seemed like the whole place was rottin alive an Karra dint have no answers. Werent gunna keep em at bay long. Them stupid fucken ladsd let Gus, the only wun what knew all of em by sight, get kilt in the street. Right in the middle of em. By none other than the Block hisself who were supposed to be dead an buried out on the sand. It were a fucken disaster, thats what it was. That fucken idiot Gusd deserved to get it. Sellin Block out an then fucken up so bad that nearly all of emd got away. Bout the only consolation was that

Blocks place was nuthin but cinders but Karra knew it werent a place he'd got to be wary of, it were the yungens what had lived there an right now they was probly plottin away on how best to open him up. He were reminded of the old fellas sayin. Yeah it were less than fucken ideal alright. He were tempted to open up the grog but he needed all his wits about him right now he reckoned. He banged on his desk an a lad come in standin in front of his desk. Karra looked hard at him, watchin him shift his weight from foot to foot an the shifty eyes an broken teeth.

Where are the rest of your fellas?

The fella spoke with a crack in his voice, like he was expectin trouble.

Sum of em laid up, sum outside waitin on what to do next. Russ aint gunna make it, got the blud poison. Could take his leg off but he aint survivin either way.

He know it?

He knows.

Thats on you.

I unnerstand boss.

Do ya? You was supposed to be out there yaself last night. Supposed to be lookin after my lads an where was ya? Smashed on clear wine an spewin in yer boots. I should have ya staked out already but I got wun chance for ya to make it right.

I will boss.

Good. First thing ya gunna do is get out there on them hooks an bring me Block, or his head, by mornin.

213

70

It were bluddy heavy an she were glad she werent carryin it far. She turned again to make sure it werent slidin off the *Wide Open Road*. She were in harness again an towin the ship with the yellow suit folded up as best she could and stowed loose on the deck. It were real stiff an when she looked at it close it had sum kinda metal woven through it real thin an layers an layers of sum clear stuff she aint never seen before. Whatever it were, it were strong. All them faded pictures showed the years on em but the suit dint look like itd been sittin in that glass case since the old times. She werent sure if she should already be wearin it but it were so hot she figgered it were best to put it on when she reached where she were goin an not before, if she wanted to make it there at all. Werent no towin the ship wearin that bluddy thing, that were certain. She turned an looked back up at the sheds on the hill. She'd half expected em to be gone but they was still there, sky clear through em.

The track she were on was gettin close to the strange grey stone out in the middle of the rocky field but the big flat red buildin she'd seen from up on the hill was still a ways off. That were where she was headed. The ground either side of the track was uneven an gettin weird around her an she knew she werent gunna be able to take the ship out with her to get a closer look. She anchored it an took a long, still look at the thing a hundred yards in front of her. Shaped kinda like a road marker but squat an heavy. The ground were burned like she'd seen before on the journey in but there was big arcs of what looked like glass glitterin in the dust an she could see when she caught the right light that they formed great rings reachin out an visible in places fore they disappeared. They was covered in places with dust an sand but she could see the curves well enough on either side to figger they must reach all around an make a great circle sumhow an in the middle was her marker. She hadta be careful on the ground, it were loose an not proper settled an each step it tried to twist her up. She got to the marker it an crouched down, seein the worn writin on the side of it. Wun side were near all gone, musta faced the wind for a coupla hundred years but the other side were still there an she read the words careful, tracin her fingers.

TEST SITE TARANAKI
A BRITISH ATOMIC
WEAPON WAS TEST
EXPLODED HERE ON
9 OCT 1957

She looked again at the other side an the near invisible sign etched into the concrete, of the circle broken into threes again. Most of them words meant nuthin to her but she knew. This were the spot. This were the spot where wun of them beasts was let out into the world without care for them that lived here or them that was comin after. She stood back up an looked around her an it came clear she was standin in a dip. Shallowlike, near hidden but sum great gouge had been taken from the earth an filled in an that were why the ground were loose an broken because it werent the ground that were meant to be here an she stood in the heart of a

215

scar now with this thing to mark its place. She looked back at the Open Road an then off in the distance, feelin a pattern to the place an a hurtin in her heart. All them uncounted years she knew to have passed. The words an numbers she dint have no knowin of but the ground couldnt lie to her. Couldnt lie to nowun.

★

Closer an closer together the glassy rings were until for a bit it were like she were walkin only on the dusty slippery surface an the Wide Open Road was slidin around as she dragged it behind her. She reckoned she musta crossed the centre of another great circle though an soon enough she saw more rings of glass in the dust but now they was curvin the other way. Yep, she were across the centre but there were no marker this time and she was edgin close to the flattopped red pyramid ahead. Around it the desert stretched out flat an blank as dust all round her, not a single bit of scrub higher than her knees in all directions just the shimmer of hills in the long distance. The sky were a pale grey she werent used to, like all the colour were bled out of it an her extra senses that usually lit her up when nuthin else was firin were dead like burned brush. There werent even a proper smell to the place.

★

It were the bones that gave it away in the beginnin. First she saw a ribcage half buried in the dirt an bleached by the sun an wind to a perfect white. Then it were the heavy bones of the leg scattered like sum creatured had a go at em an here an there some cloth or were it flesh still on em. Then more an more an she started seein skulls of fellas lookin up at her from the dust an they werent as old as she woulda liked neither, specially considerin they was out here bein blasted by the sand. An these were just the wuns what the desert had given up. She reckoned if she looked deeper she might find she was walkin on a carpet of bones hidden just under the surface of the sand. Found herself followin the bones, realisin they led to the wall an there was no escapin. She were deep in hostile lands an no mistakin it. The air seemed to be tryna cut her breath short an the terrain gave nuthin away. She knew she werent but a moment away from losin all idea of direction an the sun seemed to have been direct overhead for hours, givin her faint idea of where West even were. She saw more shards of grey bone stickin out the dust an she reckoned soon enough her own might be joinin em. She stopped dead an felt the lack of anythin, the big, reachin, creepin vastness of the space around her. The wall rose up in front of her, smaller than it looked from a distance but made of rock an stone put together with sum care. A pile maybe, not a wall an flecked with glass an who knew what but sumwund built it wun time an here it stood. She took the slack of the Open Road an looked, seein a path to the side of it, an old road maybe an railings, rusted off an rottin but markin a path. She grabbed the ship again an started across it, figgerin it were leadin sumwhere, an she turned the corner of the big red structure an saw a maw cut into the site of it an the blackness within.

★

The suit were stiff an it smelled like sumthin poisonous itself but she'd wedged herself into it after stowin the Open Road an zipped it in all the right places. It were too big for her, built for a bigger fella, but she could walk in it at least. She left the hood off an started walkin towards the dark square cut into the red rock wall. It were a Glow of sum kind she realised. Sumthin she'd known near her whole life but this one were different to any dark she'd seen. As she got closer there was more an more bones an it looked like there been sum kinda fight out here or maybe years worth of fights an near enough all of em was torn to bits. The way they was flung about looked like sum giant beast had thrown its great claws about, not carin where they landed. Her old mate the razorback mayhap.

Or Karra's blokes. Ghosts mebbe. Her guts was turnin watery an her foot crunched an she looked down to see itd gone through the top of a skull she hadnt seen half buried in the dust. It musta been twice as hot in the suit but she were workin hard not to shake. She pulled the hood up an over her head an zipped it slow an clumsy, her breath foggin the mask almost straight away, makin it hard to see straight. What the fuck was down in the dark? She were about to find out. There were steps leadin down an inta the darkness. She started headin down the crumblin concrete, waitin for her eyes to catch up.

71

This were the real thing. Block knew he was livin now an it were like he'd been dead all them years. What did that say about a fella, that he werent real till he dint have nuthin else? He dint have time to think hard on the answer an he reckoned he might not like it too much anyway. They was huntin him through the System but he dint think they was gunna catch him. Block were an old hand at this game an most of them pups workin for Karra aint never seen the inside of a cipher an half their blades looked for show. He reckoned near enough most of his yungens musta got away. All but the real yungensd had the talk, they all knew the fallbacks, the dead letters, the arvees. Yeah Blockd put all them book lernins to good use over the years an there werent a fella what called hisself wun of Blocks kids what dint have a plan when things went to shit. Bushcraft, tradecraft, no nevermind to him. Them lernins of the old times dint let him down. How muchd Gus been passin across though, that were the heavy question. He'd been walkin while he was thinkin an his feet hadnt been far behind his head cos he found himself at the tyre towers again, the giant stacks loomin up an over in the darkness, the black edges only just visible against dark sky. Still too much smoke in the air an the stars was murky an only on the edges. What they wanted was a changin wind but for now the haze was gunna help his boys no end so he dint mind. Block crouched down an leaned his back against the outer wall of tyres. He whistled low an clear, singin the panic song an outta the dark come an answer. Block hit the notes again and the answer come closer an just cos he aint had a great night of it he drew his long knife slow an kept the blade down an outta any light that might show through the murk. Outta the dark come two yungens, a boy an a girl, short blades out an Block dropped his point an called to em.

Yer alive.

The relief on their faces near made him weep.

Yeah an just about is all.

Block nodded.

Good fellas. What happened?

We was waitin an workin, just like ya told us to, an Gus an Cutter was lookin after us. Then summa Karras lads come to the door an they was lookin for ya. Nowun told em nuthin but Gus went outside with em an I dint think nuthin of it cos a coupla the others went with him an I figgered they was just gunna back him up in case sumwun was pressin too hard.

The yungen faltered an Block let her breathe, knowin she'd just seen her brothers an sisters cut down in front of her an that werent no light thing.

When yer ready yungen.

Then we heard fightin an summa them tried to come back through the door but we was tryna get out to help em on the street an there was a push backanforth an Gus come back through the door except this time he was facin us an he had a blade out an he slashed up sum of us what was tryna get outta the way an Cutter jumped in the mix an got stuck for his trouble an then the place was on fire an sum of us got out the front and sum got out the back an me an Kris stuck together an we remembered where we was supposed to go an we come here an we been waitin. We dunno what happened to the lads what went out the front, we just come here an stayed low an waited for you.

Block took a long look at em. They was tough lookin but they were shook right now an the pair of em mustnt a been a year past ten each, both big eyed an skinny with hunger an fear. They was of the System though an they was family an deserved the real, no less.

I seen them fellas what went out the front. Theys all dust. An Cutter too.

The pair of em dint move at that, just kept lookin at him like any second he were gunna tell em it were a joke an their mates werent just bled out in the street. Shame to say that werent on the cards but he had summin maybe nearly as good. Leastaways it woulda warmed him back in the day.

Gus was rattin. You seen him turn. An now hes dust. Did it meself. An we're gunna do em all, all the rest too. An then their boss an Im gunna end him meself too.

72

Before

Lemme tell ya sumthin else Orphan an stoke up that fire a little will ya. Im real tired an it aint gunna get too much better for me. I know I go on an on about them old times and sumtimes Im guilty of makin them old times sound better than right now just like plenny of old fools before me I reckon. Truth is, theres a heapa ways to spread poison among people an ya just gotta look around the System to see how many ways peoples is happy to poison themselves an pay for the privilege. Im tryna tell ya Orphan that I know ya trust me an its enough to warm an Old Womans heart but Im tellin ya, there werent never a good time to be out here an long before Ghosts lived down them Glows there was ghosts out here. Ah I jus keep ramblin, dont I girl? Dont right know what Im sayin these days. Youre outta this land an plenny of them in the System is too. Theres a clean line connectin you an me an the peeps in the past runnin back longern you can even imagine an its gunna take moren any beast to disappear the System an the the folk that make it up. Wes a mix of all kinds, mongrel folk yunnerstand, yer the next thing in a long line Orphan, Ghost or not, silent or speaker, you got the Glows on ya girl. Do ya unnerstand? Dont think ya do. Do yer best Orphan, keep searchin for them things, got no more time to tell ya all I wanted. Best pack up the billy an kick sum sand on the fire yungen, we gotta head back, aint no more puttin this off I spose.

73

Her eyes adjusted quick enough and she saw that the stairs dint go far fore they met another room an at the end of that were a pair of huge doors sunk inta the ground but whatever once had been was no more an apart from the giant hinges there werent no trace of them covers. Down she went, her years in the Spirals keepin her feet movin an glad, ever glad for them brighteyes lettin her see in the gloom cos she werent trustin a torch down here. It were funny cold off the desert floor an through the front of the hood things was all blurred an fogged an she knew she were breathin too hard but sumhow it were stayin sorta cool. That dint explain the cold sweat runnin down her back though an the terror what seemed to come from the very walls themselves. There were a monster down here an she knew it now. All them bones shoulda warned her. There was sumthin down here worth killin or dyin for an sumtime in the nottoodistant before fellas had been tryna get at it. The stairs curved around an down an down again an she realised she was passin sum kinda layers, sum kinda giant rooms as she had been headin down an she could feel the space of the place expandin out into sum kinda cavern. Made sense theyd buried the beast down here, they wouldnt have wanted to dig their own pit this deep out inta the bedrock, made sense they was gunna use the land for it. They dint know they was placin evil on top of more evil though. She could taste the colour of this place now, she knew that sumthin ancient an terrible were down here with her. Her eyes was still gettin used to the dark an she could see a railin now runnin down the stairs with her an past that railin out in the middle dark was the layers an she knew if she looked out an up an down she was gunna see the concrete theyd poured down here to seal it all up an she knew without needin to see that it hadnt worked. It were like she could smell sulphur though she couldnt feel the yellow colour comin with it an she knew it were all just in her head. She went to the railin an looked out an down there in the dark she could see the shimmer of water an she knew nowun hadnt ever planned for water in the desert when they buried this place and that even a Systemraised, wasteborn orphan like she was knew that water soon enough went through evrythin, even steel an rock an concrete. She looked up again. The levels was stacked so neat in the dark an all she could think was they sorta looked like the tyre stacks she knew from home but bigger, so much bigger, maybe each layer was thirty spans thick, an she knew that the longer the water was down here the more it were gunna eat up an down an drag all the poison out. She walked down a few more flights of stairs an the black water at the bottom of the shaft were like a mirror evry time she checked over the rail an she could see the sweat startin to bead up on the inside of her face mask an fog up even more. There werent nuthin to do but try an brush her forehead against the plastic now an then to make a clear bit she could see through. She kept headin down, not realisin she'd reached the bottom until she felt the legs of the suit slosh through shallow water. She jumped back to a dry step but the bottom of the suit were wet an she stood lookin at it for a long minute waitin to see if the suit were gunna fall apart but it dint. She went back around to the landin an looked across an sure enough she saw that the side of the nearest wall were breached through but lookin close she could see it were too destroyed for it to be water. Them walls looked like they was made outta rock or concrete themselves an from what she could see there was sum kinda thick metal in em too, glintin dull in the neardark. What she were lookin at though were like itd been attacked with tooth an claw, or were it pick n shovel, like sumwun or sumthin wanted it to get busted open, like they was actually tryna let it out. A beast, or Karras scavs. Dint even matter she thought. Them poor stupid fellas he'd set to find his fortune. Just looked like another kinda Glow to them. Not wun of em could read worth a scrap but theyda dun what he told em anyway. She knew without even thinkin on it. The stripes was forever on her back markin that ya dint go against the bald man. Theyd been this way an found it an she were too late. Lookin right back at her was the destroyed wall an what looked like dirt an metal an glass from the inside was spillin out. Inta the water that was lappin around the stairs. The suit were stinkin hot now an her whole body was covered in sweat an she were feelin lightheaded an like her eyes was gunna pack it in, evrythin fadin to a speck. She fought it, hopin it were just the air in the suit but sumthin about bein down that hole was doin her no good at all an it were a real long, steep climb back up. She took a look to remember what she was lookin at an then started draggin her feet back up the crumblin stairs but she felt a heavy weight pressin on her an she knew that the beast were down there with her an it aint never left this place spite bein evrywhere. Itd crept inside her suit an crept inside herself an she tripped up the stairs an fell hands out, choking, light fadin, throat closin in its grip.

74

It'd taken him a day or were it two but he'd gathered twelve of
em in all, a grimy dozen yungens what had gone to ground an
remembered their fallbacks. There was others out there but he
hadta trust that they was safe an sound an keepin their heads
below the surface. Twelve might be enough he reckoned. Enough
to get it done. Who knew. Block were knackered from walkin,
delirious an tired but he'd met all of em on the run, listened to the
stories, told em to keep their heads up as best he could an moved
on. Werent no sense in standin still an he had to save the trust of
the wuns what was left standin. No doubt about it, Karrad done
him over good an shattered what he took so long to build up.
A coupla weeks ago his was a gang of lads to be reckoned with an
now they was scattered to the hooks an burrows and he were left
makin do with whatever he could scrounge up. He couldnt think
of the lads dead in the cut without his hands clenchin up into fists
an his heart drippin poison into his gut. This was the recknin,
Reckoner go to dust. This was what happened when he stopped
bein Block an started bein a fella of the System. This were what
happened when the Orphan took over his world. Deep breath.
What did he know for sure? Karra werent untouchable. Truth.

The great an terrible Block was out here in the dust scrabblin, dint have a plan, and at the back of his mind he knew the Orphan were still out there. Still out West an if she come back he dint know what she was bringin with her.

75

Before

Hold Orphan, before we go in the gate, lemme talk to ya wun more time. Prolly wont get to talk to ya again. I can feel it comin on the wind an I reckon Karras gunna take his chances pretty soon an there wont be no more of these trips out to the hills. Yer mighta figgered it by now but this been part accident an part on purpose an theres sumthin I been wantin ya to get ta grips with before I ask ya ta carry that weight for me. Yer see, findin Maralinga aint no joke Orphan. I been lookin for a real long time an in this whole wide open space I aint never even come close an I spent plenny of days walkin the waste an searchin for sumthin that might send me in the right direction. All in vain Orphan, nah dont tell me any different. I aint never even come close as far as I know an out there is still the poison what did for plenny of folk way back when an might just do for em again. Im gunna tell ya sumthin now what might sound like it gives ya reason to walk away from all this but Im hopin yev lerned enough. Theres a real big chance that after all these years you aint gunna be able to stop whats happenin out there. Might be the poison been spreadin for such a long time that its gunna be already in the water an the rocks an the creatures an the trees an there aint no takin all that back. Unnerstand? Lets say ya find it out there, there might be nuthin you can do to stop it spreadin. Do ya get that Orphan? Thats sumthin Ive hadta think about evry year, an evry day. All me work might be for so much pride in the end. An nowun but yous gunna know. Lissen to me careful Orphan. Dont do what I done. Ya gotta tell sumwun. Ya gotta make sure what was started secret an kept secret, ya gotta make sure it dont stay secret. It dont even matter than ya might not be able to stop the poison spreadin. Whats done is done but like I told ya, that dont mean ya cant change the past. That dont mean ya cant change things so all them mistakes instead of bein a road down to old Nick the badman, ya can make em just a road that ended up on high after all. Dont keep it close like I done. Tell people. Give em a choice. They dont need to sit here in the System just waitin for a slow death to come on em. Speak on it Orphan, from the highest place ya can. Give em the chance peeps dint have before when they let that thing loose. Ya unnerstand? Whats secret cant be secret no more.

76

She were outta the earth gaspin. Night sky an the faint light that couldnt reach nowhere near the bottom. Her visor was off but she were still in the suit an she were gaspin. Howd she got there? She were slumped against the wall of the building, sittin to the side of the big openin an in front of the flat, glassy waste with them strange rings of cooked sand glitterin in the dirty moonlight stared back at her. Them bones specked here an there like markers. The last thing she recalled were the beast takin her breath down below. What had happened? Howd she got topside? Were she dead? Were she poisoned? Her legs musta carried her up spite her mind goin. She'd been dyin in that suit, strugglin for breath all the way down but now even the dead air of this desolate spot were like cool water to her. She'd been right when she went in, there were a lifestealin monster down there an thered been a fight out here not longago an all them bones was markin the spot. Sumhow theyd got them doors open an headed down inta the pit. Prolly dint have no fancy suit like hers neither an theyd breathed in all that poison an sum of them unlucky fellas had walked out inta that water an worked with pick an shovel at the walls for who knew how long it took to get through concrete an metal like that. Theyd stuck with it though, theyd made sure they got through an that meant they kinda knew what they was doin or they thought it were worth sumthin real valuable. It were a fool whod think that stuff were gunna be good for anywun though. Theyd buried it down real deep an made sure nowun knew where it were for who knew how long. What had happened out here? There werent nowun smart enough to be findin this place an then greedy enough to be diggin into it. Anywun who knew the full tale would never do such a thing. The full story. There were sumthin funny about that when she turned it over in her head. It were quite a story. The Old Woman had spent years tellin it to her in fact. Repeatin parts of it so she dint never forget. Remindin her over an over again that it were out there an it were close. That it were an old, bad, powerful thing from a time gone past. Over an over. Sittin in the readin room at the System. While she counted stones next to the window, lamp lightin the little piles an the sun droppin over the yard. Dust on the floor. Always dust. Couldnt never get it clean, dint matter how often Karra clipped her ear. Karra. She figgered shed known for years that he were huntin the same thing as her but the truth of it were sumthin different altogether. The truth were he'd got there first an gone about it his own way.

The Orphan were standin there on the outside, doors gone an surrounded by bones. The thoughts come to her real slow but they wasnt lettin up an it were comin clear, all too dark an clear to her an she started pullin off the suit an walkin towards the Open Road all at once. She were in her own head. Lost past an present. She dint see the fella sittin on her ship until he spoke.

Sister.

Her blud turned to ice an she felt for her blade but she knew she were done. Caught up in the suit she werent doin nuthin. She looked an saw her maras come real. Ghosts behind him an ghost blade on him an she was caught cold. She was gunna join them bones an the weariness an frustration of it all hit her in the gut an she wrenched her arm out the sleeve an drew her bayonet just the same. She were gunna go out hard like she'd promised the Block since they was yungens. It settled on her an she felt her blade waver an she dint know if it was the suit, the place or that she were ready to die but evrythin swam together an she heard him speak again, markin the word proper this time though it dint make no sense to her.

Sister.

77

She were glad he'd lit a fire. She couldn't stop starin at him. Not sure what he were. Reckoner? Brother? Both? She'd heard him call her sister but it dint stick. She weren't nowuns sister no more. Weren't nuthin like that to nowun save Block mayhap an a daughter to the Old Woman, dust rest her bones. She were woozy from the pit an not sure it weren't all a dream. That she weren't dead an gone back to dust. He'd made the fire normal enough. Tinder an kindle just like she woulda done but she still couldn't fix her eyes on him proper. Her brother were long dead an this fella was claimin he were him. Too much made sense an too much dint. Why he'd let her live again an again. But how he still lived himself? He beckoned her sit opposite him at the fire an she dint know how to run or say no so she sat crosslegged, blade in reach. The other Ghosts sat watch around em like they'd dun before. Just whitish blurs on the edge of the firelight an theyd turned their backs to the brightness, their eyes dint like the flames. There were so much she dint unnerstand, so much she dint know. They sat in silence for a long time an he let her be until she were ready to speak.

You carried me out the pit? An yer me brother? Jon.

She said it a near whisper.

He took a while an she weren't sure he'd heard her but eventually he nodded.

An yer a Ghost?

I am.

All this time?

For a long time.

Another wait. Coulda been a minute but more like an hour. She weren't sure of time an what were happenin but nowanthen she looked up an it mightve been her brother sittin opposite.

But where have ya been? Why dint ya come home?

I been home.

But why dint ya come for me?

He lowered his gaze. *Dint know you was alive.*

The size of the thing hit her in the gut an she leaned forwards an retched. Brung up nowt but drool an bile an then retched again in the sand. He looked at her worried but that were worse an she hacked again, eyes waterin an head spinnin. It were like she felt nuthin from the flames in front of her.

What about Mum?

He looked into the fire a while an then met her look.

She been on the wind these three years past. She got a strange kinda sick and there werent nuthin nowun could do for her. Im sorry.

Three times an orphan.

It werent real that she were sittin here with Jon. It werent real that her mumd been alive. While she was lernin her letters and catchin the lash from Karra her mumd been in the Glows. They mighta even crossed paths down there in the dark while she was scavvin. Thinkin on it made her gorge rise an her mouth fill with spit like she was gunna chuck again. Long wait fore she spoke again, swallowin it down this time.

How come ya stayed so long with the Ghosts? Couldnt ya have got away?

I dont unnerstand.

You remember that day? All them years ago. When youse got took by the Ghosts.

Jon stared at her a long time, then looked back inta the fire like he din wanna be lookin at her when he talked next. *You poor fucken orphan. Thats what they told ya dint they? That you was a Ghost orphan?*

She just looked at him.

We wasnt never taken by Ghosts you poor fucken kid. We was taken by fellas, slavers, from that fucken place ya call home. They been doin it for years. Not enough women an kids in the System, not enough slaves. We was rescued by them you call Ghosts while they was tryna take us back. They come upon the caravan we was in an took em to pieces an brung us back to the Glows. Them Ghosts kilt evrywun of em, left em bleedin out on the sand an Im still glad they did. Them slavers was snatchin up kids and women what couldnt fight for themselves. Been doin it for years. Takin them wuns what was easiest to take. We was rescued by the Ghosts sister, not taken. An I aint never once wanted to go to yer System an yer fucken slavers an yer badfellas, special as I were certain up until not long ago that my little sister was kilt by em. Them Ghosts been good to me, was good to Mum too an we aint never forgiven the System. Soon as I could I come back out to where we was but you was gone an nowt left. We marked ya dead and et, you was so little there werent even bones left behind. Never figgered you was took. Woulda come for ya. Believe it.

He was breathin hard an he stopped talkin for an age but she knew he werent done. After a while he spoke real soft an she hadta lean in to hear him.

Them Ghosts is just fellas like any others but they been cut off an deep dark a real long time. I mean a real long time. A real long time close to the Glows as well, an sum strange things happen down there in the dark. Far as I can tell them first wuns, the ancestors callem, was fellas what dug the Spirals, an they went under to get away from all what was goin on up top. They aint real fond of the sun no more, an it dont do sum of the older wuns eyes no good. Sum of the younger wuns is OK though an theres others like me what got picked up or rescued an aint had no reason to return to the light.

235

It were all too much for her. Too much histery all at once. She looked across the fire, seein the little boy she'd thought was so tall and catchin only dust for memories. He were sorta there but in his place was a grim fella whatd lived a long time in the dark. She could only guess what she looked like to him, recknin the long years of servin an livin day by month by year in the System by her wits prolly hadnt left much of the little girl he remembered neither.

★

The sun come up an they was still sittin, parlayin now an then. Her head still werent right with all she'd heard an she knew it werent gunna be right a long time. The Ghosts around the edge of the fire had disappeared silently in the night to sum dark place they preferred. Jon started to take shape again in her head as it got brighter an sumwhere along the way she found herself errin towards callin him Jon in her head instead of the Reckoner. There were still so much she dint know an the weight of it were heavy on her heart. She wanted to know about their mum, how she moved, how she talked, evry little bit, but at the same time it were too late for all them things an she might be better off just not knowin for now. She aint even started thinkin on them slavers an all the things she thought was writ in stone shiftin an changin like the sand.

Do ya know this place?

She nodded slow in the clear dawn light, lazy smoke comin off the last of the fire as it burned out.

Jon took a long breath.

We got stories of this place, sister. In the unders we call it the Section, or Woomera or Maralinga or the Totem or the Scorch. Unnerstand? The Scorch. Fellas already been here, fellas from where yer from. Diggin. Openin. Meddlin. Theres a poison here from them old times, but ya know that dont ya? They scorched this place, burned it outta memory, off the map, an made this a place of forgettin, unnerstand?

Why Im here.

Whatcha want with it?

Make sure it dont spread again.

The fire cracked an flickered an she could see him wrestlin with himself.

Too late for that sister. Fellas come an gone.

He took a deep breath like he were clearin his heada sumthin.

I come out here to find ya, to find out if you was who I reckoned you was. To tell ya I was alive an that ya had family left. Im real sorry I dint know you was still breathin until I saw ya out there on the flats. Nearenough kilt ya an I still couldnt make meself believe it were you. That aint all of it though. I come out here to give ya fair warning. I aint gunna stand in yer way, special if comin heres sumthin ya gotta do to make yer rights with the dead. I gotta tell ya though sister, I know what they call me in the System, I heard em call it at me sumtimes when wes movin among em in the dark. I heard slavers out there pleadin an sayin Reckoner this an Reckoner that an I bled em wun an all. I aint the first wun to carry the name but they aint wrong callin me it. Theres a recknin comin for the System an its been comin a long time. Elders thats been waitin on this recknin a real long time. Thats why I come all the way out here too, so yev got yer warnin. Soon as I get back, we're comin.

Jon were lookin at her, waitin an after sum thinkin she spoke.

I dunno what to say about all them things ya told me. They ringin true but I come up in the System an I know for meself that theres sum peeps worth savin in there. Not many but a few. That aint the why of it though. I dint have no mum like you did for moren a few years an the closest thing I got to family is that fella you crossed blade with, the old fella what was me boss and the peeps that live in the Stacks. I promised meself a hundred times over that I was gunna find this place an I dunno, seal it up, I dunno, make sure it werent gunna bring no more sufferin.

Jon hung his head low like he wanted to be speakin only to the sand.

But it aint sealed sister. An it aint secret. Them what came will come again an again until they figger out how to use whatevers down there or it ets us all. I got no more time to stay the recknin. Unnerstand? Im here to give ya the word. But that place? Yer home? Theres a storm comin an even if I wanted theres no stoppin it.

They sat in the quiet a long time an then he stood up an the ashes of the fire was glowin at his feet an he were wreathed for a second in blue smoke like he werent really fixed to the earth. He looked square at her an she realised she aint seen him smile the whole time. His face though, sumthin in it made him look like the yungen that he once was an she felt all of a sudden like she were gunna cry but nuthin came.

Gotta go sister. Im sorry.

She had plenny to say, wanted to ask him to stop an wait but the words died in her throat an she knew she'd be wastin her breath anyways. He waited an when she dint speak he dipped an threw half a wave, lookin like he wanted to say more but what she couldnt guess. Then he were off, movin in that way what had become sorta familiar to her cept now she knowed what he carried on his hip an it werent nuthin to be trifled with. She went to stand but the dizziness hit her an she sat back down hard. Hadta watch him move away, knowin she couldn't follow straight away. She dint know what had happened to her down the pit but her head weren't right. Her legs was slow to obey an she felt short of breath. Dint know if it were real or in her head but she sat at the fire, desert wakin up slow, watchin Jon cover ground real good as he loped away. She were all outta shape an it were slow comin to her that he were headin back to put blade an torch to the System. She hadta follow, were gunna haveta go spite her shakes an murky thoughts. Block were back there. The Stacks was back there. Meant sumthin dint it? She watched the speck that were Jon out on the plains reckonin the Ghosts was gunna meet him out there. It were a real long shank all the way back home but she hadta admit that if anywun was gunna walk that way it were probably her brother, or the Reckoner or whatever he really were. She tried to clear her head, the heat comin over as the sun got higher until he were just a speck an then the haze hid him an it were just her sittin there head spinnin, alone again.

78

He'd been dreamin of it a long time he were thinkin. The time werent right an the Orphan were gone an the System seemed to be foldin in on itself but Block reckoned a settlin between him an Karra had been a long time comin. Maybe even all the way back to the day he'd seen the bald bastard take the Orphan off the auction block an back to the old fellas place. Maybe all the way back to when he'd seen her show up at the market with stripes on her back an he'd made up his mind he werent gunna get lashed like that an nowun else were gunna neither. Maybe the dreams of runnin Karra through went back a real long time an only now they was ready to be spoke out loud. Block had sent the others away to check the arvees again an he were sittin in the shade of a rotten old shed thatd been left to collapse a long time. He were realisin itd been a powerful long time since he'd had any kinda rest an it were startin to take its toll. On his feet four days he could count, maybe more. He dint wanna nod but there werent much he could do without a solid plan an the plan were gunna need eyes on, an right now that werent possible. Nah, best thing to do was hope the Orphan were figgerin sumthin out for herself in that dead place an that she werent rushin back. He reckoned she'd have her work set just findin exactly what it was she were lookin for an he hoped them sunshy monsters had left her be an that fella theyd faced aint come back. Even if the winds was good, he reckoned he had just a scrap of time. Just a scrap that he were gunna have to use to get to Karra an make his move. It were years ahead of time an normally he'da had his war room around him but instead he were gunna do it in the shadow of the Stacks with rats and dust an rot for company. Behold the great Block, feared an knowed all over the System an beyond. Were a joke now. He shook his head to clear it an tried to fight the sleep. Hopin the years hadnt been for nuthin.

79

Three of his fellas was standin in front of him an nun of em had nuthin worth sayin. Gone to ground they was sayin. Turned to dust, gone Ghost, out in the Glows, disappeared. Werent that many peeps in the System and they was all livin crowded cheek by jowl an now Block had turned inta smoke. Peeps was afraid they said. Stayin in, fraid of catchin whatever it were that was layin em out sick. Sum had it, sum not. The wuns that did was dyin quick though. Rotten from the inside out, blind an blackmouthed. Nuthin was makin sense. His fellas was useless. Half of em was sick themselves, werent enough left fit to hunt the Block proper. Karra kept the lads standin while he sat beind the desk. Lookin up an down the row, lettin his gaze settle real heavy on em. These fucken smartfellas were the wuns who dint get it done. Now they was coughin an hackin, eyes all red from the smoke an whatever grog theyd got their hands on. Lotta stealin the last week, lotta fellas leavin out the front gate an takin their chances an the cando men wasnt knockin on his door as much, they was too busy bleedin out an takin dust naps. Still he dint have no clue. Orphan gone an Block disappeared. One of the lads coughed hard again an it turned into a fit of wheezes that was rattlin in his chest like chains bein dragged. Karra watched as he dropped his hands to his knees an then pitched forwards slow onto the floor, racked, blud comin out his mouth. Peeps were powerful sick an for the first time Karra felt sum kinda fear of whatever it were out there. He banged hard on his desk an more boys came in. He gestured to the fella on the floor, still tryna suck in whoopin breaths twixt coughs an rattles. His hands was shakin as he signed the lads.

Get him outta here. An get as many fellas together here as ya can, sick or well dont matter none. Tell em theyre stayin here till I say otherwise. Gold in it for em. Take all the names of them that dont come, we gunna remember em.

The boys nodded, draggin the fella out by his arms. He'd stopped breathin Karra reckoned, looked for all the world like he were asleep.

80

It were funny she thought, it were more than passin strange that on the way back it always seemed to go quicker or maybe it were that she was puttin distance between herself an that terrible dead place. Poisoned an dry, bones an glass. It were a place of beasts. If she never hadta go there ever again itd be too soon but she knew it were gunna have to be dealt with sumtime, an she were the wun what hadta carry that. The Old Woman had dun sumthin to her, sowed sum kinda seeds what had come up a tough dry grass that werent gunna let her go.

The winds was favourin her, had been blowin hard from the West for days an sendin her back towards the System fast but she knew she'd took too long. Had pushed herself as hard as she dared, huntin her brother back across the flats. Hopin to see the dust trail of a ship or his tracks in front of her but he werent nowhere to be seen. She were days quicker than the run out but in the end she knew she'd been slow. Slow to come to evrythin an if she were too late werent tellin what the Block was gunna do or where Karra might be. The light was goin but she werent gunna stop now she'd figgered what was happenin. In front of her the whole time. She were blinded thinkin she were special, thinkin she were so special with all them knowins the Old Woman had given her. Thinkin she were the only wun what ever heard of Maralinga an the only wun who wanted to find it. What did she reckon? Karrad turned to proper treachery overnight, that he'd sudden woke up an just figgered to become the boss? Nah, evrywun got their plans she knew now an evrywun had their own ideas, was the middle of their own stories. Karras story was gold an havin fellas do as he told em an she knew that he werent wun to get his hands in the muck less he really had to. He dint mind a mess but if he could get sum other fellas to clean it up for him, so much the better. The Old Womand had it mixed up but then again maybe she hadnt. That place she'd come from mighta lasted a real long time. Maybe though, she were right an it was gunna start leakin stuff inta the water an the rocks and the sand real soon an they was all gunna die off, the whole lot of em. Sooner or later what the Old Woman had feared was gunna come to pass but there werent no tellin whether it were her fear that had sowed the seeds for Karra to be so hungry. Just no tellin. She dint know what he were doin with the stuff either, even figgerin his fellas found a way to carry it back to him. That fucken fool.

She could see the light from the System on the horizon now. She'd made real good time but she'd been smellin smoke in the air two days past an she thought of Jon again. How long had it been? Were the Ghosts comin over the sand like a wall of dust, eatin evrythin in their way? That were meant to be her blud. He'd seemed real set in his mind when they parted ways and she dint have enough histery with him that she could figger what he were gunna do. He were her brother though an he'd gotta know that there was folks worth savin in the System, even if they was just orphans like her. There were smoke driftin over the place an she fancied she could see sumthin gatherin like blud in the late arvo light. Her senses was all bleedin together like they did sumtimes an she wondered again just how much poison was in her already

244

an what the pit had done to her. She heeled the Wide Open Road over to skirt a shallow dip where water mighta once run in the old days an as she come closer to the walls she saw no Watch were set. At the entrance to the Silent Gates she dropped the mainsail an kicked out the sand anchor an leaned on the brake with her other foot. She stowed the Open Road up good an took a drink. It were near enough the first time in days she hadnt been up at speed, leavin a dust plume across the waste. She knew she were still weak an that her brother woulda made better time but it dint look like he'd got there ahead of her. Mayhap other business in the deep. Mayhap he'd been raisin them Ghosts up an marchin em. Whatever it were she were gunna take the time as a gift. Hadta find the Block. Hadta word him up.

*

In the tunnels she dint need to tax her mind too much. The brighteyes was back now she werent in that terrible place but in her chest was growin sum kinda fear an all what she'd seen from outside the walls was quiet an smoke an sumthin bad in the air an she were near sick thinkin what she might be comin up to when she stuck her head above ground. She hit the end of the tunnels an started up the ladder to the rubbish pit an as she got her head out an into the night air she realised she couldnt hear nuthin. None of the usual chatter that echoed round the System at all hours an also no screams, no cries of Ghost. It were real strange. She pulled herself up inta the heap, the smell of the rottin garbage fadin inta the background an she saw sum fellas, hooded up ahead an lookin like they was waitin for her. Just yungens by their looks and she thanked dust that Block were clear enough still alive an it dint look like Jond arrived yet with his Ghosts. She walked towards em, hand on bayonet an careful as she ever were an as she reached their backs they turned to her an she saw the confusion in their eyes. She dint know em by face an that werent unusual, she dint know all of Blocks lads but there were sumthin wrong an they looked real afraid of her. She got a bad feelin right down in the pit of her stomach and she had the long knife half drawn when sumthin hit her, right in the spot Jons stone had not that long ago an the world turned to water an smoke an then it were gone all together.

81

Dark

We ken it now Reckoner, we know the truth of it.

    Im sorry.

    Shes kin. Blud of you an the witch.

    Shes blud to me. Sister.

    We ken it good now Reckoner an we aint without mercy. Stay your blade an spare the blud but that place must scorch. Put it to blade an fire an yer sister be spared. Shes blud of you an the witch, dust rest her. Go now an reckon.

    It will be done.

82

Bring her in. Keep her hands tied tight, shes real handy with a blade.

Karra werent takin no chances with the Orphan. Not now, an not ever again he reckoned. His lads brought her in still knocked out an she dint stir as they put her on the floor. He used his foot to tip her onto her side, dint want her chokin afore he could have a word with her. She'd aged since he last saw her, fact she seemed to be lookin a bit grey around the face when he looked close.

Didja get anythin out of her?

Nah boss, just put her on her arse. They was comin and goin through sum kinda tunnel in the rubbish.

No wun else though? Ya dint see the Block?

Nah boss. Just her. Sent two fellas down the tunnel though an they aint come back. Been gone a while. I told em come get me when they come up.

If they come back up.

Yeah, yeah boss.

Karra waved them out the room. The Orphan lay there like a sack of rocks, just the gentle rise an fall of her ribs lettin him know she were still alive. He looked at her real close, all them little scars an nicks what come to an orphan in the world an she were carryin a whole lot. He was almost feelin tender to her while she was quiet like this an sure enough after all these years he hadta be wun of the only fellas what knew her as a real little kid. Were fucken strange how things turned out. His mind was turnin in the past an unbidden thoughts of the old fella come up an thinkin how hot the blud were when it run out the Old Mans throat an down his hand. He'd spent a lotta time over the years turnin that minute over an over but he clear couldnt think of anythin else he coulda done that would have seen him sittin here now, high as he were. Nah, regrets was for them what dint get up. He got nuthin to regret an once he'd sorted out the Block he werent gunna have to worry about nuthin no more. He waited too long he was realisin now, waited too long an let him get too powerful an now he was payin the price. Steppin on a rat instead of a roach. Still, dint have no regrets. Was still breathin an was gunna see this out. Just had to figger how best to play the Orphan. Were she bait? Or were he best to just take her out the way right now. Knife her up or have his lads take her outside the walls an bury her in dust. His head was achin an there werent no room for clear wine or nuthin to ease the pain. He werent at his sharpest an he knew it, swingin between decisions that oughta be easy, an he were feelin like the Orphan had sumthin to do with it. That an the fellas what kept showin up sick. Them fellas he'd sent out huntin for him come back all shaky. The fellas what swore theyd seen clean bones gone to dust an et by beasts out there in the West. The bluddy smoke in the air from the burn pits was gettin in his eyes. Shoulda been used to it by now. The Orphan were stirrin a little an he walked over to her from behind his desk an turned her on her back, watchin her eyes flinch an glimmer as the lamplight hit her. She werent in a good way. He were enough of a healer to know that. His lads musta hit her hard but he sposed he should be grateful they hadnt kilt her. Then he wouldnt have no choices at all. Werent no talkin to her until she opened up her eyes good anyway, that were sumthin about the hands, they werent no use in the dark or to the blind.

83

They got her.

Who?

He knew an he dint wanna hear em say it.

The Orphan. Karras lads got her. We seen em draggin her away, too many for us to take.

Block took his time breathin. She were back again. An he aint got to her. She were on that bluddy block again. Outside the wind were pickin up an he could hear it whinin through the wires, whippin up dust an blowin down hook and cut, seemin to come from all directions at once. There were a sandstorm comin. It were bad blud stirred up an made red in the air.

Whered they take her?

Straight to the bald bastards place. Took her inside. She were out of it, reckon they belted her or sumthin.

Werent nuthin for it. Hadta move things along he reckoned, before that bastard figgered he had sum kind upper hand an used the Orphan for bait or whatnot. The fella was keepin hisself surrounded with blokes just like always.

Listen good. Yer gunna go check all them spots I told ya an fetch up all the yungens whatve gone to ground. Unnerstand?

They nodded.

An then yer gunna come back here an we're warrin. We're doin this now, not tomorrow or the day after, now. Unnerstand?

Again, the glassy nods. They dint have no idea what was comin. Werent nuthin for it though. Hadta chance his hand.

84

She were dreamin of family, she knew it. Dint wanna wake up though, it were better in the dream. She dint know when the arvo ritual started or when she began lookin forwards to it but sure enough she did. The sun were comin down over the System an outside the dust in the air were makin evrythin a bit softer than it normal was. Werent too much cryin out an the ciphers was silent for once. Most of the lasses an lads was gettin a feed of sorts an a few was cardin real quiet an summa the clever wuns was lernin their letters. She let the curtain fall an turned back to the room she an Block was in. The roof was rustin bad she saw when she looked up, dust comin in. Dust evrywhere. She was gunna have to get up there an fix it for him wun of these days she reckoned. She crossed the room, Block not lookin up and she let herself sink down inta the second chair he'd had brought in an she picked up the papers she'd scavved the last time she were down the Glows. It were all he seemed to want, paper an rounds. She swore it were more important to him than the gold an food an whatnot they traded it for. First thing he always asked when she come back from the waste was did she find any lernins, or readins. Blocks eyes werent gunna lift from the pages for a while she reckoned, this were the quiet time. Her eyes drifted back up to the roof an watched the fine sand comin in like an hourglass cept it werent markin nuthin, just vanished into even more dust on the floor.

85

The yungens he had left was standin round him an it were nearly like them times from the near longago. Couldnt think too much on that. Too many faces missin.

Orright.

There was a rumble from the lads an lasses around him an Block nearly smiled.

I know ya mournin ya bluds like I am. Yer family an aint nuthin more important. I took each of ya in an plenny of ya come up in the System same as me. We was caught short an thats on me. Sold out an down by wun what we called family an there aint nuthin worse than a snake cept a rat. Gus were both. An he werent on his own.

He had em now. All eyes was glued to him an he looked around the yungens, meetin the eye of evrywun of em.

Ya all know Karra, ya all know hes the big fella of the System an he do what he wants. I knowed him when he were a belongin an I know that he aint as gully as he reckons he is. He took sum of our fellas and left our lads in dust an now hes took the Orphan an got her at his place right now. Ya done good stayin alive an dust knows right now I aint got much right to be askin more of ya. But family is family an I want this bloke. I want blud. Tonight in the dead hours Im goin in to snatch his life an get the Orphan an any of ya wanna come with me is welcome. I wont hold it against ya if ya reckon its all gone too far an ya just wanna fade but if yer family, this is how its gunna be. Im goin in there for the fellas what got ended, goin in there for Cutter and for the Orphan an honest, Im goin in there for bluds sake. An I will not lose. Its endin tonight an we're either runnin this place tomorrow or we're dust. Thats the way it is.

86

The back of her head was on fire an she could feel the layers of
pain pressin on her eyes all the way through. There were a howlin
in her ears an she could hear a sound like Ghosts an wind screamin
together. Sum big pressure was buildin up there an she blinked
in the low light, eyes comin to rest on a familiar face. Karra. She felt
her guts drop. The howlin werent stoppin, it come from the wind
outside an she could hear a big dust storm brewin. Her eyes closed
again an she couldnt help a grunt of pain comin out. When she
opened her eyes again he were half leanin over her lookin down
an it were almost like the years bled away an he were wakin her
up to go fix the boss's tucker or head down to the hook to trade.
She tried to shift her hands an felt them come up short. They was
tied fast behind her back. Yeah, almost like old times but not quite.
There werent no point pretendin she were out of it she reckoned so
she grunted again an moved her legs round, sittin up half slumped
against the wall. There were sumthin big weighin on her but her
head was fogged. The Block. Needed to see the Block. Reckoner
comin, brother comin, storm comin. She needed up an out. Hadta
be out there now. He were comin.

Orphan.

Real soft with his hands, like he dint wanna rile her up. Too late fer that though. She took her time, rollin her tongue round her mouth, feelin real thick but wantin to make the words right.

Karra.

Its still boss to you, Orphan.

Karra.

She said it again, wantin him to know.

Whyd ya do it? Whyd ya go lookin for that poison? Boss were tellin the truth, werent nuthin but a beast.

He sat back then, rockin on his heels an suckin in his breath. His clothes seemed like they dint fit too good now, like they was gettin too big for him an she wundered just how much he really knew about what he was doin. He took a long time gettin his hands in order.

What are ya runnin yer mouth about now, Orphan?

It were gunna be like that.

There werent no gold, Karra. Werent never no gold or treasure out there, or anywhere as far as I knew. The gold died with the old fella. I told ya that. That werent gold out there Karra.

He were lookin at her face like he were concentratin and she realised for sure that he was sick. That he might not know for sure what he had done. Knew it were bad but that might be all.

His hands whispered, like spiders. *What're ya talkin about ?*

It were the poison ya bastard. It were the poison an it were real. It werent a story, it were real. You an yer fellas been sick havent they? Yer fellas brought ya sumthin back dint they? Sumthin out the ground. Theres moren more fellas gettin sick out there, aint there? What didja do with it? Wheredja put it?

Karra shook his head. *Burned it. Burned it on the pits. Were rubbish. Weren't nuthin.*

She dropped her eyes, takin deep breaths, feelin the blud pound in the back of her head. Looked back up at him, crouched in his robes in front of his desk.

Yev kilt us all. Yev kilt the System.

87

It were dead hours an the wind was whippin up sumthin terrible. There were a dust storm real close an the air were gunna be full of iron, he knew it. Might be a good thing for a bad nights work. Never knew. Been a while since the last big wun an itd ripped the System half to bits. He looked at the lads mustered up. All of em. Not a wun was missin. In the alleys around Karras place they was watchin and waitin. Block dragged his finger over the burrs in the sharpened hook blade an rolled em out on a thimble, straightenin the edge like hed done evry day since he were a littlun. In the shadows of Karras door he could see a coupla fellas lurkin. His ladsd make short work of them he reckoned. All he hadta do was get inside an get upstairs. The lay of the place werent tricky. In an through an up an to the left, round the stair an then inta the door at the end of the hall an hope the bastard was between him an the Orphan. A bitter gust blew sand and rubbish across the cut an the wind picked up even more. The stars was gone altogether now, no sky to be seen an the air was comin down all close an dull. Like the place was holdin its breath.

88

Karra werent his old self now. All the puffed up bullshit were gone an he were lookin at the Orphan like she might help him an she knew she couldnt an dust forgive her she had nuthin in her heart for him. He were gunna get evrythin he deserved an maybe more when he started rottin from the inside out. Just a question of how many others was goin the same way. Karras hands was movin real slow an even though she knew it were probably gunna take a long while for him to go, she fancied the blud thatd drained outta his face made him look like he was dyin right there in front of her.

Whered ya burn it?

West edge, by the Stacks.

Out near the lowest of the low, the orphans an Ghost kids an the wuns what looked after em. Of course they did. But the stupid bastards dint care that the poison smoke was gunna blow back over the place and they dint know what they was burnin neither.

We gotta get evrywun outta the System.

Karra looked up at that. *Nowuns goin nowhere.*

The Orphan shifted again, easin the pressure on her wrists. *Yer not gunna have anythin to lord it over if ya dont get evrywun out. Dont ya get it ya dumb bastard.*

Karra leaned across an slapped her hard in the face. The sting of his hand takin her all the way back to the old days. She'd felt that hand plenny of times but it dint hurt much no more if it ever did. She wondered if she oughta tell him he was gunna be dead soon. How were a man gunna take that news. She dint reckon he was mournin nuthin but himself in his heart. She dint reckon he cared nuthin for the System deep down. It were just a measure to him, a yardstick of how far he thought he'd come.

Nowuns goin nowhere. If we're all gunna die, then we're goin out together. You an me, an all the fucken dregs in this place.

The rope was bitin into her an from outside the door to Karras office she heard a commotion. He dint even look like he was hearin nuthin. He just stared at the Orphan like he were willin her to disappear but she werent movin. Not even if she could.

89

So it were his sister, no mistakin it no more. An the reckonin were comin. He'd covered good ground an his brothers an sisters had come out the deep dark an sum of em what could stand the sun had met him on the sand. The wild wuns aint come, they was blud unto themselves an he dint know what the olders mighta said or who was sent for just that it were time the reckonin be done. The System were sittin out there like a blight waitin to spread. His sister were out there playin with things she dint unnerstand an he could see that down the line she were gunna unleash sumthin she couldnt control.

Theyd covered good distance. They was made in the dark and the cool an they flowed over the sand like smoke, like they was livin up to their names in the System. He marched em hard, but they was slower in the day, not all could ship up an it were shanks most of the way. He were strapped with sling an blade, an they was lean an hungry an wrapped in rags against the light. Just before dawn they made camp as best they could an the sun come up. He'd seen plenny go sunblind for good an he covered those what needed it best he could an they sat out the long day in shadow while he waited for cloud or sumthin to break the glare. When the sun

261

dropped low they turned their backs to it an they never talked but ten of em turned back to the Glows. Jon watched them marchin away, his hand restin on the handle of his parang. Sister or no sister, he was gunna go in an burn that place an all them slavers an dogs an poisoners. She'd live, she were smart. He dint care nuthin for none of the rest.

90

Block an Karra facin each other. The Orphans eyes was wide open now an the two of em stood just starin. Block werent movin he were lookin just like his name. Karra was keepin eyes on, werent flinchin, werent movin none either. Block had blud on him from a cut in the chest but he were holdin onto the short hook blade proper enough an Karra had his own parang danglin easy by his side. She shifted against the rope an the pipe she were tied to shifted a little but neither of em even cast her a glance.

Karra.

Block spoke to him but the bald bastard dint waste no time with the hands. He knew what itd come to. He snaked the long blade out an Block slipped around it but the Orphan fancied he were movin a little slow an she wondered where that blud comin through his shirt were leakin from. It were never gunna last long though. Karra went hard but he aint spent the time in the road Block had. The blades clashed dull an metal an they came apart, Block crouched an she seen him heavin from the pain an Karrad picked up a nick on his knife hand, nuthin much but he were touched. Block were still low an breathin hard when Karra took a big swing an the Orphan watched as the Block did what he'd been doin a real long time an stepped inside the blade, stoppin Karras hand at the wrist an pullin the fella close like he were gunna kiss him. The hook came up almost lazy like an he punched it once, twice into his chest an Karra looked surprised an then not surprised at all. The Orphan watched it all an she felt tight in her chest an hot water comin from her eyes an she dint know why until she figgered that sum part of her was goin with him, even after all them years an the scars on her back.

Block set Karra down on the floor an the commotion an shoutin outside got even worse. Blocks lads was carvin through an the noise of the wind screamin through the hooks was gettin louder an louder. She could hear iron flexin an slammin an things goin over in the wind.

Untie me. Im tied to the wall.

Block came to her an cut the cord but he stayed kneeled over his head hung low an she could see the blud poolin next to him on the floor, mixin with the dust. She got her hands free, not lookin at Karra, not lookin at their blud mixin together on the floor, just plain not lookin at nuthin but searchin for Blocks eyes. He raised his head up an she saw how skinny he were but his eyes was smilin at her even though his mouth werent quite there.

We done it Orphan.

Block I gotta tell ya sumthin.

His shoulders heaved an sum more blud come outta him an when he spoke it were like he were short of breath.

What is it?

The Reckoner, its my brother. Hes blud Block. Kin. Unnerstand? The Reckoner is blud to me an he's comin here to put the place to the torch. Do ya unnerstand me?

91

The wall of sand'd come up behind em like it were meant to be, an in the cloak of dust and dark theyd met no trouble. Theyd picked a spot on the wall an them few that was still with him had gone up an over not seein a soul as their heels hit the packed sand. He'd pushed on through the streets, takin flame from their own fires an put a torch to their shacks an the wind was doin the rest, spreadin it from roof to roof an people was runnin here an yon in a panic, the dust an fire blindin em to their end. There was wasted bodies evrywhere in the shelters an shacks an he saw dozens of peeps stumblin in the dark, fleein from sumthin, like his recknin had started without him. Werent much for him an them with him to do but see it were done proper. They burned as they walked, carryin fire with em an settin it against house an scrap alike, just burnin as they walked an he dint see no sign of his sister. Evrythin were parched an ready to spark. The dustd cut the distance down close an the flames was glowin an eerie red, blasted this way an that by the wind. It howled in here, different from the outside. The gusts shot an blasted through rope an down between their narrow tracks. Jon checked his back. Din have nuthin but a coupla lads with him now. All but the yungens had lost their taste for it as they come close but he werent forgettin. He were made from rememberins an he owed a reckonin. He could feel they was workin their way into the centre of the bastard place, runnin out of things to burn an the flames was catchin up to em an leapin the rubbish piles an catchin on anythin dry which was near enough evrythin. He walked with his blade out, but even though there was people movin towards the East an runnin along some of the tracks to the left an right nowun paid no special attention to him an his two yungens. When he looked close the place looked part destroyed already. He wondered just what were goin on here before him an his kin had come. It was fallin apart, a shadow itself. The three of em came around a curve in the road, walkin slow an stoppin to smash sum bottles into the fastmovin fire an they went up with an blast, filled with sum kinda clear stuff that werent water that were certain. The two lads with him could walk plenny good in the day or night but they was driftin along, startled at the place. Jon guessed theyd never seen so many fellas packed together under the open sky. Werent many who could come as far as the System an fewer who wanted to. He figgered the pair of lads with him were seein it all new an wonderin what it was they was burnin.

Been a long time comin to this place, dont shed no nevermindin tears for em.

The boys looked at him an back at the destruction, seemin bewildered. They came further round the hook an the road ended in a square of dirt, surrounded by high dwellins. The flamesd overtook em now an the smoke and dust was gettin real thick, blowin across them, sendin rubbish and metal flyin through the air but he hadta see the middle of the place, to know it were all done. Out of wun of the buildings right in front two figures was standin all lit up by the flames an he hadda sinkin feelin deep in the pit of his guts. He'd been hopin they was gone an outside the walls but it figgered they was last to leave. Werent no turnin back now anyway, nuthin to do but stand.

92

The Orphand never seen a storm quite like it. Heavy like she'd never known. The air were the colour of blud where it were lit by the burnin System. Evrythin was glowin, like the whole place was on fire an she could smell the scorch of burnin tyres an knew the Stacks, her home, were finally burnin too. The wind made a noise like screams an under it she could hear the faint sounds of people an panic but she couldnt see moren shadows of it in the haze. She were near blinded by the gusts but she pulled her wrap up over her mouth an leaned into it. The Orphan hefted Block again, pullin his arm around her shoulder an the two of em supported each other to the door where there was fallen fellas from both sides, tangled with each other so you couldnt tell who mighta been fightin for what, or who. As they come through the door the heat of the flames hit em hard and she could feel sumthin shiftin, sumthin real bad comin. She peered through the smoke and dust when the wind blew swirlin clouds sideways an she could see people, looked most like women an yungens, draggin each other across the road an towards the East gate. That were gunna be the safest place outside the circle. Wun of Blocks fellas come up to them, lookin askance at Block who had his head down an the blud spillin in ropy draughts outta his side.

Boss OK?

Gunna be fine.

What you want us to do?

Go round up anywun else from your fam an then run around the ring an get evrywun ya can out the gate. Dont leave nowun behind yungfella, yhear?

The kid nodded an was off, dirty soles of his feet kickin up dust, an she saw him grab another young lad and disappear up the cut into the fire and haze. A good kid she reckoned, an the best she could do all considered. She hadta get the Block outside an get sumthin in his wound. Block were still carryin the parang he'd taken off Karra an around the pointer finger on his other hand was the bitta jute he usedta always keep tied around the hook blade. She remembered that wun from a long time back an near smiled. The hook were in his pocket now but he always kept the string wound like a reminder. Fucken Block. Gettin stuck for his troubles. Gettin stuck for her. She pulled him up again as he started to sag an dragged his arm further over her shoulders. He dint weigh much, that were lucky, an the days out on the sand had toughened her up for just this kinda thing. Were bout the same as draggin the Wide Open Road she reckoned, cept Block dint have no sail. She knew she had the madness on her, like she were just holdin on. She dragged Block out inta the little square an towards the mouth of the road. He were half standin, nearly helpin her an she looked down to give him a lift an when she looked up there was three fellas comin towards her, all black against the glow. They was masked up but there was sumthin familiar about the bigger wun in the front an it din take moren a few steps for her to recognise him an for all the pieces to fit. She felt Blocks head raise up to see why she'd stopped an then all of a sudden he were standin upright an on his own two feet, eyes sorta clear after all that. His voice were hoarse though an she hadta lean close to hear his raspy whisper.

Thats the Reckoner aint it.

It werent a question but she answered anyway.

Yep.

Hes burnin our place down aint he. Just like he promised ya.

She dint answer. The smoke was all around them now, makin her eyes water an the breath catch in her throat.

93

He'd been sayin his whole shortlong life that the game were chess not checkers an when it all come to it he figgered it werent neither of them, it were just between what he knew he had to do an what he wanted to do. Woulda been easy to sit it out, the Reckoner were a badfella that much he knew an just as he'd got rid of a bad old bastard, another wun sprung up right in his place. Block were glad he aint never had the time to become the bad old bastard hisself an it had plenny to do with the Orphan he reckoned. She'd been there most his life, an it were strange how theyd all come back together like sumthin more were workin that day down at the auction block. Couldnt never put nuthin past the old fella an he knew well enough like most of em did that there werent no such creature as coincidence livin in the System. Here she were, standin right beside him, just like she had been for a long time. He guessed he loved her, reckoned he did for certain now. Loved her better than any of the other lads an lasses whatd been part of his crew. Too late for any of that nonsense now though. This were his System an he knew he'd gotta stand for all of em or he werent nuthin better than the last. He straightened up his shoulders an spat into the dust.

Dont do it Block.

The Orphans voice were real low.

Please dont. Ya cant save this place. Its already done for.

He looked sideways at her.

Gotta try though Orphan.

An he straightened up, walkin forwards real quick, swingin Karras parang in a loop an keepin the hook blade level an steady as he came up on the Reckoner. The blades met dull an Block clean forgot the blud leakin out of him an lost hisself in the knife fight like he were in a cipher. Roll right, move left. Slip an cut. He were movin like he were yung again an he were beatin him back. The Reckoner were faster than anywun he'd ever fought but he were gettin tired fendin off the Block an his two fellas behind him werent movin an if they did he knew the Orphan were gunna be moren a match for em. The place was burnin around em an the dust was chokin but Block were seein clear an breathin in clean air sumwhere from outta the roilin clouds' of poison. This were his place, this were where he were always meant to be, defendin this place against all comers, leadin em outta this muck. Leadin em back to them places he were always readin about in the papers, takin em back to the stories he'd been collectin for years. Stories where they din always live in dust. Outta the dust. That were where they was gunna head. Outta the dust.

An it were done.

He looked down an saw the Reckoners blade in his chest, near the same place that he were already bleedin an he looked up at the Reckoner who was bleedin from a ton of small nicks an breathin hard but still standin, still holdin the hilt of his blade an lookin kinda surprised, covered in sweat an ash an dust.

Blockd been dreamin. Always been his trouble the dreamin. Even in a knife fight. That were Block all over, he knew hisself. Could always fight sleep, but not the dream. He looked up at the Reckoner again an saw the Orphan come from the side, nowun

271

else movin, an saw her punch a short blade into her brothers ribs over an over again until he fell sideways in the dust. Block an him fell at the same time an he heard the terrible wailin cry of the Orphan as she cut at the Reckoner an sliced his hands as he dropped his blade an put em up to fend her off. He lay sideways in the dust an watched as she sat over her brother, put her knee into his ribs an pulled his head up, ready to drag the blade across his throat an he saw her stop an he knew it were gunna be okay.

94

Buildins was burnin in a great ring around em an she sensed a movement behind her. Karras place was burnin but from the alleys next to it come six or seven lads, armed up an led by the wun she'd sent to get people out. They musta seen whatd happened an they was walkin ready for blud. She took her blade away from Jons throat an stood up, backin away an lettin him fall back into the dust. She dint right know whatd stopped her but she were done. She dint want this no more. The yungen she'd sent out lookin for folks came up to her an stood lookin at her an her bludy hands and made a move to walk past, blade up an out, fear an murder in his eyes. Evrywun was masked up an there werent no tellin who were who. She couldnt see moren twenty metres anymore an they was lit by fire reflectin off the dirt in the air.

Hold.

Her voice came out strongern she thought she were able. Jon were lyin on his back bleedin in the street an Block were face down in the dust an it were all still for a long minute. Jons two lads hadnt moved neither an she was caught between em in the wind. It werent gunna come out right, never did an this werent no cipher an there werent gunna be nuthin to win at this rate. Nuthin but keepin the lives she had left in her hands.

No more. We done. No more burnin. Get out there an get whoevers left out the East gate. All of you fellas, you too.

She gestured towards Jons lads.

Get evrywun out.

The Ghosts looked at Jon, his face a mask of pain an he nodded.

Lissen to her, shes blud.

Blocks lads hesitated an the yungen whod taken charge came in close to her.

He just kilt the Block, we gotta end him.

She stared into his eyes an after a moment he dropped his gaze an it were like she'd come home, like she'd found sumthin she dint know was lost.

You gotta look after the Blocks peoples. Thats all of em left alive in this place. Dont go killin them other fellas over there. I said no more blud, no more. Go save who ya can like I told ya an get em outside the walls. Block put these peoples ahead of hisself, now do the same. Go do what I say.

The yungen raised his eyes up an looked at her afore he nodded real sharp an took his boys off into the smoke again. She'd see em outside the walls she reckoned. She hoped. See em with whoever was left alive. Karrad done for this place long before Jon had come. An now Block were dead an she dint even have time to mourn him. He were face to dust like a dog an she were gunna have to leave him here. There were an almighty crash behind her an Karras place came down, spittin embers at her back an makin Jon on the ground flinch and moan at the heat. Her shirt caught an she slapped out the cinder.

Get up.

Jon rolled to his side, gaspin with pain but he sat hisself up an climbed to his feet, blud runnin through his fingers from the holes she'd put in him. She dint feel nuthin lookin at em, just turned an looked at Block. It werent right. She stepped to him an rolled him over in the dust, wipin the red earth off his lips an closin his eyes proper. She left the earth on his brow, werent never afraid of dust were Block, never feared the earth or nuthin that walked on it. She took the hook and laid it on his chest fore pressin her lips to his, tastin the iron, her brow against his, markin herself with his sweat an the dust. The wind whipped around them an she looked down at him, tryna commit it to memory. Blade up, that were how he were gunna stay. Lookin up through the smoke at the stars, with his hook close an in the middle of the place he belonged. He'd got there in the end. He'd got his System. She turned her back an started through the smoke, barely breathin, an she figgered that sumwhere behind her, Jon were followin.

95

After

She were sailin on the South roads, further than she'd ever gone. Weeks out from the System. Far enough that she couldnt feel the ache now an then. At the point where she woulda headed for the Glows she'd held her line an kept the bow pointed South East an then she came upon the blacktop. Them old roads was perilous now, the asphalt cracked an worn down, fallen into dry water courses and gullies, cracked by the cold and the heat and the time. This wun had red in it, like the iron an the earth had got into it when it were made. They was still useful as a guide though an she knew that if she kept close to the snakin road she'd gotta hit the Edge eventually, if all what the old fellad told her was true. She kept the Wide Open Road runnin alongside the remnants of the highway, mostly preferrin the packed sand that she knew. The dust and the rattlin of the ship soon fell away and her mind was driftin through the waste, wonderin on what were ahead and behind but most of her keepin an eye on the road an the waverin horizon. This were country she hadnt ever seen before an as she travelled the greenery got more common, more spinifex an the occasional tree turned into clumps of washedout green that marked sum underground water. Here an there she saw that things was growin, shoots an gourds in the long grass. She saw a mob of roos at dusk an then another an the trees was a quiet green that tasted of salt an she were reminded of her ma fore she hadta push the thought away. The road kept runnin South an the sun was always droppin, shadows gettin long and the wind droppin just as it were gettin too dangerous to sail anyhow. The trouble with the South runnin was she werent exactly sure how far she was goin. She made camp and took a cold tea an sum damper but she werent carryin much more than a few days supply anymore. Werent nuthin to skip a few days worth of food an the coupla skins of water she carried was a lot more important but she dint fancy gettin weak from hunger either. She were gunna need to scav sumthin along the way but from what she was seein maybe there was food to be had. Maybe sum kinda life.

★

Before the sun come up she were out on the wind again, catchin the first gusts that come with dawn an stoppin only once in the day to scope out a shed that came up fast on the horizon. She hitched the Open Road to a post and furled the mainsail, takin her time an doin good recce until she was sure it were abandoned an alone. A wall on the far side of her approach was missin altogether an the rusted walls was just waitin for a good blast of sand to collapse the whole place under the weight of the burnin sun. She took her time goin through the rustin inside, findin sum scraps of wire and sacks of what mighta once been seed or feed but were now just dust. Sum handles of tools with rusted heads, nuthin she weighed good against what she'd gotta carry. She dint stop again that day, just kept gunnin south, no need to eat an a coupla sips of water was all she was getting, all she figgered she had time to take. Then again, she dint have nowun really waitin on her she sposed. Another cold camp, her food supply down to the last scraps of roo an bread now an not enough water for a billy or nuthin warm. Were alright. She'd set a trap tomorrow. Dig a soak next to wun of them green stands she'd been passin an see what the water were like. She slept loose furled in the sail under the Open Road an she'd had worse nights out on the sand. Sum of the high dust cleared an she saw a few stars overhead, castin a starshadow of her ship over her an eventually she slept, dreamin of Karra an the Block like it were old times an the old fella comin to her to say sumthin but the words never quite arrivin.

★

When she woke again she could smell sumthin different on the wind but it werent nuthin she could pin a name on. After breakin her fast she hit the road. No moren a half hour in the Orphan saw another track of black asphalt crossin the wun she was trackin an broken poles that looked like trees stripped of branches come up outta the sand and stretched into the distance. In the near haze she could see the blacktop was scorched an blasted an by the side of the road was burned out squares of what musta been buildins but was now only ash, drifts of tailings, blown this way an that by the uncarin wind. Here an there were hulks more like the big beasts she seen underground in the Glows than the wuns scattered inside the Boundaries. Piles of ash an charred bones inside the burnedout shells, skulls lettin her know that she werent in no dream, these was bad times she was courtin an in the before peopled been fleein and runnin from whatever she were headed towards. She pressed on through the burnedout squares, crossin grid after grid of blacktop an on the horizon she started seein a low smudge of sumthin an the wind died down an she found herself in harness, towin the ship until she saw the outline of a city or town ahead an she stowed the Open Road in cover an started skirmishin ahead in broken lines, takin her time. She could smell sumthin else now, it were a colour she dint know, a blue an grey she aint never tasted. There were hills up ahead scattered with burned trees thatd turned to stone in the sun an by the time she'd crested the low rises the sun were high in the sky an she took her breath, lookin down on the blastburned remains of what musta been a goodsized town back in the longago. That werent nuthin compared to the Edge though. She werent no stranger to open spaces but this were sumthin else. Across the whole horizon was a greyblue haze an the smell of salt in her nose made sense an it were only through her book lernin that she knew what she were lookin at. That were the sea. It were water. Water you werent supposed to drink but water still. She took a minute an just looked at the vast mouth of it. Swallowin up the earth it were. She reckoned it werent moren a few miles from where she stood now an between her an the blue was what looked to be the town an now she looked closer she could see it werent all burned and blasted. There were a whole bit to the East of where she stood that looked near enough intact, like the fire or whatever it were hadnt reached its fingers out that far. There were buildins and shacks an long low sheds that reached out towards the water an she could see that in sum places the buildins ran down an disappeared into the water an the old fellas stories came back to her about how the seas had rose up an et the land and how it got hotter an hotter an then it all got burned an swallowed up by the fierce ocean that dint care nuthin for nuthin. True as dust it were, she reckoned. She were lookin at the proof right now an the blacktop ran right into the sea as far as she could tell like she was gunna walk to her grave. She thought of the Block then. Thought of the burnedout System an the scattered folk campin in the desert. So manyd burned but even more was alive an scroungin, close to starvin, sum sick mebbe werent never gunna heal. Jon an his fellas had headed back to the Glows but she told him she'd be comin soon. He were healin up from their fight but she werent ready to face him yet.

*

She took her time checkin out the town. Dint know if there was any fellas livin in the place but she werent gunna find out the hard way. She was usin her bushcraft, comin through the gullies an stayin off the ridges an up above her now an then she could see halfcollapsed walls an she hadta skirt around the wrecks of more burnedout beasts. She never knew just how long ago the longago was but judgin by the bones she passed an the ash that was built up in drifts itd happened long before her mum was born, looked like the works of people was blendin back into the land an soon enough all that was gunna be left would be broken an unformed memories in the heads of them that wandered the waste. Werent no way she could wrap her head around how these fellas musta lived, all she could do was scav through the wreck of their times. Werent never gunna get that back again she reckoned, it were all dust now, she dint know the way back to them times an nowun did. She were gettin hungry now. It were sumthin she were used to an she knew it must be gettin bad if she was noticin it. Funny though, she dint feel weak an she knew there were food back the way she'd come if she wanted to find it. The idea of the town was drivin her on she figgered. She'd never been this far from the System, never even thought to come to the Edge even though the old fellad talked of it plenny back when he'd been of a talkin disposition. She could hear the sea now, if that were what it was. A dull hiss an a quiet out in front of her. She were usedta the noise of the land, the hum of the ground and the wind on the dust but out ahead of her was a great animal she dint know nuthin about. She crossed more an more burned blacktop an after a while she werent so watchful. This were a dead place. No animal tracks, no birds calling. Nuthin had been alive in this place for a terrible long time, nuthin had disturbed the dead but the wind. She came over another hill, walkin now in the middle of the road and there it were, the water no moren a few hundred metres away at the bottom of a long slope, the road runnin clear into the grey an the skeletons of what she knew musta been ships was stickin out of ruined houses and it were all swayin gently in a way that made her feel unsteady on her feet. The salt smell was heavy now an it were all mixed up with a faint smell of rotten wood an the rotten stink of the sea itself under the clean of the salt. There was plants an dead drift in the water, sloppin back and forth through smashed out windows an open doors. She walked slow down to the Edge itself, shiftin her ruck on her back an takin off her boots. She hitched her pants up and rolled her sleeves, tyin her blade up high an walked real careful into the swayin water, just ankle deep. It were cold like nuthin she'd ever felt an the pulse of it were alive but just barely. This were a thing. This were a beast that was restin, or maybe sick, but she could feel that it werent always like this. The suck an swirl of it around her legs had a power that was hidden, she knew it sumhow. Maybe them old books had done the work the old fella intended cos she knew that in spite of the quiet it were wild. All around her in the scum an splinter of the broken ships an houses was the truth of the lie the sea was tryna tell her. She shuddered an had the urge to run from the ocean but she made herself walk out backwards, never turnin her back. She sat a little up the hill an put her boots back on, tightenin up her straps an bindings, rollin her pants back down, an then she sat quiet, watchin the Edge for a long time till the motion of it were makin her sick an the grey water blended with the grey horizon an she knew if she dint stop lookin it were gunna eat her.

*

High up on the hill she looked down on the bay. She'd climbed up the windin asphalt, through broken streets an buildings an glass that was startin to go back to the ground. Evrythin was rusted, rotten. Signs she couldnt read'd fallen off rustweak hooks an splintered on the ground. She worked her way up towards the long low buildings what looked like they was mostly untouched. She figgered it long before she went inside but she made herself check anyway. They was fulla people whatd never made it onto the blacktop. Layin in rows, big, small an evrythin in between. Skin dried out an parched like paper, kids under cots, twisted up like they was sleeping. Wuns whatd never had the chance to head into the desert away from whatever had blackened this place. Wuns whatd never had the chance to find safety for whatever thatd been worth. Maybe these were the lucky wuns but she dint really believe that. Maybe it were her what was the lucky wun but she couldnt quite buy that neither. She oughta head back. She oughta be helpin settle the wuns what had left the ashes an ruins of the System an now were just more debris, blowin in the wind. She was gunna bring em out this way. She knew it now. Not all the way to the Edge but to them greener lands she'd crossed to get here. It'd been slow comin to her but she knew it now. She aint just carried what the Old Womand given her, it were her own weight now. Spite all them tellins an all them knowins she reckoned the Old Woman dint really know what'd gone on in the longago an chances were nowun ever would. Might be now that she herself knew moren the Old Womand ever dug up about them bad places though mayhap she were getting a little ahead of herself. What she knew for sure was that them fellas whatd made the System had run too far an theyd never knowed what they come across. By chance or bad luck they built their place on a secret an it were a terrible wun. All that bad blud'd come back up though in the end. The Old Woman had told her you could change the past with a thought but she were gunna have to wrestle with that wun she reckoned. It were sumthin she woulda liked to chew on with the Block. Them what was left was gunna need help survivin though, workin with the Ghosts where they could. It were gunna be a new time but she werent sure what part of it she were gunna be. She'd lead em to a new place. Find em shelter in them hunting grounds she'd passed. Get em outta the worst of the dust but then, she dint know. Dint even know if she could look at her brother yet, still a hole in her heart where Blockd been an it werent gunna fill soon she reckoned. She walked back outta the place filled with the dead an then sat down on the hill up high. Sat a long time. Let her eyes stretch out over the grey sea, seein sumthin out there, far out past the dead town an the quiet waves.

Acknowledgements

I'd like to acknowledge that this story was written on Cadigal Wangal land and is set in Maralinga Tjarutja country.

Thank you Lex Hirst, editor, co-conspirator and fellow believer. Thank you for championing this story from the very beginning and for making it immeasurably better. I am so fortunate to have you as my editor and my dearest wish is to work together again.

Kate O'Donnell, I am in awe of your attention to detail and talent. You made this story stronger and so much more coherent and I am extremely grateful, thank you.

Emily Cook, thank you for all of your help in publicising this story.

Laura Thomas, for the amazing cover design, thank you.

Michael Rayner, one of the greatest adventures and joys while writing this story was travelling to Maralinga with you. Thank you – I'm looking forward to the next trip.

Michelle Tan, thank you for your kindness, your talent and for making me look like an author.

Jimmy Murray, what if we hadn't gone to the Vic? I don't even want to think about it. Thank you again.

Theresa Bray, thank you for the encouragement, support and feedback as this story took shape.

Richie Hull, thank you for introducing me to *Riddley Walker*, to which this story owes a considerable debt.

Cam Shea, thank you for reading an early draft and being a very early fan. GBC represent.

Robin Matthews, thank you for guiding Michael and me around Maralinga, the history lessons and the incomparable storytelling.

James d'Apice, thank you for helping me, a long time ago, find the title of this book and for helping me, not so long ago, with your kind counsel.

I'd like to thank and acknowledge NaNoWriMo, which spurred on the writing of the original manuscript. Every November is National Novel Writing Month and I can't encourage writers enough to give it a go. Thank you Darren Wells for the tip.

Thank you to my wonderful family, friends, colleagues and teachers for encouraging me, reading early versions and understanding when I had to drop everything and write. I am very lucky to have had your support.

Finally, but most importantly, thank you to my kind and wonderful partner LeaLea. You were the first person to read this story and you have believed in it, and me, from day one. Words can't do any justice to how much you have contributed to this story but it wouldn't exist without you. Thank you, I am forever grateful. We did it.

Dan Findlay is a historian by training and editor by trade. Dan has over ten years' experience editing Australia's leading youth magazines. He also has over a decade of freelance experience as a writer and photographer for *Rolling Stone* as well as contributing the odd music story to the *Sydney Morning Herald* and writing for a wide variety of other pop culture titles. *Year of the Orphan* is his debut novel.